STRIVING AFTER WIND

The DeJarnette Sanitarium Killer
-Book One-

S.W. YANCEY

ISBN Paperback: 979-8-9892177-1-7
ISBN E-book: 9979-8-9892177-2-4
Hardback: 979-8-9892177-0-0
Publisher: Susan W. Yancey
Edited by: www.bookdoneforyou.com

DEDICATION

For Matt, Andrew
and the Vision.

FORWARD

While *Striving After Wind* is a fictional book, DeJarnette Sanatorium in Staunton, Virginia, which housed James Martin, was real and administered to patients for over sixty years. Joseph DeJarnette was the director of the nearby Western State Hospital, a state-run asylum, from 1905 to 1943. His philosophy was a far cry from that of his predecessor, who had been a disciple of the "moral medicine" movement. DeJarnette was involved in conducting heinous social experiments and was a big proponent of the eugenic movement. Joseph DeJarnette opened a semi-private mental hospital for paying patients in 1938, adjacent to Western State Hospital, where he remained acting director. He reigned over his namesake until 1947. In 1975, the state of Virginia took over DeJarnette, which became a child/adolescent hospital until its closing in 1996. The ghostly historic structure, has remained on the hill for over ninety years, looking down in defiance.

PROLOGUE

I told you not to have that damn baby," he said, throwing his third beer can across the kitchen in the direction of the already overflowing trashcan. "I told you to get an abortion!"

He looked at the sink that held stacks of dishes and floating bits of food, which was now spilling over onto the decaying Formica countertop, and made a sound of disgust. Passing on his way to the refrigerator, a strong whiff of curdled milk drifted from the sink. He brought his fingers to his nose and blew air out in an attempt to get rid of the smell that had settled in his nostrils.

He cursed at the dishes and raised his arm in preparation to hurl them onto the floor but stopped himself and instead went to the refrigerator for another beer. The remaining beers rattled as he yanked open the door. Grabbing another, he popped open the top and allowed cool air to get rid of any lingering odor. After taking several long swallows, he did a quick scan of the refrigerator's contents: beer and butter. He gritted his teeth and slammed the door shut.

"F—" he stopped mid-curse surprised by the small figure staring up at him. He smiled, bent down, and ran his hand across his son's hair. "What a shithole this place is, huh James?" He didn't wait for confirmation. "Things were a lot better when it was just the three of us, wasn't it?"

The boy nodded, not wanting to disappoint his father.

"Yeah," he chugged the rest of his beer and tossed the can in the direction of the sink.

He leaned down and looked directly into his son's searching eyes. He said, "I'll see ya, boy." He opened up the refrigerator for the last time, took another beer, and opened the back screen door, ready to leave. Holding it open with one hand, he turned and yelled into the air, "I'm not working my ass off to feed a kid I don't know is even mine!" He let go of the hinge-less screen door, and it slammed behind him.

James watched silently as his father walked out of his life.

It had been months since he walked out. Initially, she believed that things might improve without her husband's hostility in the house, but things had only gotten worse, especially her relationship with James. Tears streamed down her face as she remembered holding her firstborn son with such love and hope. Now, he would barely look at her. The revulsion from his father had passed down to their eleven-year-old son. She now held the only ally she had left, hoping for another chance at renewed love from a child, and closed her eyes to hold on to her memory. She was brought back to the present by the sense of James standing in front of her.

Before she could put any thoughts together, he asked, "When is Dad coming back?"

She lifted her head at the sound of his voice, her eyes welling up. She had been waiting for the question but still did not know how to soften the answer. "I don't know James. I don't know if he is."

He looked straight through her. She watched him go into the kitchen and heard the slamming of the cabinets. She shuddered and bent her head down to focus once again on the sleeping innocence in her arms.

Inside the kitchen, James opened the cabinet to pull out a bowl, but all the dishes had piled up again. He took one out of the sink, rinsed it off, and set it aside to dry as he went to get cereal and milk. There was no cereal. Opening the refrigerator, he saw there was no milk either. Hungry and angry, James searched for something to eat. He stood on his tiptoes and dragged the lone jar of peanut butter toward him. Opening the drawer, he pulled out the last clean spoon, opened the lid, and stuffed several scoops of smooth peanut butter into his mouth.

Looking around, he mimicked his father's words. "What a shithole." He picked up the empty bowl, which should have been full of cereal and milk, and slammed it against the wall. The sound of shattering glass evoked a response from the other room.

"What broke?" his mother called into the kitchen.

"Nothing," he answered.

"Well, I know it wasn't nothing, James. What was it?"

"It won't matter soon," he muttered under his breath and stormed out of the kitchen. The door banged behind him as he headed to the small shed.

"James?" she called his name several times with no response. She was growing used to his silence, so she shrugged, continued rocking the baby, and eventually dozed off.

Then, she felt the jolt of the rocker from behind being pushed. Not sure what to make of it, she decided to give James the benefit of the doubt. She leaned her head back and smiled up in his direction.

"That's nice, sweetie, thank you," she said. Turning her head to accept his gesture, she was met in mid-turn with a crushing blow of a hammer. Soon, there was a rip in her scalp, a round depression in her skull, and blood everywhere. Her body instantly slumped in the chair, and her grip loosened. Her sleeping baby dropped to the floor.

James wasn't sure if his mother was dead or not. He assumed from all the blood and the way she fell that she was. He didn't know about those things. He looked down to see if any of that stuff had gotten on him. He didn't see any, but went to a mirror to check his face. Picking up the moldy rag in the kitchen, he wiped his face and smudged his mother's blood. He wiped harder, fueled with hate and a desire to shut up the crying object in the other room. He picked up the red gas can from the shed, the one his mother had wanted him to use to fill up the lawnmower later today.

"This," he said to the gas can, "is better than having to mow that stupid lawn again." He made a trail of gasoline from the kitchen to the curtains in the small living room. He figured they would go up fast. He took the can over to his mother to pour the remainder around her. The can was empty.

"You couldn't even have a full tank of gas!" he screamed at his mother's motionless body. He threw the gas can across the room, stood in front of his mother, and began rocking the curved part of the chair with his foot, slowly at first, then faster. Then,

he stomped his foot to the floor; the rocker stopped, lurching his mother's body forward next to her crying baby.

James reached into his pocket, pulled out one of his mother's cigarettes, and lit it with a lighter. He took a few puffs while looking around the room. Only a few minutes ago, his mother had been rocking his baby brother while he was standing in the kitchen, hungry. He took one last draw and flipped the cigarette next to her body. Nothing happened. He waited. There had only been a few drops of gasoline. He had visions of everything going up in flames. Angry, he stomped back into the kitchen and rifled through a drawer until he found a pack of wooden matches. He went closer to the curtains to accelerate his new life. *Whoosh!* Now that worked.

He fled the house while feeling the heat on his back, ran to the edge of the property, and hid.

He lifted his head when he heard a frantic voice yelling and saw a man leap out of his car. "Call 911!"

The man ran straight into the burning house without a thought and emerged within seconds with the crying baby in his arms.

"What the...?" James peaked around the tree to see where this possible intruder could have come from.

The car door was still open, and he could now see a second figure running up to the man holding his brother. Together, they huddled by the car and waited for help.

Hearing the sirens, he snuck further into the woods to hide. By the time the fire department reached the small country house, it was almost burnt to the ground. He could see the firemen unfurling the hoses and heard them shouting directions to each other. One of the firemen was talking to the strangers.

He was shaking from cold and anger, uncertain of what to do next. Getting restless, he moved just enough that the firemen walking the back to the truck saw the movement in the woods.

"Hey," he shouted, "over here!" Waving his arm, he took off running in James's direction and was rewarded by finding the boy huddled next to a tree, knees pulled up to his face, his face hidden. The firefighter scooped him up and ran towards the obligatory ambulance. They wrapped him in a blanket while speaking to him in soothing tones. "Son, is this your house?"

No response.

"Do you live here?"

No response.

"Was that your baby brother?"

No response.

1

THIRTY YEARS AFTER

Dr. Kem Hunter sat behind the wooden desk in front of an oversized chalkboard. His steel blue eyes were fixed as he profiled his new graduate students coming in to take his wait-listed Psychopathology Course. There were rumors about his relationships with his female graduate students, but not enough to cause him trouble with the school. In some ways, it elevated his mystique.

He watched and waited until he thought he had heard the last of the rustling papers. He got out from behind the desk, his hands behind his back, and watched them until there was complete silence.

Only then did he begin speaking. "James Martin was an eleven-year-old boy who was found outside of his childhood home in Staunton, Virginia. His house had been burned to the ground with his mother inside. His mother had been bludgeoned to death by a hammer, and the fire was arson."

He paused and glanced up at the class before continuing. "To this day, no one knows if it was James, his estranged father, or someone else, but when the firefighters found James in the nearby woods, he did not speak. Since there were no living relatives, James was sent to DeJarnette Center for Human Development in Staunton, Virginia, a facility for children and adolescents. No one could ever rule him as a possible victim or the perpetrator because the entire time he was at DeJarnett he could not or would not speak."

He paused again to absorb the energy from the students. "James Martin's diagnosis while at DeJarnette was a severe form of elective mutism. By definition, this is the refusal to speak in almost all social situations, or in his case—at all."

This time, when he paused, he waited until several of the students moved forward in their seats in anticipation of his next words. "Complicating the matter further was the lack of family history. There was no way of knowing if James had ever spoken, but he did, however, comprehend what he was hearing. He was given the WISC. If you remember from your testing class, you know that it tests a child's cognitive abilities. James had a score of 146, making him highly gifted. His IQ score was 160, which placed him in the genius category. Granted, the psychologist had to adapt the tests since James was non-verbal. James Martin did not utter a word from the day he was admitted to the time of his escape at age seventeen."

Several of the students gasped, and he smiled back at them, amused at their reactions, until they brought their attention back to him.

"No, no one ever caught him, and to this day, no one knows what happened to him. This is a real case from the archives of DeJarnette, and although I understand it might seem more interesting to you to delve into the psychopathology of James Martin, for our purposes of this class, we will use this case to study elective mutism."

He heard several expected groans from the class but ignored them and continued. "I will start by telling you that in 1994, the terminology was requested in the DSM-IV to change from elective to selective mutism." He waved it off. "To me, that is more heavily associated with anxiety issues, and although I think there is room for both, alas, I was not asked my opinion." There were several obligatory chuckles in the room. "For our purposes, we will use Torey Hayden's four subtypes of elective mutism."

Dr. Hunter turned his back to the class and began writing on the chalkboard while continuing to lecture, "The first and most common type is symbiotic mutism. It is the most prevalent and stereotypical: a domineering mother and absent father. You know, classic mommy issues." He paused as he heard several students laughing.

"The second and least common is speech phobic mutism— often brought about by the fear from hearing a recording of one's own voice," He continued. "It is also more associated with OCD and theories of a child who is told to keep a family secret."

"Reactive mutism..." he paused briefly, noting bobbing heads frantically writing to keep up with the lecture, "is more self-explanatory—a reaction to trauma and or abuse. And then, finally, we have the fourth. Passive-aggressive mutism is where the silence is more likely to be manipulative, meaning they can speak but won't." He underscored the term several times. "Now, assuming a thorough medical workup has been done, which subtype would you place James Martin in and why?"

"Reactive mutism," a clear-cut male voice called out.

Dr. Hunter circled the item on the board, "Very good. Now why?" he asked, turning toward the unknown student for further confirmation.

"Trauma. Even if he killed his mother, it was still a trauma."

Dr. Hunter nodded, satisfied. "That's all I have for today's class. We'll pick it back up next time."

"Professor, excuse me," A female voice in the back said before the professor could officially dismiss the class. Not waiting for acknowledgment, she plowed ahead with her question, "Why wouldn't this be passive-aggressive mutism?"

After asking her question, Catherine leaned back slightly and waited for a response.

"Excuse me? Who asked…"

"Catherine," she stated holding up her hand.

Dr. Hunter moved in closer to the class, his penetrating eyes scanning the students. "Go on?"

"In passive-aggressive mutism, silence is usually a display of hostility and can be connected with antisocial behavior." She stopped, exhaled, and waited for the humiliation that was about to fall on her.

He shrugged slightly as he inspected the wide-eyed questionable doctoral candidates. "You have a valid point."

Awestruck, Catherine slowly picked up her belongings and headed toward the front, receiving pats on the back and envious glances from her female classmates as she passed them.

"Catherine, is it?' Dr. Hunter called up from his position.

"Yes," she stopped.

"Oh, good. I got it right," he said, quietly smiling at her. "Could you come here for a minute?" he asked.

She nodded. As she approached the desk, she could smell a hint of his cologne. The odor evoked a strong, unexpected, visceral response, and suddenly, she fought to remember why she was walking toward the intriguing floral, woody, warm scent. With each step, the aura drew her closer to him. She automatically stopped short of the desk, unsure what to expect. Immediately, she saw the steel eyes that had summoned her, soften.

"What are you studying, Catherine?" he asked. His smoky voice mixed with his cologne and made Catherine reflexively tilt her head and run her fingers through her strawberry blonde hair.

Blushing, she projected a kittenish smile. "Excuse me?"

The slight cough from behind her allowed her to focus. She had not noticed the petite blonde sitting crossed-legged and bouncing her leg up and down in the front row, glaring at her. Catherine attempted a smile in her direction—the blonde snarled, looking away.

"I asked you, what are you studying?" he repeated.

"Um, I'm concentrating on clinical psychology with perhaps an emphasis on forensic psychology," she answered.

"Clinical psychology," the unidentified coed mimicked while rolling her eyes.

"Enough, Amber," the professor ordered. "You can wait for me outside if you like."

"No, I'll wait." The blonde stuck out her bottom lip and crossed her arms, accentuating her plunging cleavage.

"Why is it that you want to go into forensic work, Catherine? Why not just stay with the clinical aspect?" he asked, returning his attention to her.

"Um," she plucked her lip, fighting for a justifiable reason. "I just want to help police catch criminals."

"A valiant reason, I'm sure, but where does that come from, for you?"

Catherine lowered her head, shaking it. "You don't have time…"

He placed his elbows on the desk, hands together, resting his chin, his eyes focused on her. "I have plenty of time, Catherine."

Her eyes moistened, and she held back tears. "Um, well, my father was a police officer, and he was killed in the fall of my freshman year in College." Shifting her weight from one foot to another, she continued, "He was killed in the line of duty. I, I," she stammered, "I just want to catch the bad guys who inflict so much harm and sadness onto people they don't even know.

"Hmm, now that I can understand," he smiled. "A bit naïve, but I understand." Pausing he continued, "I brought you up to let you know that I can already see you are taking my class seriously enough to question me on your first day. Most students would not do that. I understand how intimidating it can be, and I was interested to find out what your motivation was in taking my class. Thank you for telling me."

"Thank you, sir. I just needed clarification." She looked down at the book she was cradling in her arm.

"I would, however, suggest that you move up to the first row, Catherine. I believe you will get more out of it than sitting in the back."

"Yes, sir. You…" she was interrupted by the hurried heels clicking up the aisle.

Amber had thrown open the door with such force it hit the back of the wall in the outside hall and created an echo in the now-empty room.

He put up his hands and shook his head, his eyes following his inamorata out of the room. "She is my TA." He paused, shaking his head. "Who appears to be a bit too possessive. He lowered his eyes and looked back at Catherine, "I might have to rethink that one." He smiled at her. "Who knows? Would you be interested in being my TA?" he asked not waiting for a response before continuing, "If you continue the way you have started, you show definite promise."

Her heart skipped a beat, and she found herself at a loss for words. She was grateful when he got up from the desk, gathered his papers, and said, "I will see you Wednesday."

Catherine continued to treat the rest of the semester in Psychopathology as if it were her only class. It paid off. On the last day of class, Dr. Hunter called her to his office. She strolled through the faculty halls, glancing inside the open doors. Most of the professors had made their offices into cozy studies that were welcoming to students. She was trying to imagine what Dr. Hunter's study was going to look like when she found herself in front of the closed door. Preparing herself, she raised her knuckles to the door, ready to knock, when suddenly it flew open, almost hitting her. The petite blonde figure emerged, storming down the hall while completely ignoring Catherine's presence.

"Amber?" she called out after her.

Jolted, the barnstormer stopped, took a few steps back, and peered at Catherine through swollen eyes. "I guess you are his new pet now. Be careful." she warned and wiped her eyes as she continued down the hall.

Confused, Catherine lightly knocked on the door. "Enter," came the familiar voice.

"Dr. Hunter," she called out, slowly opening the door.

"Catherine." He stood up, waving her in.

The room was filled with the scent of his cologne; otherwise, there was nothing that made the stark room personal. The walls were empty, unusual for academics who cherished placing their ivory tower accomplishments on display. A metal bookshelf half full of books and two wooden desks with accompanying chairs supplied by the University were the only pieces of furniture.

"Monsieur Dupin," she said under her breath, looking around the sparse room.

"You read Poe?" he chuckled. "Yes, I suppose if I did have a window, I would drape it with a dark curtain."

"The Murders in the Rue Morgue was one of my favorite books."

"I believe Poe and Doyle spurred many an inquisitive mind." He remained seated behind his desk and quickly changed the subject. "I suppose you saw Amber?"

Catherine moved closer to his desk, plucking her lips and unsure what to say.

"Let's get you started," he said and reached into his desk to pull out a white binder. "Here you go."

He handed it to her before continuing. "I want you to read this. It's the syllabus for next semester. I have tried to mix things up a bit. I thought I should maybe spend more time delving into other case studies of psychopathology. It may be out of the norm, but I would like you in the classroom with me first before you move on."

"Thank you," she said, plucking her lip at a possible faux pas. "I think that would be great." Catherine winced at her rudimentary word choice. Attempting a recovery, she added while patting the binder, "I guess I know what I will be doing over break."

"I guess you do. I will see you Tuesday,"

"Tuesday," her eyes widened, "I thought I had at least all next week."

"Well, it looks as though you thought wrong, Catherine. I will see you Tuesday?" he asked with a slight inflection in his voice.

"Of course," she stood straighter. "I understand there is a lot of preparation. Thank you." Pivoting, she started to walk out but turned halfway to the door to say something…but he was already engrossed in what was in front of him.

Catherine had worked hard to get into UVA and was a focused student, but the death of her father during her freshman year caused her to question everything. She was uncertain if she even wanted to return to school, but with the help and support of her mother and her roommate Anne, she decided to do so.

Anne helped her to focus and put aside the things she could not change. She was her rock. Together they graduated UVA undergraduate and were now attending graduate school while renting a small two-bedroom house off of Park Street. They shared a dream of working in Anne's father's practice together in Northern Virginia and that one day, they laughed, would take it over.

Anne walked into the living area and found Catherine burrowed in the binder on her lap; papers were spread on the coffee table.

"Are you going to come up for air?" Anne asked, knocking lightly on the table.

"Probably no air for me till Tuesday," she looked up glassy-eyed, lifting her head long enough to give a quick smile.

"I know you want to make a good impression, but you do need to eat and sleep,"

"Don't worry, it's just a few days. It's a great opportunity. Anne, be happy for me," she said.

"All right. I get it. Dr. Hunter definitely can open doors…" Anne stopped herself and shook her head. "I'm going to get something to eat. What do you want?"

Tuesday morning, Catherine showed up with a fully loaded backpack and ideas. She was ready to begin the next phase of her career as a budding psychologist. To her surprise and Dr. Hunter's credit, he listened to her ideas and even implemented some of them. Her confidence grew, the weeks passed quickly, and the work impassioned her as she gained deeper insight in areas of her field.

She enjoyed discussing ideas that would not be covered in a classroom and thrived on her in-depth conversations with Dr. Hunter. Catherine had always doubted Amber's accusations, believing the neophyte had either been a woman scorned or that she simply did not know enough or did not have the talent to do as well as Dr. Hunter would have hoped.

Over time, Catherine began to feel more like a colleague than a TA and began to believe that together they were molding their class.

"I think that the class is enjoying the deep dive into the psychopathy." She said once they were back in his office after one such class.

"Everyone enjoys being a voyeur into the dark side of the mind as long as it doesn't affect them."

"I guess that is very true, but don't you think that people also want to find an answer as to why certain people commit such horrific crimes?"

"You believe there has to be an answer?" He questioned.

"I guess when people hear about certain crimes, they have a basic need to want to understand why or how it happened. Maybe it is a sense of control," she said. "To try to make sure something like that does not happen to them."

"It's different now," he said. "The motives used to be very basic, Catherine—anger, greed, lust, or revenge. We have always had serial killers, and people have randomly killed for other reasons, but the numbers were not as large. Thus, the ability to solve the crimes was greater. Now it is much different."

"I suppose once you take out the logical reasoning behind a killing, like what you said about lust, greed, anger, or revenge, it becomes more difficult to understand the why."

"There are more murders committed today by those with a mental disorder. Not to mention that, as a culture, I believe we lack valuing human life."

"I was doing an internship in a psychiatric hospital in Northern Virginia, and a young man about twenty was brought in for attacking his mother," she said. "His mother was also concerned about his drug use. I did the initial intake on him and throughout his six-week stay observed him in both individual and group therapy. My instinct was that his behavior and ideations had not been drug-induced, but that he needed further psychiatric evaluation and treatment. The psychiatrist, however, chalked it up to the drugs he had been on at the time. I came in one day to find he was being discharged in two days. His mother was so distraught she came in and begged me not to let him out. She was in fear for her life and did not believe the attack on her had been drug-related at all. I relayed my concern and the mother's fear, but I was just an intern, and who was I to question authority?"

Catherine sighed as she remembered the case, and the arrogance of the psychiatrist. "Three weeks later. I found out he had killed his mother."

"Hmm. Our profession can certainly be imperfect, Catherine," he said. "I believe that some have an innate gift for therapy while others secretly selfishly seek to heal themselves. These are the people who are most often fooled and manipulated by their patients."

"What makes it even worse is that after he committed this crime, he was thrown in jail, then prison, and will most likely never be properly evaluated and get the treatment he needs."

"Tragically it seems that the jails and prisons have started to become the new mental institutions." He looked over at the clock. "It is getting late, Catherine. Would you like to go grab a bite to eat with me?"

She did.

They walked down to The Corner for a quick bite to eat.

As they settled into their seats, she ordered an iced tea.

"You don't want to have a glass of wine with me?" he asked.

Catherine eagerly changed her order to a merlot, grateful for the chance of letting it ease her anxiety about sitting across from her esteemed professor.

"May I ask a question?" Catherine asked as she twirled her wine glass back and forth on the white cotton tablecloth.

"You may ask away." He gazed at her, intrigued, holding the wine to his lips.

"Your cologne. What is it?" she asked, suddenly uncomfortable by the attention he was giving her.

"Hmm. My cologne. It is Clive Christian No. 1. Along with it being one of the most expensive men's perfumes, it comes in a lovely crystal Baccarat bottle." He took another sip of wine before musing, "Its namesake has an intriguing story, which is perhaps how I became interested in his perfume. When I lived in England, Clive Christian started as a freelance interior designer but turned that into Clive Christian Furniture. I remember liking his designs and became curious when the furniture designer decided to purchase one of the oldest British perfume houses. His constant evolution intrigued me, and I was drawn to the scent. I have been wearing it ever since."

"It is singular," she said as she moved her wine glass to make room for her dinner plate.

As the weeks progressed and they shared several more meals together, Catherine began finding that she wanted more from their relationship. The more Dr. Hunter stimulated her intellectually, the more she wanted from him physically. Her deep desire for him was growing daily, and she began to replace her conservative wardrobe for tighter-fitting clothing, shorter skirts, higher heels, and plunging necklines.

"I have been meaning to ask you a personal question," Dr. Hunter asked out of the blue.

Catherine focused on the paper in front of her on her desk, her heart fluttering. She did not trust her voice. "Sure."

"We have been working together for a while, but I don't know that much about you personally. Where is it that you are from?"

"Right here in Charlottesville."

"Hmm. You haven't ever ventured too far from home then, have you?"

"Well, my mom is still here, and ever since my dad was killed, I want to be close to her," she said while twirling her hair, "except I guess I haven't seen her too much lately."

She smiled at him.

"Yes, I am truly sorry about that, Catherine." Undeterred by her comment, he continued. "Do you know the details of how your father was killed?"

"Um…he died in the line of duty," she looked up, not sure if she was relieved the question was not more personal.

"I remember that is what you said. I was just wondering how. Call it professional curiosity."

"He had just gotten off of duty, but he always kept his radio on until he got home—used to drive my mom crazy. She never understood why he had to keep it on," Catherine said, looking off into the distance. Tears welled up in her eyes. "As he was driving home a call came over the radio of a home burglary. He was the closest to the scene, and so, being my dad, he went in without waiting for any backup."

"He went in alone, off duty?"

"He knew how quickly those home invasions could escalate. So, yeah, he went in alone and was killed. But from what I was told he saved the people inside. I think it was a mother and her two children. I think." She paused, a lone tear drifting down her cheek. "Regardless, he was a hero."

"Did they ever catch the perpetrator?"

"No," she looked down at the small droplet on the paper where her tear had landed.

"Again, I am so very sorry,"

"Thank you," she said, changing the subject. "Is there something else you need me to finish up today?"

"Are you in a hurry?" Dr. Hunter asked, smiling. "We could order something in for dinner."

"I guess I am not in a hurry, but I just need to make a quick call."

"What are you doing? You blew me off again." Anne asked when she walked into her room in the morning while Catherine was applying her makeup.

"I'm getting ready for work," she said brushing her cheeks with blush.

"Oh, is that what you're calling it?"

Catherine twisted around glaring. "What is that supposed to mean?"

"You're never around, you cancel anytime we have plans, your mom now calls me, and your other classes have been slipping. I haven't even heard you say one word about your dissertation, which is pretty much why we are here."

"I am not sure how you would know my classes are 'slipping'," Catherine said, gritting her teeth and making air quotations.

"Because I am in the same program as you are, and I know how much work I have to put into my classes, and I don't see you doing it."

"We are not the same, Anne," Catherine threw down the makeup brush, watched it bounce to the floor, and stormed out the door wearing a short black skirt and heels that were higher than comfortable.

She could feel Anne, her closest friend, watch her as she wobbled hastily out of the room. When she reached the front of the house, she slammed the front door shut and flinched at the sudden noise.

Perched at her desk, Catherine stared down at the same paragraph and read it several times. The underlying sexual tension that was developing made it increasingly more difficult for her to focus on her work.

Later that afternoon, as they were stacking extra books onto the shelf, she closed her eyes and took in a deep breath of his cologne, her chest heaving up as she exhaled. She heard the book drop next to her. Stunned, she opened her eyes as they both reached down for the book, their eyes locked.

Slowly focused only on each other, they stood in unison. His eyes undressed her as he looked at her with a lust and longing Catherine had never experienced. His lips parted, and she closed her eyes in anticipation. She trailed her fingers down her neck to her cleavage. She waited, but nothing happened. When she opened her eyes, he had brushed past her, put the book back on the shelf, and returned to his desk to grade papers.

Humiliated and ashamed, Catherine gave a slight cough as she smoothed her dress.

"Um, I'm going to call it a day if you don't need me." She stood in front of him, plucking her lip, her bag in hand.

"I don't think I have anything else for you." He marked one of the pages with his pen.

She drove home in tears and, throughout the weekend, replayed the scene several times in her mind. How did she misread what was between them? She paced back and forth, unable to let her feelings of rejection go. She needed resolution. She tried calling Dr. Hunter over the weekend, but when he answered, he was curt and quickly hung up the phone. Catherine attempted several more times in hopes of getting some sort of answer from him, but she received the same response if he even answered the phone at all.

Monday, as she entered the office, his eyes remained on the papers in front of him. "Catherine, I have a new TA coming in next week. Today is Monday, so you can choose to finish the week or you can have your things packed up today. That is entirely up to you." He looked up briefly, awaiting her decision. It had been the first time he had made eye contact with her since their encounter Friday.

She closed her eyes, stunned, willing herself not to show her tears. "I'll finish up now, Dr. Hunter, and come back tomorrow for my things."

"I can have them packed up for you, and Jessie will have them out by the door."

She was determined to leave with some dignity. "Dr. Hunter," Catherine stammered, plucking her lip, "um, I'd like to thank you for the opportunity."

She walked out. Shutting the door behind her and leaning against it, she squeezed her eyes together, determined not to create the same scene as Amber.

As her illusion became a reality, tears began to stream down her face, and she unglued herself from the door, "What a rookie mistake," she berated herself.

Catherine had not spoken to her mother in weeks, the relationship with her best friend was contentious, and she let all her other studies fall behind in hopes of sleeping with her professor. She walked down the hall for the last time, the solitary sound of her heels echoing through the empty hall.

At long last, Catherine and Anne sat together in the uncomfortable rented folding chairs, giddy with the excitement that came with reaching the culmination of their hard work. They were surrounded by classmates smiling, hugging, and giving out high fives to each other. Beaming, Catherine watched the procession of professors entering the stage when a sudden flush from her past came over her. Her mouth dropped as she saw Dr. Hunter enter the stage with the Dean of Students and the President of the University. She had not seen him since that fateful day in his office but was aware that he had received the position as acting Head of the Psychology Department. Of course, he would be here. She remained poker-faced, determined not to let this interfere with the importance of the day.

"You alright?" Anne asked leaning over, leaving her head on her friend's shoulder.

"I'm fine." She flashed a fake smile in her direction.

Before Anne could say anything further, the President took the microphone and introduced the Commencement Speaker.

"Good Lord, let's get on with it," Anne whispered, rolling her eyes. "Honestly, I think our parents will be the only ones who remember what this guy is even saying."

"You are probably right." Catherine stifled a laugh.

"Graham Ashton," the first name was finally called. Their collective heads perked up, and all eyes returned to the stage as each student waited for their name to be called.

Catherine stepped forward to the stage, eagerly climbing the steps to the approaching hands reaching out. The last hand slowly grasped hers too tightly and rolled her slightly into him. He was close enough to whisper. "Forgive me, Catherine. I should have never let you go." He released her hand and handed her the diploma.

2

KEVIN AND CATHERINE

Spewing up dirt and gravel, Catherine pushed the boxy BMW M3 down the twisted driveway toward the white wooden farmhouse. It had been six years since she and Anne left Charlottesville and joined Anne's father's thriving clinical practice in Northern Virginia. He had just retired and had been ecstatic to leave his practice in the capable hands of his daughter and her best friend. It had been a Godsend for both of them and allowed them to be further along financially in their profession than most at their age.

After a long day of seeing patients, Catherine was glad to be coming home. She was even happier when the front door opened, and the large yellow lab bounded down the brick walkway to meet her as the car door opened.

"Hey, Marlo!" She reached down and hugged his thick neck as he blocked her exit. "Come on, buddy, you gotta let me out," she said, slightly nudging him out of the way to get out of her seat.

Playfully, the dog followed her, bouncing up and down behind her as they headed toward the house.

Kevin, Catherine's husband, stood in the doorframe smiling. After three years, he never seemed tired of watching the dance of Marlo and Catherine.

"Hey, you," he said and leaned down to kiss her as she reached the top step. "How was your day?"

"Good, but long." She closed the door behind them, headed up the stairs, turned midway, and said, "I'm going to take a quick shower, change, and be back down."

"There'll be a glass of Merlot waiting for you," he called up after her.

"I look forward to it," she said, trotting up the stairs.

He had already finished half of his glass by the time she entered the dark paneled den dressed in comfortable Lou and

Grey loungewear. She plopped down in the blue leather wingback next to Kevin, crossed her legs, and reached for the wine on the table between them.

"You know me so well. Thank you." She took a sip and returned it to the table. Leaning her head back into the chair, she lifted her neck and chest toward the ceiling, closed her eyes, and let out a deep sigh. "Long day."

Kevin smiled and scrolled down his phone, giving Catherine some time to decompress.

Being a clinical psychologist, at times, could be a solitary existence. She lived with the trauma of others, absorbing some of it vicariously and involuntarily, with no one to talk to about it. Ironic.

After a few minutes, Catherine opened her eyes and reclaimed her wine.

"The book is on its way to the publisher," he said.

Her neck snapped toward him, and a smile stretched across her face. She leaned over and met his glass with a clink. "Kevin, you're kidding. That is fantastic news!"

"That is pretty much what Steve said, except his words were, 'It's about fucking time,' or something along those lines." Steve was his old college friend turned agent.

She uncrossed her legs, went to her husband, and threw her arms around his neck. "My niche," she said, playfully snuggling her head into the crook of his neck. "More wine?"

"Why not?" he snickered before asking, "What do you want to do for dinner?"

"I'm torn," she said. "Part of me would love to go out and celebrate, but I do have an early morning."

"Lombardi's pizza it is," he proclaimed, making the executive decision. "I'll call it in."

After they polished off the meat lover's pizza, they sat back in their chairs, sitting in silence, sufficiently stuffed.

"I am really proud of you." She looked over, breaking the silence.

"Well, you can be proud that I'm finished. Let's wait and see what happens next."

"I am assuming that now you will finally allow me to read it?"

Kevin had made a decent living with his technical writing, but he had always wanted to try his hand at writing a novel. "Everybody has one restaurant, one book, or one song in them," he would say, but once Catherine told him about the case study of James Martin, he found it so compelling that he wanted to fictionally complete the story. Kevin had been protective of his writing and had not shared any details with Catherine other than what the inspiration had been. He seemed afraid to disappoint her.

Writing was, like any other creative process, his own inner art. Ideas and words on a piece of paper in front of you were one thing. They could remain there and be as great as you imagined them to be. But once someone else reads them, the delusion could be gone. Some were never willing to take that risk of vulnerability.

"My character has been with me for a long time," he sighed. "But I have to admit I often wonder what happened to the real James Martin. It's just so hard to fathom that this kid grew up in an institution and never spoke for six years. It's also just as crazy that he escaped, and no one ever looked for or found him."

"I'm sure it was a lot easier to vanish in the 90s than it would be now with today's technology. Now, you would need some expertise to stay off the grid," she said, tapping her phone and smiling. "That or be like my mother, who still has a flip phone and has never touched a computer. I'm fairly sure she could be considered off the grid."

"True," he chuckled at the mention of Catherine's mother's aversion to anything electronic. "I think I would like to envision James Martin escaping from DeJarnette and living a quiet and productive life."

"Is that what you wrote in the book?" she asked, mimicking a fake yawn.

"I'll see if I can get you an advanced copy, and you can see for yourself. I did a lot of research on that institution. It was fascinating."

Kevin had been a history major in college and enjoyed digging deep into any subject he was covering.

"That place has got a twisted history," he said. "Do you know anything about it?"

"Not really, other than it is in Staunton, Virginia, and has not been operational since 1996," she said, pouring herself another glass of wine, before nestling back in her chair, smiling and awaiting a history lesson.

"It's creepy namesake. DeJarnette was one fucked up dude. He was a mix of Dr. Frankenstein and Gosnell. Everyone wants us to believe that the only dark time in American History was slavery, but what you don't hear about is the belief and practice of eugenics. Even though we don't call it that, it is still happening today."

He recapped his research on the practices and personality of Dr. DeJarnette.

"Human behavior has not changed," she added. "People in power truly believe that they know what is best for you. It's how we become dependent and stop thinking for ourselves. So yes, in the clinical historical way, it is fascinating, but in reality, it is chilling."

3
KILLER

Parking the car further down the street, he navigated his way in the dark to the familiar Cape Cod. Reaching the waist-high picket fence, he unlatched it, climbed the steps to the back door, and knocked quietly. Through the window in the door, he could see the young boy running, waving, and hurrying to open the door. As the boy opened the door, he looked up and smiled at him.

"Hey, Johnny," he said, knocking down on the brim of his baseball cap with his knuckles. "I hope you don't open the door to just anyone." Not waiting for a response, he walked through the kitchen, glaring at the stacks of dishes waiting to be washed. Clenching his fists and shaking his head, he looked down at Johnny and asked, "Have you had anything to eat?"

He was pleasantly surprised to see the boy nodding his head up and down. "Well, that at least is something."

A youthful, disheveled woman appeared in the kitchen doorway cuddling her infant. Her mussed hair, like the dishes had not had any exposure to soap or water.

"Ellisa." He leaned in to give her a quick peck on the cheek before withdrawing quickly, "Don't you ever put that thing down?"

"Never," she gave a slight giggle, unfazed by the slight. She returned her gaze to the baby in her arms.

He gave a slight cough, reacquiring her attention.

"Oh, where are my manners?" she said. "Come in and have a seat." She pointed her head in the direction of the scantly decorated living room.

Ellisa made a beeline to the wooden rocking chair, and he took a seat on one of the two other ladder-back chairs. He settled on the edge of the seat, attempting to focus on Ellisa as she launched into her usual diatribe of the difficulties of being a single mother.

"The bastard just left, walked out after the baby was born." Her voice began rising with each sentence.

He sat silent, deviating his attention only when Johnny ran into the room with a baseball bat. "Look, look what I got." Proudly showing it off to his newly arrived companion.

"That looks like a good one…" he remarked, grateful for the interruption.

His mother turned and gave Johnny a look that collapsed his momentary jubilance.

He seethed as he imagined how many times Johnny had had to endure that withering look. Glancing around the room, he saw no visible signs that an older child also occupied the house.

Through a tightened jaw, he turned to the older boy and asked, "How about you show me some of those baseball trophies I heard about?" He looked over at Ellisa. "Do you mind? It will only be a minute." He got up, not waiting for permission.

She shook her matted hair with pursed lips, resentful of any time not focused on her.

He followed Johnny down the hall into the room of a typical boy's room, which consisted of covered walls of baseball pictures, trophies, and team pictures adorning the wooden dresser.

"You sure do like baseball." The visitor sat on the end of the bed.

"Yeah, and I'm pretty good at it, too," he said, enthusiastically pulling down one of the trophies and handing over one of his prized possessions, "See," he said, plunking himself down and dangling his feet off the bed.

He looked down directly into Johnny's eyes. "This is great." He took the trophy, turning it over several times in his hands. "You know I never got to play baseball when I was young."

Enjoying the attention, Johnny maintained his eye contact. "Why not?" he asked with childlike confusion before carefully taking his trophy back.

"It's a very long story." With a foreboding smile, he leaned over to Johnny and, with one accelerated movement, reached over to the small, trusting figure and snapped his neck. His small body immediately fell back on the red and blue baseball comforter.

He looked down at the sudden lifeless body, stroking his hair. "It was fine when it was just the three of you…" his voice trailed off. He was filled with a mixture of remorse and rage. Adrenaline pumping through him, he looked around the room and grabbed the baseball bat Johnny had put back in the corner. He smacked it hard into the palm of his hand, advancing quickly back into the living room. Her back was to him, rocking back and forth. She did not hear him coming.

He could not contain his anger. "You couldn't leave well enough alone, could you?" He swung the bat.

She collapsed and dropped her baby to the floor. The baby began to cry. Enraged by the wailing, he fled to the back door to retrieve the gas can he had brought with him. He doused the curtains with the accelerant, lit a match, and ignited the room in flames. *Whoosh*. Tossing the gas can into the fire, he left the way he came in, not looking back.

4
KEVIN

Elevated on a temporary wooden stage, Kevin positioned himself in front of the generous crowd gathered for his first book signing. Anne, the cheerful proprietor, stood next to him, laying witness to her hard work finally coming to fruition. She had given up her lucrative counseling practice with Catherine to pursue her dream of opening a bookstore. Fresh Ideas was bustling with a sense of community where people browsed the extensive inventory, socialized with a glass of wine, or simply relaxed.

"Welcome to Fresh Ideas," she said loudly, breaking up the idle chatter, stretching her arms wide, graciously greeting her guests. "I am delighted." She paused for effect before turning toward Kevin. "No," she said correcting herself. "I am ecstatic, to introduce my good friend and the soon-to-be best-selling author Kevin Richards."

"*Acceleration,*" he began after the applause quietened down, "is loosely based on a true story of an eleven-year-old boy who was institutionalized for allegedly killing his family. The whole time my character, Ethan, is at DeJarnette, he never speaks. He escaped and continued his killing spree until he was eventually caught. Kevin read a few designated parts of his book to draw their attention.

"There it is. That is the *Readers Digest* version of the book." Some in the audience chuckled, while others looked confused at the reference.

"In writing this book, I became acutely aware of a growing portion of our population that is underserved-people with mental illness." He looked out at the audience and saw the majority nodding in agreement. He continued, "My book involves both historical and fictional aspects as my character travels through and deals with his mental illness. I'm going to give you all a brief background of two facilities that were historically pivotal in Virginia's mental health progress. In 1828, the Western Lunatic Asylum was constructed in Staunton, Virginia. The building was built by Thomas Jefferson's protégé, Thomas Blackburn." He paused for a sip of water. "A quick side note. This building is now recast into the majestic Blackburn Inn. It is structurally a beautiful building, maybe even more so to us Virginians. It is fabulous and well worth the visit." He smiled.

"Down the road, a second Hospital was built in 1932 and was named the DeJarnette State Sanitarium after the psychiatrist who ruled over it for forty years. The hospital has a dark past. One rooted in horrific psychiatric experiments and eugenics. Dr. DeJarnette would conduct experiments using blood transfusions between patients on the opposite end of the psychiatric spectrum as well as lobotomies. These were just some of the atrocities that took place here. In total, there were over 60,000 sterilizations in America, and 8,000 of them were in Virginia. Why? Because those who make decisions deem certain people "unfit" because of their life choices, ethnic background, and mental illnesses. DeJarnett's strong belief in eugenics, after all these years, is still adopted nationwide, and even globally. It may be carried out in different ways, under different names, but it seems that disposing of the people we don't agree with or are inconvenienced by has a long history of being funded by the rich and powerful worldwide."

There were several gasps of disbelief from the audience.

Kevin held up his hand. "Stay with me."

"In 1975, One Flew Over a Cuckoo's Nest was unleashed on the big screen," he continued. "Hollywood pushed out a horrific portrayal of American mental institutions, and I don't believe that the system has ever recovered from it. The decrease in mental institutions has been devastating. Institutions are and were a reality and necessary. DeJarnette was certainly in line with the depiction in the movie, and while it is a good thing to shine the light on failing institutions, not all were bad. However, the uninformed public received its knowledge from the silver screen and believed all these places were cages for people that were unnecessarily placed in them. It played on their emotions, and the pendulum began to shift toward deinstitutionalization.

Civil Rights leaders, politicians, and the media latched on and did what they do best, making the problem worse in trying to solve it. The final blow came in 1987 with the stock market crash. The mental institutions were one of the hardest hit."

Kevin took another sip of water and drew a circle in the air. "Now, bringing this back full circle, one could wonder if the character in my book would have received better treatment if the funding had been there. More facilities for mental illness are vital, and dumping people on the streets or in prisons is inhumane and does not work. We don't need to reinvent the wheel. We just need to fund it and improve on past mistakes. I hope that in time, the pendulum will fall somewhere in the middle."

He extended his arm to the right and then to the left before bringing it back to the center and bowing.

"Thank you for your time," he said over the clapping audience.

He gave Catherine a quick hug before getting behind the table and took a seat in the chair set up for him. There were mounds of books at one end and a payment system set up at the other. As the line formed, Anne excused herself from Catherine and went to the end to facilitate the checkout.

Reaching down into the breast pocket of his blazer, Kevin plucked the Mont Blanc fountain pen in preparation. The stylish pen fit comfortably between his fingers as he graciously began to sign his book. Nodding, smiling, and writing, he wasn't sure if his face would freeze or his hand would cramp, but either way, he was grateful for all the support.

"Excuse me?" a strained voice questioned. Kevin put down his pen, looking up at the rumpled figure in front of him.

"Excuse me, I said," the man repeated louder than necessary. "Your book. It reminds me of them murders in Staunton a few weeks back."

Kevin scanned the placid crowd, tightened his gaze on the stranger, and asked, "I'm sorry. I have no idea what you are talking about. What murders?"

The stranger changed tactics, bending over quietly and asserted, "It's mighty funny how just before your book comes out, there are murders just like these in my city." He took the book in his hand and threw it at Kevin.

"I'm sorry," Anne said, giving a forced smile, "but we need to keep this line moving."

"I'm going."

Rattled, Kevin looked at the line, flashed a smile, and said, "Next," but he struggled to redirect his attention to the remaining supporters awaiting his John Hancock.

After the last person left, Anne locked the door, dimmed the lights, and rotated four chairs to fit around a farmhouse coffee table. "Y'all have a seat. Catherine, will you help me?" They ambled back to the temporary bar draped in a white tablecloth and retrieved four wine glasses and two full, opened bottles of wine.

"Here we go," Anne said, placing the bottles down. "I give you choices."

"Anne, this is a great place you have," Steve said, admiring the bookstore as he poured himself a glass of Cabernet and nestled back. "And these chairs are very nice."

"What good are books if there's not a comfortable chair?"

"And wine," Catherine added leaning over, pouring herself a glass of Merlot.

Once they all had full glasses, Anne hailed while raising her glass, "A toast. To a successful day for all and continued success, Kevin, on your tour."

There was a clinking of glasses, and Kevin stood up. Bowing, he tried his best Elvis impersonation and said, "Thank you. Thank you very much."

"Good crowd." Anne smiled wistfully and leaned back in her chair.

"Speaking of crowd," Steve said out loud, "What was up with that one dude?"

"I don't know. It was weird." Kevin recalled the conversation. "The guy said something about some murders that had happened a couple of weeks ago in Staunton and then said that they were like the ones in my book."

Steve reached into his pocket and pulled out his phone. "Well, let's look it up on the information highway." After scrolling a bit, he said, "Here it is, June 23. A house fire in Staunton, Virginia, took the lives of three victims. The medical examiner was able to make an eventual identification from the badly charred remains of the mother and her two children. Ellisa Wilson, thirty-five, and her son Johnny, eleven, and infant child were killed before the fire was set. No other details were given, and at this point, there are no known suspects. The police have ruled this a murder and the fire arson and ask for any help from the public." He put his phone down and turned to Kevin. "Dude, that is fucked up."

"Yeah, which part? The fact someone is using my book to commit murder, or we just might have had the murderer here taunting me?"

"When you put it like that, then both." He picked up his glass and rested the rim on his lips, deep in thought.

"I know that look," Kevin turned to Steve. "What are you thinking?"

"Actually, this could easily be turned and could be used as good publicity…"

"Steve, that is a horrible thing to think! Using a tragedy to promote a book," Catherine hissed. "I know you're an ass, but you just took it to a new level."

"Don't shoot the messenger, Catherine!" He raised his hands in defense. "Look, I know it's awful. I'm just saying that we could use this to our advantage as well. Never let a crisis or a tragedy go to waste."

"That is a horrible thought," Anne interjected.

"This whole thing opens up the possibility of James Martin being out there," Catherine whispered.

"What? No way that is possible. The guy was never heard from again," Steve proclaimed while leaning back in the chair. "Not possible, Catherine."

"As much as I don't like to agree with Steve," Anne said, winking in Steve's direction, "but—why would after all these years he just appear out of nowhere? Even though the book wasn't out on the shelves per se, Steve has done a hell of a job getting this book hyped."

"That I have." He leaned over and grabbed his wine glass.

"I suppose this could be just some depraved copycat using this as an opportunity to become famous himself," Catherine mused.

"Or maybe just some horrible coincidence." Kevin hoped out loud.

5
KILLER

"Fin de siècle," he said out loud. He sipped scotch with the open laptop in front of him. In the past, he had the benefit of a prior relationship with his victims, but the risk of getting caught was beginning to outweigh the ease of this arrangement. Realistically, he knew it was time for a new chapter, and it required a whole new level of research. Looking at the paper and drawing upon his knowledge of the area, he pulled up Google Maps while juxtaposing it with his potential list of targets. Skillfully, he zoomed in and out of various neighborhoods while finding the landscapes that adapted to his objective. He needed a denser brush with larger lots that would limit prying eyes.

Finishing the third scotch, he ultimately decided on two older, more established neighborhoods. Not knowing the inhabitants of the neighborhood would require an evolution in his process; surveillance would now be remote. Closing his eyes, he played out several new scenarios in his head. He had to amend the original blueprint of when he knew his victims.

He opened his eyes when a fresh idea came to him and sprang into action. He got out of his chair and set about to gather everything he would need for his kill kit. It would roughly be the same items, with just a few more additions. Rummaging through the downstairs closet, he snagged an empty khaki canvas duffel bag and threw it into the hallway. He moved several items on the shelves until he found binoculars, a baseball hat, and gloves. He shoved the items into the duffel bag, grabbed a baseball bat, and took them to the garage, where he continued to stuff the bag with a filled water bottle. Taking a second bottle, he dumped out the contents in the sink and took a few granola bars and anything else needed for a long wait. Opening the driver's side of his black Toyota Corolla, he checked the glove compartment for matches. Check. Then, he modified the lights so they wouldn't turn on when he opened the door or trunk. Lastly, he snagged one of the red gas cans that were lined up against the wall, placed it in the trunk, and tossed the baseball bat and duffel bag in the front seat. Satisfied, he closed the door and went upstairs to bed.

The alarm did not need to go off; he was wide awake and determined. He took a shower, slipped on black jeans, a black t-shirt, and a dark blue plaid flannel shirt, and then headed straight to the garage. Fully stocked, he plugged the first address into the GPS, opened the garage door, and began driving in the dark to the more rural part of Fairfax County. Arriving at his destination, he parked the black Corolla, careful not to park under large trees or between houses, which he had read could draw more attention to the stationary vehicle. Being out in the open was the best form of concealment. Having a good visual of the large colonial brick house with the circular driveway, he settled in as the sun peaked over the rooftops. He witnessed the sudden movements of the birds flying and squirrels scurrying away as doors opened and closed. The ebb and flow of the morning suburbs caught him slightly off guard, and he slid down in the car seat, reaching into the bag pulled out a baseball cap and a sheet of paper. He held the scrap paper in front of his face and looked over it slightly while pretending to stare at it as the neighbors came out of their houses.

He soon found he had nothing to worry about. Their heads were bent down, immersed in their phones until they reached their car, and by then, their concentration shifted to the rest of their day and not the unwanted car hiding in plain sight.

Once the surrounding streets were quiet, he placed his full attention back onto the house, quickly noting that the layout was slightly different. Some of the overgrown shrubbery pictured on the map was gone. Undiscouraged, he pressed forward. He had plenty of time to find a new way of gaining entry with the least visibility. He sat peacefully observing the house for more than half the day. Entertained by brainstorming several different scenarios in his mind, he eventually found himself lulled into complacency.

Abruptly, he was brought out of his trance by the sound of screeching tires. A blue convertible Mazda had infiltrated his target. He pivoted forward in his seat for a closer look at the intrusion. A man, much too tall to have been comfortable in the car, had emerged from the driver's seat and was met by a bounding figure with swinging hair racing toward him. She seemed to have appeared out of nowhere. Standing on her tiptoes, she gave the man a peck on the cheek and, in teenage mastery, adroitly elevated the keys from his possession. In what seemed like one swift movement, she was in the driver's seat, zooming out of the driveway and gunning past him. The man stood in the driveway smiling as he watched the car disappear. His happiness was fleeting, for moments later, the voice of an exasperated woman called him inside the house. The man walked up the stairs, wandered inside the house, and shut the door behind him, unaware that his presence had saved his family.

Stunned, wide-eyed, and clenching his teeth, he smacked his fist hard onto the seat next to him over and over, each thwack harder and harder. Something had gone wrong. There was supposed to be a single mother and younger children. How could his information have been so far off? Was it too old? The questions began to spiral, and he could feel himself getting out of control.

Focus, he told himself. He took a deep breath in and out. *Focus.*

"The best-laid plans..." he said, talking himself down. He sat for several minutes in an attempt to regain his composure. Once calm, he placed the second address into his GPS. The map popped up on the screen, and he smiled when the next destination was not far away. Starting the car, he left the neighborhood and the fortunate occupants of the colonial in the rearview mirror.

Acknowledging that surveillance was vital, he was still embittered with this whole brand-new process. Reaching the second site, he examined the area, deciding to park on the corner of the cul-de-sac, catty-corner to the off-white Cape Cod. Within minutes of turning the engine off, a yellow Fairfax County school bus pulled up behind him and stopped. Taken aback, he promptly reached back, pulled out the bat from the backseat, and began coming up with a ruse for his presence in the neighborhood. Two boys with backpacks emerged from the bus deep in conversation, seemingly unaware of the intruder. They walked down the cul-de-sac, dragging their backpacks behind them. Once they reached their respective front doors, they turned to give the other an exaggerated wave goodbye before they went inside.

His mood elevated; this day was not a complete loss. He decided to stay and find the neighborhood pattern for nighttime by watching when and which lights went on and off. People were creatures of habit, especially where children were concerned. They tended to stick to tighter schedules. At eight-thirty, the light went out in the upstairs room. He looked across the street at the friend's house. One of the upstairs lights went dark. No doubt the boys compared schedules. He continued to wait long past what was needed, making certain there were no surprises. At two a.m., he turned the car on and left the sleeping neighborhood in peace for one more night.

Returning before the sun was up, he parked in the same spot as the night before. He leaned the seat back until he could comfortably keep his eyes focused on the house. Once the sun cleared the last rooftop, the doors opened, and the boys flew out of their houses. They darted across the street toward each other, unaware of any danger, and ran up the street with their oversized backpacks swaying from side to side. When they stopped at the corner, they were feet from his car.

He again devised the unneeded story, but the boys busied their time searching for things to throw, unaware of anything but their own existence. He refocused on the house. The door was still ajar from the boy leaving when suddenly a woman emerged and began scanning the street, eventually resting her eyes on the boys.

She smiled, went back inside, and materialized within seconds with a baby stroller and an elderly yellow Labrador tethered to her wrist. Moving slowly to keep up with the toddling dog, she barely reached the sidewalk when the bus appeared and the doors opened. One boy leaped onto the bus while the other boy paused, gave a big smile, and waved to his mother. He waited until she waved back before he boarded the bus for what would be his last day of school.

The man held his breath and waited to see what path the woman would take. She was still moving slowly in his direction. He threw the baseball bat in the back seat and came up with another explanation for his presence, knowing the one that would work on boys would not work on a mother. His pulse quickened as she crept toward the car. He leaned down towards the floorboards as if looking for a lost item, timing her steps in his mind with his search. When he poked his head up, he was relieved that she had turned back toward her house. Thank goodness for old dogs, he thought.

In the afternoon, the school bus re-appeared and dropped off the two friends, who, to the man's relief, repeated their exact same movements from yesterday.

Groundhog Day in the suburbs was quickly going to change.

He waited and watched.

At eight-thirty, the light he was focused on turned off. By ten o'clock, the surrounding doors opened and closed, and the lights began flickering off one by one as they had the night before.

The only light that remained on was in the Cape Cod. Nighttime, for new mothers, was sometimes the only time for peace and quiet.

He waited. The single light remained on. By twelve-thirty, he decided it was time. He did not see any lights on in the surrounding houses, just the one faint light of his target. Opening the trunk, he pulled out the gas can and placed it next to the duffle bag on the passenger seat. Scrounging through the side pockets of the duffel bag, he pulled out a pair of blue latex gloves.

Opening up the glove box to retrieve the matches, he swore under his breath as the light went on. He forgot about that light. He would have to attend to that when he got home. He wedged the matches down into his front pocket, put the car in neutral with the lights off, and coasted closer to the house. Reaching into the backseat, he grabbed the bat and clutched it in anticipation. Before beginning the walk to the back door, he snagged the bag and gas can.

Glaring through the top of the glass, the dimmed light allowed him to be able to see into the long, narrow room. He put down the can and bag. Holding the bat, he decided to try his luck on the door. He was able to fully turn it. Slowly bringing the door back towards him, he was startled by the older dog's unexpected presence. Its ears perked up. The animal stalked into the room towards the sound of the opening door. The man opened the door wide and brought the bat over his head in anticipation of any trouble, but once the door opened, the dog found new energy. It trotted right past him and down the stairs. The man snuck in with only the bat and gingerly shut the door behind him in case the dog returned. Once inside, he saw a plush green sofa, a blanket, and magazines piled high next to it. A white wicker bassinet was almost within reaching distance. He walked in further, bat poised, as he heard a woman's voice approaching, "Molly?" the woman called out. He stood waiting.

"Molly?" she called again. "Where are…" she walked from the kitchen straight into the bat. She dropped immediately and blood began pooling around her. He held onto the bat and peeked into the bassinet. It held the sleeping infant. He picked up his stride, careful not to step in the gushing blood, and made his way up the stairs into the room he had been watching from the street. The dim nightlight illuminated the room just enough for him to see the smaller figure snuggled comfortably under the multicolored car comforter. He placed the bat in the corner. The dark shades were drawn, and several pictures of boyish memories and dreams hung on the wall. Looking around the room, his eyes settled on a puzzle that spelled his name; David. He moved toward the unsuspecting sleeping child. Bending down over him with ninja reflexes, one swift movement was all it took to snap his neck.

It was done. The man sat next to the body, pulled the glove off his right hand, and brushed the boy's hair with his fingers.

"I am so sorry she did this to you, David. I understand." He kept brushing. "I know what it's like. It's better this way."

He sat for several minutes as the rage began to fill in him. Placing the glove back on, he hurried down the stairs to finish what had to be done.

He opened the door to retrieve the gas can, half expecting to see Molly. The dog had not returned. He carried the can into the dining room, doused the curtains, and turned his attention back toward the kitchen. There were piles of clothes next to the washing machine. Angrily, he thrust an armful in the direction of the woman's body. The fabric began to soak up the surrounding blood. He picked up the can and, in jerking motions, spilled the little remaining on the floor as he walked to the door. Returning to the dining room, he got as close to the curtains as he could and threw a match. *Whoosh.* Immediately, the flames shot up the walls. The room was filled with orange and red bursts of color as it consumed the room. He darted to the frame of the outside door, staying as close as possible to watch his living masterpiece. Soon, the scorching heat radiated through his body and began to sear his skin. He picked up the duffel bag and tossed it as an offering to the hungry flames.

Reluctantly, he retreated down the stairs and took a deep breath from the parching smoke. With each step, he continued to feel the warmth on his back as the fire attempted to follow its creator. He could also hear the crying from the basket, his ears filled with the screams of an animal meeting its death.

Ducking between bushes to keep out of sight, he made it undetected to his car. He started the car and stopped it at the corner of the cul-de-sac. He got out, turned to face the blaze, leaned back against the car, and watched as the house began to take on a life of its own. He figured he had a little more time. Night generated a slower response time. It took people long enough during the day: a lot weren't home, and if they were, it took time to fully process what was happening.

He had time. He waited and watched his creation until he heard the distant sound of a siren mixed with the popping sounds of the windows being blown out. Flames escaped, shooting out to get higher. He watched. The flames were his. Dancing for him. Satisfied, they would continue, he started the car and headed in the opposite direction of the first fire trucks.

6
DETECTIVE MCALLISTER

As the sounds of three distinct sirens blared, the red and blue lights filled up the starless sky, assailing the previously quiet neighborhood. The responding lights paled in comparison to the force of the blaze. Doors began to fly open. Families poured out of their homes to find the source of the intrusion. Their eyes fixed on the jetting flames. Their movements instinctively froze as the inferno before them forever destroyed their sense of security. The intensity of the heat burned so hot they could feel it from across the street. Their nostrils were overwhelmed by the smell of smoke and burning debris, and they would always remember that smell.

The residents of the street stood helpless. The first responders acted with choreographed efficiency. The police set up a physical barrier between them. None of them knew why the house was on fire.

The last police cruiser pulled up and parked a safe distance away from the frenzy. It stopped, and both doors simultaneously opened. The passenger leaned back into the car and retried a video camera. He left his door open and walked to meet the driver behind the car. He leaned down to listen to her as she pointed toward the gathered crowd. He nodded, pressed the button, and began to film, panning left to right. Detective Mattei McAllister stood beside him, hands on her hips and her eyes following the camera. After several sweeps, she gave him further instructions, went over to the open door, and pulled out a notebook. Flipping the pages, the detective walked over to the uniformed officers who had set up the temporary obstruction. She displayed her credentials, slipped under the tape, and made a beeline toward the woman in a pink fuzzy robe. Her hair had been pulled back in a quick ponytail, and she was standing with neighbors in front of the house, directly across the street from the fire.

"Is this your house?" the detective asked, pointing behind her. The woman nodded, tightening her robe.

"I'm Detective—" she was cut short by the looming figure in blue hospital scrubs, who stepped protectively in front of the woman.

"I'm Detective McAllister, from Fairfax," she repeated, not taking offense to the hasty encroachment. She understood traumatic events compelled people to be even more protective of their loved ones. She looked down at her book, then back up at him. "Mr. Robinson, you called this in, sir?" she asked.

"I did." His body language softened, looking at her in hopes of an answer.

"I just have a few questions," she said.

"OK," he said, his hopes of an explanation dashed.

"I see here that you made the call at one fifteen this morning. What alerted you?"

"We had the windows open, fall weather, you know. Supposed to be good sleeping weather." He gave a sarcastic chuckle and looked across the street. "I'm a light sleeper," he continued, "so when I smelled smoke, I got up to find out where it was coming from. When I figured it wasn't coming from anywhere inside the house, I looked outside and saw the fire."

"Is there anything else?" she paused her writing to look up at him. "Anything at all?"

"You mean anything else besides my neighbor's house catching on fire? No, I would say that's about it."

She continued to look at him until he tightened his lips, shook his head, and looked around at his exposed neighbors in their pajamas on their front lawn.

"I'm sorry…" his attention suddenly turned to his front door opening as a young boy in red pajamas ran headlong into his mother's waist. She stumbled by the force and bent down to the level of the frantic child. His hair tussled from sleep, his eyes bulging from fear.

"Mommy," he howled, pointing to the fire. "That's David's house! Where's David?"

Both parents gaze directed toward Detective McAllister, hoping for the best but knowing the reality. She returned their answer with her eyes closed slightly and shook her head as she mouthed "no" through pursed lips.

Looking to the sky for answers, tears began flowing down the face of the young boy's mother. His father picked up his terrified son.

"They were friends?" Detective McAllister placed her hand on the thick, fuzzy bathrobe as it was retreating.

"The best, walked to the bus every morning for years." The mother answered through her tears.

The detective reached into her back pocket and handed the woman two business cards. "This is my card, and the second card is of a psychologist who can help."

"Thank you. If there is nothing else." Wiping her eyes with the sleeve of her robe, she turned and walked back into the house with her family.

She watched them as they closed the door and knew they would be forced to have a conversation about the painful realities of life too soon for a young child to hear.

After speaking with a few more neighbors, she crossed the street to her colleague, who was watching the now smoldering remains of 157 Aspen Way.

"Have you heard anything else?" she asked.

"Nope," he replied.

"Why is that the only answer people seem to be able to give, Jim?" she put her notebook away.

The firefighters were beginning to come out of the house, stripping themselves of their Bunker Gear while some began to roll up the hoses, the choreographed dance of first responders in reverse. She patted Jim on the arm and motioned him to follow her. The pungent smell of watery soot meant her job was just beginning.

"Anyone seen Carlos?" She asked loudly to anyone who would listen.

Stepping out from the passenger side of the fire truck, the Fairfax Fire Chief emerged. "Somebody called me?"

"Carlos," she said, grateful to have someone she could count on to cut through any inner disciplinary BS. He always allowed her on the scene as soon as possible.

"M," he said, using the nickname he had for her.

"Anything you can tell me before we go in?" she looked over at the remaining officers who were securing the area with distinguishing yellow tape. The next group of forensics was standing behind it with their equipment waiting to be cleared.

"It looks pretty clear cut-murder and arson to cover it up. You ready?"

"Yep," she waved her hand, and the forensic team dipped under the tape and followed her inside into the crime scene.

They walked through the opening of what was left of the front door. "We found three bodies," he said, pointing two fingers toward the kitchen, "and one upstairs. By the pattern, we were able to tell an accelerant was used. The arson investigator may be able to tell us more. But it looks pretty cut and dry. Usually, people try to hide the fact that the fire was arson, but this SOB left the gas can."

The forensic team nodded and dispersed. Finding the clearest spot possible, they opened their numerous apparatuses and began getting to work.

The fire had stripped the walls and beams and now all that was showing through were pillars of black coal. The smell was still pungent, even though puddles of the water that was used to put out the fire could be found throughout the house. Amongst the black and gray canvas, several bits of color poked through from the debris, revealing the life and vitality that existed before the destruction.

"He didn't use the accelerant in the upstairs, which is why it is slightly more intact. But see…" Carlos paused, shaking his head. He pointed to one of the melted bits of color. "There it is."

"Pretty in your face," the detective said as she stooped to examine the remains of the gas can. Once finished, she looked up at Carlos. "Nice of this asshole to do some of our work for us."

Feeling the vibration in her back pocket, Detective McAllister reached for the phone.

"The ME is on his way," she said after reviewing the message.

The following day, Detective McAllister leaned against the corner wall of the morgue and scanned the sterile, utilitarian space. Her mother's favorite saying, 'a place for everything and everything in its place', certainly applied here. Mattei crossed her arms, hugging herself. She was not dressed warmly enough for the climate-controlled room. It was a balance. The temperature needed to be cool enough to help preserve the dead while allowing the living to work comfortably. In the end, it did not matter how cold the room was once Dr. Jack Lynch began cutting into the body.

The stench of decomposition saturated the area, and the emanation of the putrid flesh hit her nose and began trickling down to her throat. She was not unfamiliar with the odor, and there was an excellent state-of-the-art ventilation system, but each time she got her first whiff of a dead body, she was taken aback by the initial assault to her senses. She knew it was the older child he was working on because the fire had not reached its destruction to the second floor, and his body had not been charred like that of his mother and baby brother. She waited out the few minutes it took to get used to the smell, blowing out her nose several times. Dr. Lynch did not allow vapor rub in his room because he believed that it could mask the smells that could be potentially important in the investigation of a crime.

She had questioned his reasoning on her first visit and been told, "There was a case that the family was convinced the husband had died from a heart attack. He was in his late sixties, overweight, with a history of high blood pressure. It seemed cut and dry. But there was something about the wife's affect that bugged the police, and so I conducted the autopsy. Initially, I went along, thinking it was a waste of time, until I smelled a trace scent of almond, which made me take a second look at his fingernails. He had Mee's lines and white bands on the nails. Those two were enough to rule his death a murder. His wife had indeed poisoned him. My point is that I have to smell everything."

He was fastidious, and Detective McAllister felt fortunate to have him as the ME she worked with. A good ME can help guide the investigation in the right direction and is a good ally to have.

Although Dr. Lynch encouraged law enforcement to attend the autopsies, he did not encourage them to invade his space while he was working. The rule was, he would make time afterward. But in some cases, her attending the autopsies process was more beneficial to the investigation, and this was turning into just that sort of case.

She remained, leaning against the chilled wall while listening to the familiar sounds of the morgue; an occasional whirling saw, click of a camera, and the dulcet voice of Dr. Lynch as he dictated his findings into a recorder. The young, gowned assistant, or diener, methodically pulled the crisp white sheet up over the last form of the day. Dr. Lynch went to the corner of the room, took off his gloves, and began finalizing the day's work on the mounted computer. As the assistant began rolling the body out the door behind him, he turned to her and thanked her for the long day's work. Completing the paperwork, he pulled off the blue-issued cap, mask, gown, and booties and shoved them into the designated bin.

He was now down to his dark blue scrubs. The surgical cap had left his hair pressed in the imprint of the hours he had completed. Shutting the computer, he picked up his well-worn brown leather briefcase and walked toward the door, finally stopping in front of Detective McAllister.

"We did all three, so if you give me a minute to shower and change, I will meet you in my office."

Dr. Lynch's office was at the end of the hall, in a large, spacious corner room. She stopped at the familiar nameplate and opened the unlocked door. The sun from the west-facing window poured out into the hall. The warmth of the doctor's office was the antithesis of his other workspace. The Oriental rugs, along with the Chippendale desk, wooden bookshelves, and dark brown leather wing-back chairs, replaced the state-issued furniture and disguised the institutional flooring.

Diplomas from West Virginia University, MCV, and certificates of achievements, as well as various sailing pictures with his family, adorned the umber walls building upon the bonhomie of the room. Dr. Lynch was adamant in his desire to have those who entered feel as comforted as possible under such tragic circumstances.

Taking a seat, she pulled out her phone, grimacing at the numerous unanswered notifications. Scrolling down, she answered the essential texts and emails, and then put the phone on the desk in front of her. The framed pictures of his children peeked through the scattered piles of papers. Over the years, the pictures of his boys had doubled in numbers, replacing any pictures of his wife after the divorce. Mattei picked up a picture of his son Kyle on his sailboat.

"That's an old one," she heard his voice say behind her.

"Good looking kid, beautiful scenery too," she said, putting the picture back and looking up as Dr. Lynch entered the room.

He picked it up and stared into the picture. "Indeed. Those were some wonderful memories; we used to take trips all over the world. That was taken in either Ireland or Scotland."

He was dressed in khaki pants, a white buttoned-down shirt, and a lab coat with his name embroidered in blue lettering on the right pocket. The fabric had frayed on the top corner from the weight of the items bulging out.

"How are you doing, Pockets?" she smiled, referring to his nickname.

"Fine, fine." He took a seat behind his desk and pulled out his laptop from his old tattered Berluti briefcase.

"One of these days, we are going to chip in and buy you a new briefcase," she said.

"Everyone's a critic." He smiled, his eyes wistful. "I guess there's a part of me that just likes holding onto a small part of my past," he said, referring to the overpriced briefcase his wife bought him when he first became the ME.

"I understand." Mattei remembered how difficult the unwanted divorce had been on him.

"Thank you for waiting." Dr. Lynch opened the laptop, and Mattei waited to hear the familiar sound of the MacBook Pro turning on.

"No problem. I got some stuff done," she said, patting her phone.

"The traveling office," he replied while looking at the screen. "I still haven't decided if it's a good thing or not."

"True. Convenience can get very demanding and inconvenient."

"Indeed. OK, let's get to it. It's been a long day."

"I appreciate you getting all three done today. You went above and beyond."

"I have a good team. I also wanted to keep this fresh in my mind after visiting the scene."

"Yes, and thank you for that too."

"OK," he said, his eyes fixed on the screen. "We did a PMCT on her and the baby, which is how we were able to give her mother the ability to identify her daughter."

"PMCT is a scan?"

"Correct, basically a CT scan for dead people. It is a post-mortem computed tomography. Charred bodies add on extra layers of a challenge, and this gives us a pictorial essay if you will."

"As you know, we have a positive ID of the family from the victim's mother. That poor woman lost her only child and two grandchildren."

"Right, she had to identify the bodies because her son-in-law was killed in Afghanistan a year ago."

"Isn't that why we do this?" He paused and looked over at the inscription from Voltaire hanging on the wall, '*To the living we owe respect, but to the dead we owe the truth.*'

She nodded as she pulled out her pen and notebook. She glanced down at the words she'd written on the pages before speaking again. "Let's start with the mother. Mary Tabor, age thirty-two. I have here that blunt force trauma was the preliminary cause of death finding?"

"Indeed, but the term blunt force trauma can sometimes be an easy out, and this is again where the PMCT came in handy. I have seen many trauma wounds misinterpreted, especially in the cases involving fire. At ground zero, where she was found, the skull's content can boil and explode like an unattended egg in boiling water." He touched his fingertips together, then pulled them apart in an exaggerated motion.

"Got it," she mouthed, wincing at the image, and went back to writing.

"The blow fractured the left side of her skull and crushed her spinal cord."

"That is a lot of force."

"And since the wound was toward the front of the head, it appears that she walked right into it."

"So, he was standing in wait." She pulled both hands in a fist across her body and swung to the other side.

"Kind of like that."

"We didn't get anything that could have caused that near the body.

"Just my guess, but perhaps a baseball bat or a golf club."

"A baseball bat." She repeated the words, wrote them down, and underscored them.

"You with me?"

"I was just remembering David's room, and I am one hundred percent certain that there was a baseball bat in there," she snapped her fingers. "Right. In fact, when we saw the remnants of baseball memorabilia, we just figured that it was his bat that he kept in his room,"

"My one son played baseball for years, and his bat was never up in his room. It was usually in the car or garage, so maybe this was a weapon of convenience?"

"I doubt it," she said. "This guy looks too well organized. I don't think he would leave things to chance. He brought his gas can, and I will bet you that he brought his own bat as well, staging it in the boy's room. This piece of shit seems to want to show us how helpful he is. Fucker."

"It is something to think about." Dr. Lynch paused, waiting for her to continue. When she didn't, he shifted his attention back to his findings.

"All right, then let's continue on," he said. "David Tabor, age nine. I didn't find carbon monoxide in his blood or damage to the trachea from heat or smoke, so it became clear that he was dead before the fire."

"I thought for certain it would have been smoke inhalation."

"Initially, I did too, but like I said, when there was no CO in his blood, we had to dig further."

"And?"

"The COD is a cervical fracture."

"So the guy…"

"Snapped his neck," he completed her sentence.

"Like a fucking ninja?"

"Indeed, that is the movie version, but it is more difficult in real life."

"But you said that was the COD."

"I said more difficult, not impossible, especially if you have the leverage to twist the head. Therefore, the spine will not be that hard to snap. Plus, there was no resistance because David was most likely asleep."

"Not to mention the size difference."

"The infant Jason Tabor, four months, was not as fortunate in death as his brother. The super-heated gasses will cook the lungs quickly, but painfully, before getting into the respiratory tract."

"That's awful," Reflexively, she took a long, deep breath, placed the notebook in her back pocket, grabbed her phone from the desk, and said, "We need to do some more probing, but as of yet, I don't believe that this was an arson to cover up an underlying homicide. This family was squeaky clean. It also seems pretty apparent that this asshole wanted us to know he set this fire. So, if I'm right, this may not be the last time we hear from this bastard."

She thanked him and left.

Once in the parking lot, she called the station. "I need someone to go to the Tabor crime scene and get the baseball bat from the boy's room upstairs. Take it to forensics. Get anything you can off of it." She knew it would be an act of futility.

7

CATHERINE

The morning sun streamed through the window, drenching her in sunlight. Tilting her head toward the heat, Catherine soaked up several more minutes of warmth while dreaming of the beach before reaching toward Kevin's side of the bed to bring him along on her fantasy. Patting the bed several times before opening her eyes, she found his side of the bed empty. She let out an audible sigh and shifted back toward the sun to bask in the remaining rays before starting the day.

The two pouncing black cats forced her to abandon any further relaxation. Propping herself up, she looked over at the clock.

"Seems you're a bit late this morning," she told the poised intruders.

Throwing off the covers, the cats jumped off the bed and rushed down the hall toward the room that held their food. She grabbed the phone next to the bed and snuggled into her grey cashmere robe, a luxury she bought to help ease into mornings. The cats circled back to meet her halfway down the hall, convinced she had forgotten which room they ate in. She opened the correct door, put more food in the bowls, and shuffled downstairs.

Pleased to find coffee made, she poured a cup and stepped down onto their newly enclosed porch that ran along the backside of the house. The brick flooring kept the temperature cool in the summer and warm in the winter, and the floor-to-ceiling windows let the light in without the heat. The room was long enough to make into two of her favorite rooms in the house. At one end, against the window, stretched the down-filled floral sofa with two overstuffed, colorful, matching plaid chairs facing it. Anne had helped her pick them out, and much like her bookstore, there was a long, weathered coffee table to complete an intimate gathering place.

No matter how big or small your house is, there always seems to be a room you gravitate to the most. For Catherine, this was it. With a big grin on her face, she walked toward Kevin, who was stretched out on the sofa. His eyes opened at the thumping of Marlo's tail, signaling Catherine's' arrival. Kevin sat up, rubbing his eyes, and quickly made room for her.

"You look beat," she said.

"I didn't sleep well last night. This touring stuff is harder than I thought it would be," he said, dragging his hand down his face and reaching over to pick up his cold coffee. He took a sip, made a face, and put it back on the table.

"Well, you're home now." She leaned over, giving him a long, deep, coffee-breathed kiss.

"Yes, I am," he said, returning the kiss. He gently slid his hand under her robe and up her pajama top just as his *AC-DC* ringtone 'If you want blood' blared.

Mixed between finishing what they were starting and taking the call, he leaned over and took the phone. "I'm sorry." He frowned, when he gruffly began speaking into the phone. "Hey, Steve, your timing is impeccable, buddy."

"So, by your greeting, I guess I still have that asinine ringtone?"

"Yep."

They both laughed out loud.

Steve used to call at all hours with unrealistic deadlines, thus creating more stress for Kevin, and so, as a result, they searched for a suitable ringtone.

"Take me off that damn speaker," he barked.

Kevin obeyed. Catherine reached for her coffee while smiling and nestled back into the sofa. She was observing the profile of Kevin's face during the one-sided conversation when he flew up from the sofa without looking at her and darted over to the table. Frantically, he flipped open the computer screen and poked at the keyboard while cradling the phone tightly against his neck. Punching in a few more keys, he stared at the screen with both eyes and mouth wide. A broad smile overtook his face. He never spoke and put his phone down while continuing to stare at the computer.

"It's number one," he finally said out loud. He turned in Catherine's direction and repeated, "Number One on the New York Times."

Jumping up, she ran over to him and threw her arms around him. Kevin remained rigid and unresponsive.

She let go, backed up enough to see his face, and asked, "This is good, right?"

He put his hand on the table for stability. "I…I," he stammered. "I can't believe this." He ran his fingers through his hair and looked at Catherine as though suddenly aware of her presence. Opening his arms wide, he pulled her close to his chest and rested his chin on top of her head.

She could feel his heart and the vibration as he spoke, "I love you."

Both of his parents were dead, and since he was an only child, she understood all of his intensity was for her alone. She melted deeper into him, grateful to share the moment with him.

Moving her back from him slightly and looking deep into her eyes, he asked, "What should we do to celebrate?"

"We can go out to dinner, but unfortunately, I have a full day of patients." She hesitated as his smile faded. Immediately feeling as if she had just kicked a puppy, she whispered in his ear, "I can think of something right now we can do to celebrate." She took his hand and directed him back up the stairs.

8

CATHERINE

Blissfully but regrettably, Catherine drove the half hour to her office. She glanced over at the other lane, thankful she was going against traffic. After both she and Anne decided to sell her father's practice, Catherine found and rented a smaller office a little closer to home. The commute each day had started to get to her. She was thankful that most of her patients had moved with her new practice, and in the end, that was all Anne's father wanted: his patients to be well served.

She parked in the back lot of the older wooden house that was now two office spaces, climbed the three rickety stairs, and opened the front door that led to her office on the first floor. The small space provided a therapeutic intimacy the larger practice did not have. The six chairs that had been her grandmother's were spread evenly between two walls. She had warmed the waiting room with floor-length drapes and a wooden bookshelf that held books and magazines for all ages. The walls were darker beige and highlighted the colorful Georgia O'Keefe-style prints.

Catherine opened the drapes and allowed the minimal amount of natural light in, then walked into the second room— her therapy room. The color and décor carried throughout. A small spindle desk with a large Monet impression of a sunrise print above was directly against the wall. Two plaid club chairs complimenting the colors of the print were on either side and could be moved around depending on the therapeutic situation. A sofa ran across one of the walls, and she had placed several small tables with easy access to tissue boxes strategically throughout the room. All of the furniture she had was hand-me-downs from her family. All the pieces were comfortable, but not too comfortable.

Closing the door, Catherine sat in the Herman Miller office chair, the only furniture item she had purchased, and although it looked out of place, its modern design was both comfortable and functional. Settling in, she pulled out her appointment book to review the day's schedule. She smirked inwardly at the thought of all her friends, colleagues, and even Kevin, who mocked her for not being in the digital age. Catherine had seen too many of them lose valuable information, and she appreciated the reliability of something that could not crash.

Flipping the pages open, she heard the creaking of the waiting room door open and close. She glanced at the clock, thankful that, despite how leisurely the morning was, she had maintained her schedule to arrive extra early when she had a new patient. The patient and his mother were 30 minutes early, earlier than most, but for a first-time appointment, it was not that uncommon. Many patients had an eager desire to be fixed.

Rolling up closer to the desk, she yanked the drawer open and took out the clipboard with the new patient information. The desk was rickety, but Catherine's grandfather made it for her when she was very young, and she had used it throughout every stage of learning in her life. Even the residual crayon marks in one of the drawers were still present. Each time she heard the nostalgic sound of the wood rubbing together, she could almost hear her grandfather talking to her.

She stood and walked into the waiting room, "Hi, Mrs. Robinson," she said to the woman. Then, she addressed the child. "Joey, I'm Dr. Richards," she greeted them warmly, bending over slightly while holding out her hand.

"I'm Judy," the woman said as she sprung up in response to Catherine's outstretched hand. She looked to be in her mid-thirties. Underneath her a bobbed haircut, her eyes brimmed with tears. She wore an oversized dress that didn't fit her properly, almost as though she had not been shopping for herself in quite a while. Joey remained seated, immersed in a video game, but at the mention of his name, he quickly glanced up, nodded, and returned to it.

"We have some time, so if I can get you started by filling this out," Catherine said handing Judy the clipboard.

Judy obediently grasped the clipboard, poised with pen in hand, eager to begin giving up any information needed.

"I'll give you a chance to fill this out," Catherine said reassuringly, then returned to her office.

Back behind the desk, she saw that Detective McAllister had referred them, but there was no further information. She felt very fortunate that the Fairfax Police Department had used her as one of their referring psychologists throughout the years.

Re-focusing, she flipped through her phone, sifting through messages before she started the session. There was a text from Kevin with tentative plans for the evening. After replying, she took a deep cleansing breath and went back out to the waiting room.

The finished paperwork was on the floor, and Mrs. Robinson's searching, wide eyes were focused on the outside door.

"Judy, why don't you go ahead and have a seat in the office," she said walking over and pointing in the direction of the open door.

Fidgeting with her necklace, Judy's eyes darted toward the room, then back to Joey, and then rested on Catherine for assurance. Catherine smiled, gently walked over, and locked the outside door in hopes of allaying some of the concerned mother's anxiety.

She knelt in front of Joey. "I'm going to talk to your mom for a little bit," she said, "Then I am going to have you come in with us too. If you need anything, we are right in there." She pointed to the room.

"K," Joey said. He looked up, briefly making slight eye contact. Judy picked up the clipboard and handed it to Catherine, gave Joey a reassuring smile, walked guardedly into the office, and sat down in a chair closest to the desk and the door.

Catherine quickly perused the finished paperwork, attempting to gain some insight into the reason for the Robinson's appointment.

"All right," Catherine said as she placed the clipboard on the desk behind her. She was relieved to see that sexual abuse had not been the reason for the referral.

She swiveled the chair within an arm's length of Judy's doe-like gaze. Judy was perched so far on the edge of her seat that it looked like any sudden movement could cause her to fall off.

Catherine began. "Detective McAllister referred you because of your neighbor's house fire..."

"Where everyone died!" Judy blurted out. The hopeful look was now replaced by uncertainty and the realization that no one could take this pain away. "Joey's best friend David was in that fire. They were all murdered." Tears streamed down her face as she reached for a tissue. Catherine waited. Judy waited. Therapeutic silence.

"I'm so sorry this happened. Was this just a few days ago?" Catherine said as she restarted the conversation.

"Yes," Judy said, barely audible, face down toward the floor.

"I'm glad you brought Joey in."

"Me too," she said, lifting her head. "My husband said I should have waited and that these things work themselves out. You know, that whole belief that children are resilient crap. Maybe he's right. I mean, Joey is out there with his head stuck in that damn game without a care in the world."

"This was a traumatic event, an extraordinary event. Children process trauma differently from adults. Sometimes, adults perceive that children have an innate ability to bounce back. And it may seem that Joey is disinterested or doesn't care because he is playing on his game, but everyone processes things differently. Children don't have the vocabulary or frame of reference that adults do. We will evaluate where Joey is in dealing with David's death."

"David's death, that just seems so...so surreal. He was only nine." Judy leaned back. "It was late at night, and we were all in bed asleep. My husband smelled smoke and called the fire department. He woke me up and we went out to watch as the Tabor's house burned. It was so morbid. All of our neighbors were outside. Why do people do that?"

Suspecting Judy was not waiting for an answer to that question, Catherine asked, "Was Joey with you?"

"No." Judy shook her head vehemently. "He was asleep, or at least we thought he was, until he came running out asking about David." She began sobbing.

Catherine waited until she could compose herself. "I'm sorry." Judy looked up, her face soaked.

Catherine handed her more tissues. "And then what?"

"And then I had to explain to my nine-year-old son that his best friend was dead," she said in a raised voice.

"Talking to children about death is tricky. It's difficult enough when grandparents or pets die, but a friend's death makes it even harder to explain. It isn't the natural progression of life."

"It isn't, is it." Judy shivered slightly and wrapped her arms around herself.

"Do you remember the words you used to describe his death? Was it 'David died', or 'he's gone'…?"

"Gone," Judy answered assuredly for the pop quiz. "Death is more of a grown-up conception," she added.

"It does seem excessively harsh, I know, and it is understandable because most adults want to shelter their children from the realities of death. The finality of the word may seem severe when talking to a child, but using the correct vernacular does help them to understand a bit better. He is nine, and I'm sure he has his concept of what death is by now."

"How could he? He has never known anyone who has died before. We haven't even had a pet goldfish that has died." Judy sat back in the seat, crossing her arms in defiance.

"Adults, parents, we believe we can shield children from death by not talking about it and using euphemisms." Catherine leaned forward., "To make it easier for us, really. But the euphemisms, like David has 'gone away', 'gone to a better place,' or is 'sleeping,' are all very confusing to them. How many pets have gone to 'the farm'? It can create an unrealistic fantasy about being able to visit that person in a better place. The unintended consequence is that not knowing can cause undo anxiety in a child."

"I never even read Joey any fairy tales when he was younger. I just wanted to protect him. My husband said I was ridiculous.

He said that was how kids learn about life. I guess I was wrong." Judy's head dropped, and she slumped down in her seat.

"Judy, there is no wrong or right answer in this at all. You brought Joey in because you want to do what is best for him, and even though death is a reality, it is hard for everyone no matter what age. We all handle it differently".

Sitting up and uncrossing her arms, Judy's tone softened. "He didn't ask how David died, and selfishly I'm glad. I think he might have created a reason in his mind, but I am too much of a coward to talk to my nine-year-old about that. How can I when I don't even understand it? He was always at our house. I'm devastated. I miss hearing him and hearing their voices." She closed her eyes, and a single tear dripped down the front of her face.

"You were hit with a double whammy," Catherine raised her index finger. "The first is David's death and the death of his family." She raised her middle finger. "The second is the house fire. Those are two very traumatic events. One of these things alone can cause severe anxiety in a child, let alone two."

"I never thought of the fire even being part of it. It seemed so incidental after David's death…you know," she said. Shifting uncomfortably in her chair, Judy grabbed for one last tissue.

"And we want to safely confront his fears. So, right now, it is important to reassure Joey by showing him where the smoke alarms in the house are and developing a plan of escape if you don't already have one. We can wait until he has specific questions about David's death. It is a tricky balance between giving a child enough information and giving them too much information. A lot of times, we don't say things to children for fear of putting unwanted images in their head because we certainly don't want to give them something to think about that they hadn't thought of." Catherine tilted her head, reached over, and laid her fingertips on Judy's knee. Looking up into her bloodshot eyes, she said, "I can assure you that is naiveté on our part, especially in this day and age with all the technology and social media. Parents are still the front line and need to be in control of what information their children initially receive and not use the Internet to avoid a conversation. I can give you some ideas after we meet with Joey and assess where he is and his understanding of the situation. I will give you a book to take home to read together."

"Thank you." Judy gave a weak smile.

Catherine stood up, "Let's bring Joey in." Opening the door she called, "Joey, you ready?"

Joey nodded and put his gaming device in his pocket, trotted in the room, and plopped down next to his mother who had moved to the sofa.

Catherine asked him simple questions about his game, what grade was he in, and if he liked school.

"No," Joey shouted, "I won't like school anymore."

Judy looked at him, "Joey, that's not true; you love school."

Catherine put her finger up and asked, "Why don't you like school anymore, Joey?"

"Because David is not going to school anymore. Who am I going to sit on the bus with?"

Catherine spent the remainder of their time offering suggestions for dealing with the new anxieties that Joey faced. She gave them the book to take home to read together, set up their next appointment, and let them out the locked door. She was relieved that no one had been outside waiting.

Returning to her desk, Catherine jotted a few things down in the new file and made a quick phone call.

"Hey, Detective McAllister, I just wanted you to know that I just saw the Robinson's, and wanted to give you a quick follow up. Mom and Joey were just here. Thank you for the referral."

"Glad they reached out. Mom was very anxious about her son, as you can imagine," Detective McAllister replied.

"Any extra light you can shed on that fire? I'm guessing his friend, David, died from smoke inhalation?"

There was a long pause. "You haven't seen it on the news?"

"I have enough reality at work, thank you. I try to stay away from it as much as possible."

"Don't I know it. Unfortunately, I'm usually the one involved in at least part of the news cycle. The Tabor family, which consisted of the mom and two children, were all killed, and the house was set on fire."

"Judy said something about murder, but I was assuming she was using it as an exaggerated figure of speech."

"You didn't hear anything from me, but look it up. There is a lot out there, and it looks like the media may have gotten something right this time."

"Murder and a fire?" Catherine said under her breath.

"Yeah, no hyperbole on this. It was bad," the detective said. "Listen, Catherine, I need to run. I have my hands full. Glad they came in. Talk soon."

The phone dropped to her lap. Catherine leaned back in her chair and stared through the poster of Monet's sunrise while taking several deep, calming breaths. She heard the front door open. Her next patient had arrived. She braced her hands on the armrests and lifted herself out of the chair, her heart still racing.

"Be present," she said to herself several times before turning the knob to bring her next patient in.

Catherine was packed up by six-thirty and darted out the door to her car so quickly that she almost forgot to lock up. Driving home, she blared music from the eighties channel, trying to figure out how she was going to tell Kevin tonight about the similarity of his book to another set of arson/murders. If the murders in Staunton were connected, and she had no doubt that they were, there could be a serial killer out there. She gripped the steering wheel tighter and placed the gas pedal closer to the floor.

Zooming down the driveway, Catherine saw immediately the decision had prematurely been made for her. There were at least ten extra cars parked haphazardly in the driveway.

"Party on," she said out loud, parking the car and placing her head on the steering wheel for several minutes. Catherine repeated her phrase of the day. "Be present"

Eventually, she forced herself out of the car and walked up the steps to the front door. When she opened the door, Marlo bounded past her, eager to escape.

Kevin leaned against the doorframe, wine in hand and gave Catherine a crooked, boyish grin. "I kinda forgot to let him out."

"I see," she said with a smile.

"I'm also kinda having a party to celebrate." He waved his glass, but quickly added, "It wasn't my idea though…"

Reaching the top step, Catherine realized everything else would have to wait. She gave him a peck on the cheek and relieved him temporarily of his wine glass to take a sip. "Mmm, tastes like we went high end," she said returning his glass.

Catherine heard Anne clopping down the hall before she saw her.

"Finally," she said, loudly brandishing a full wine glass and giving her friend a quick, light hug. She whispered sheepishly into Catherine's ear, "I hope this is OK."

Before Catherine could answer, Anne changed her tactic and clicked Kevin's glass with hers. "We had to do something. This is a big fucking big deal, C. Anyway, you were working, and…" Anne rattled on before Catherine stopped her.

"No need for explanations. I'm glad you did this." She looked around at the pop-up party. Beaming, Anne took her friend's arm, and they smiled their way to the back porch, losing Kevin along the way. Bouquets of flowers were displayed on various tables, tubs of champagne and wine were on the sideboard in the back room, and an abundance of finger foods sat on the table.

"Looks great," Catherine said while pouring a glass of champagne.

"It helps to have a friend who is a chef. As well, you know, the secret to all parties starts with…" she paused for effect. "Costco!"

"Party in a box," they said together, laughing.

Steve stepped down from the kitchen to give Catherine a hug which almost spilled her drink. "Can you believe it?" he asked and turned to wave at a tall, slender blonde woman in the kitchen.

"It's been the Steve show," Anne whispered, rolling her eyes before the woman reached them.

"Catherine, this is Melanie." he introduced her by grabbing her waist to bring her closer.

Catherine smiled, but before she could say anything, Anne asked, "Now, where are you in school, Melanie?"

Steve gave Anne a nasty glance before he and Melanie moved on to the next group of people.

"Anne," Catherine scolded her friend. Their incessant sparring had always made her suspect there had been some history, but Anne never let on, and Catherine never asked.

"Oh please, he won't remember, and besides I doubt we will see that one again." She winked.

Kevin stumbled into the back room and made a beeline to the wine. Steve chuckled and went over to retrieve his intoxicated friend. He placed his arm around his neck and bellowed to the crowd, "Since Catherine is here, I think it is time for a toast."

He raised his glass and said, "To my oldest and best friend, Kevin."

Turning to Kevin with his glass, he continued, "I have known you since our first day at track practice in college. We raced each other in the four-forty, and both of us fell to the ground when it was over and sized each other up. We were either going to be the best of friends or enemies."

Kevin nodded, smiling at the illustration. "You got me by what, nine-tenths of a second?"

"Yeah, but I still won." Steve lightly punched him in the arm. "Doesn't matter. The point is, we became the best of friends and have been through a lot together, including getting a D from Mr. Liquerman in our first year of English. I never would have imagined that we would one day be standing in your beautiful home with your beautiful wife celebrating you writing a number one bestselling book. Here's to Kevin." Steve concluded by clinking his glass and giving his friend a heartfelt embrace.

Catherine raised her glass in Kevin's direction while taking in all the merriment and goodwill in the room and placed the moment in her heart. She was afraid within the next few days that all of this would soon be coming to a crashing head.

9
KILLER

Convinced he had a long night of work ahead, he opened his laptop and poured a glass of scotch from the nearly empty bottle. Rubbing his hands together in preparation, he unfolded the dog-eared paper from the bottom drawer of his desk. It had taken extensive research to get the list of birth announcements and other needed information. It wasn't like the old days when birth announcements were in the paper. Some information was easy to find, and some took a little more digging. Programming in the correlating addresses with the names on the paper, he waited to see what popped up. There were more to choose from, but the houses were a greater distance apart, meaning more surveillance. The thought of that unnerved him.

"Fuck." He slammed the computer top down and balled up the paper, squeezing it so tight his knuckles turned white. He threw the crumpled ball across the room, grabbed the bottle, and poured the remainder of the scotch, not noticing when it began spilling onto the desk. Running his hands over his face, he thought briefly of returning to his original game plan but knew the gamble was too high. Closing his eyes, he took several deep breaths. First things first, he needed to clean up the mess on his desk. Jerking his eyes open, he hastily grabbed a few papers and arranged them on top of the spill. Problem solved.

Back to work. Nothing worthwhile was ever easy. He hated that fucking phrase. Maybe because he had heard it so many times, or maybe because it was true. He took a long swig from his drink, got up to retrieve the wadded paper, and smoothed it out on the desk. This was the way it was going to be. He leaned under the desk, moving several bottles until he found an unopened bottle of Ardbeg.

He poured the light gold liquid into a new glass, swirled it around, and smelled the intensity of the smoky fruits. Leaning back in his chair, he savored the taste of the fresh pour.

The smooth, peaty flavor coated his throat, changed his mood, and elicited the memory of the first time he had tasted the rich, smoky flavor in the Isle of Islay, the southernmost island of Scotland. It had been years since he had been there. "World Whiskey of the Year," he said, twisting off the top again.

Now, he was better able to focus on his task at hand, which resulted in him finding several homes in the Clifton, Fairfax Station area.

Like a new homeowner, he scrutinized the landscape, the distance from the road, and the proximity to the neighbors. He dove deeper by searching the Internet to find out about the makeup of the families. It took quite a bit of research, but once focused, he settled on two places.

The first hurdle complete, he began organizing his kill kit. First, he looked in the closet for a baseball bat. He didn't find one, nor did he have a spare duffle bag. Then, he remembered throwing the bag into the fire. What had he been thinking? He slammed the door shut, thankful that he had already readjusted his mood. He had allowed himself to get caught up in the moment, but he was not going to let that happen again. He debated going out tonight to the store to keep on schedule, but after looking at the scotch bottles, he decided not to take the risk. Instead, he took the remaining half glass up to bed.

He remained there until the loud alarm tone on his phone went off at seven a.m. After silencing the phone, he perused through his emails. He deleted the majority and responded to the few that needed his attention. Throwing the phone on the bed, he showered and dressed in black jeans, a non-descript grey t-shirt, and a baseball cap. Leisurely making his way downstairs, he opened the refrigerator, poured a large glass of orange juice, and left it on the high-top table to get the morning paper. Strolling to the end of the driveway, he waved to the neighbor, who was also completing her morning ritual. He took the paper back inside, perched on the bar stool, sipped his juice, and attempted to read the paper until the stores opened. All the stories blurred together as he kept glancing at the wall clock. He wasn't interested in any of this crap. At long last, it was a half hour before the store opened, so he sprang into action. After grabbing his car keys and the flannel shirt on the coat rack, he got in his car and sped down the road.

He drove to the largest sports chain store in the area, parked the car, and was relieved when the door opened. Navigating through brightly fluorescent-lit aisles, he reached the vast array of baseball bats: one-piece, two-piece, aluminum alloy, wooden, and composite. He went straight for the wooden bats. It was nostalgic and always got the job done. Plucking it out of the rack, he hit the palm of his hands several times and took the batter's stance, gripping the bat with his top hand. The aisle was too narrow to swing, so he closed his eyes and imagined the recipient of the blow. "Now, that's a power hitter," came a voice behind him.

Startled, he turned to see the slouched unshaven six-foot lanky adolescent smiling behind him. "Yep, it sure it," he said, lowering his voice and his baseball cap.

"Are you in a league?"

"Um...no, I'm not; it's uh, for my son," he said, gaining confidence with his story. "He's trying out for JV this year."

"Where does he go to school? I play at Madison! Maybe I can help him out. Give him a few pointers."

Shifting his weight back and clamping tight on the bat, he wondered how in the hell he came across one of the few adolescents who actually spoke to an adult.

"I'm trying to earn extra money, so..." the young man droned on.

"No," he blurted out too quickly. Realizing his mistake, he added in a calmer voice, "I'm just here on business and thought I would surprise my son."

"Where are you from?"

"I'm from Pennsylvania." He didn't wait to see if the flunky had any friends or family in the state. "Thank you for your help." He bustled past to the front of the store.

"Well, good luck! You picked a good bat for him," the helpful voice called after him.

"Jesus," he muttered under his breath while pulling the baseball cap even further down over his eyes. He focused on the self-checkout in front of him.

Once back at the car, he threw the bat in, slammed the door, and scoured the shopping center. The kid had flustered him, and he forgot to buy a duffle bag, but it was probably a good thing. Not buying two items at the same place was probably for the best. At the next store, he settled on a cheaper black backpack to replace the duffle bag.

Impatient and behind schedule, he decided to drive out to the rolling hills of Clifton to do a cursory inspection of one of the properties.

He easily found the address and did a slow drive-by to make sure Google Maps portrayed the lot correctly and to examine the area for adequate surveillance spots. The phone chirped he had received a message on his phone. He looked down at the text and swore under his breath. It appeared he was about to be interrupted once again, and he would have to cut this journey short.

The other half of his life couldn't be ignored, so he responded in the opposite way of how he felt. *Sure. Be there at 2.*

Convinced he could not do all that he needed to do in the shortened amount of time, he turned the car around and drove towards the Historic Town in search of parking. He turned the car off, took off his baseball cap, and inspected his appearance in the mirror. He looked in the backseat and exchanged the flannel shirt for a light blazer. Narrowing his eyes, he ran his fingers through his hair and got out to have lunch before he had to make his unexpected appointment.

He made one other stop and placed several more items in his kill kit before heading off to take care of his other duties.

The following morning, he was awake before the phone sounded the alarm. He had showered, packed the car, and drove to his pre-ordained spot where he was able to have eyes on the modern white farmhouse. Most of the houses were set on several-acre lots. His parking needed to be strategic since an unfamiliar car could be viewed as out of place by curious neighbors. Confident in his positioning, he settled in and committed himself to the monotonous artistry of surveillance.

The overcast sky cast shadows on the houses, making it feel earlier than it was. Before long, a yellow school bus passed and stopped at the end of the driveway. It waited several minutes until a bounding young boy who was carrying a toy airplane reached it and climbed aboard. The man sat and watched, but the only movement that came all day was the school bus that returned in the afternoon. The kid was still holding the plane, and he flew it up and down toward his house. About a half hour later, the boy reemerged with the plane again and propelled it toward the man's car. A worn-down mother carrying a crying infant in her arms followed behind. She barely glanced at her son, even as he buzzed the plane by her and tried to talk to her. She opened the back door, put the baby in the car seat, got into the driver's side, and was ready to start the car when she felt the knock on the back outside door.

She'd forgotten to let the boy with the airplane into the car. The man's eyes narrowed as her hand flew to her forehead, and she mouthed the words, "Oh shit, Jimmy."

Shifting slightly forward, he looked more closely at the boy as his mother took him to the other side of the backseat and buckled him in. He did not seem to be his stated age, and his actions were that of a much younger child. Upon further scrutiny, he could see that the child had Down syndrome, and the mother was not paying any attention to her older child even though he needed her sole attention. He watched as they got into the car and drove off. Almost two hours later, the car returned, and he witnessed the same scenario of her older son as he playfully ran around the front yard. She carried the still-crying baby inside and called back to her son to come inside.

As night fell, he watched as the lights went on in the house. There were two upstairs and two downstairs. He waited and watched, occasionally turning to see what the other houses were doing. Finally, one went off upstairs, and fifteen minutes later, the second upstairs light went dark. It was almost midnight— all the surrounding houses were dark.

There was only a faint fluttering glow from the window downstairs. He had been stewing all day and decided he was not going to wait. Putting the car in neutral, he coasted in silence as he moved closer to the house. Reaching into the backpack, he rummaged in the outer pockets for the matches and gloves. He stuck the matches into the pocket of his jeans and put on the gloves.

It was time.

He crept down next to the oversized boxwood that lined the side of the house and crept to the back door. Placing the can, bat, and bag down out of sight of the glass doors, he tried his luck and jiggled the door handles. They were locked. Unzipping one of the side pockets of the bag, he pulled out a bump key and a rawhide mallet. After inserting the key into the lock, he pushed it till it stopped, then slightly pulled back before delivering a hard tap with the mallet. Click. He turned the knob. He was inside.

He put it back into the side pocket of the bag for future use, grabbed the bat, and opened the door. Raising the bat to his ear, he followed the flicker of light until he reached the front of the house and saw the big screen TV. *Law and Order* was playing. America's television backdrop.

He saw her sitting motionless on the dark brown leather sofa her head casually back, eyes closed, mouth slightly opened. He snuck up behind her, took the time to position his feet shoulder-width apart, repositioned himself, and then raised the bat with both arms elbows bent. Only then did he come down straight onto the center of her head. Blood began gushing and quickly soaked the couch, but her body was still. Moving the coffee table, he reached down and grabbed her legs. When he pulled her off the couch, her head thwacked loudly on the floor. Ignoring the sound, he dragged her in front of the TV.

Casually proceeding up the curved stairway, he gave a cursory glance to the numerous family pictures going up the wall. When he reached the final step, he heard the familiar dun-dun-dun that signaled the beginning of the next episode.

He entered the first room that had a glimmer of a nightlight. The older boy was asleep, still holding his prized possession. He walked over directly to the sleeping child and looked at him long enough to determine his body positioning before leaning down and, with one quick and silent motion, snapping his neck. Taking off one glove, he sat on the bed, watching the release of the airplane from his small hand. He ran his hand through the thick brown hair, while there was still warmth in the motionless body.

"Jimmy," he said aloud. The room was filled with books, posters, and toys that mostly consisted of airplanes and trains. Putting his glove back on, he got up and walked around the room, pausing to hold several bronze track and field medals that were hanging off the curtain rod. He smiled as he read the back of them. There were quite a few pictures and ribbons displayed on the dresser that captured all the stages of Jimmy's life in snapshots of joy and laughter. He picked up one of Jimmy and his mother, tightened his jaw, and threw it across the room, shattering it into pieces.

He returned to the bed to sit with Jimmy again. "I'm sorry she did this to you."

He pulled the covers up around him and felt the adrenaline resurging in his body. He marched down the hallway. Placing his arm against the wall, he forcefully dragged it along down the stairs, smashing the family memories to the floor.

Filled with rage, he could not bring himself to look at her body. Instead, he went directly to the back door to reclaim the gas can and backpack before taking it back into the television room.

Calming down slightly, he leaned over to feel her body temperature. He decided to give it a bit more time and dropped the backpack next to her body. To pass the time, he chose to sit in the recliner closest to her body and watch the television. He pushed the lever, reclining in the chair as he prepared to watch the remainder of the *Law and Order* episode. Not surprisingly, he had seen it before. He shrugged, leaned back, and settled in to watch anyway. At the conclusion, he glanced over at the body and could see some mottling of her skin as gravity pooled the blood toward the floor. He supposed it had been enough time. He didn't want blood everywhere.

Kneeling down, he recoiled as if touching a hot stove and plucked her clothes in the position he needed. He opened another pocket of the backpack and carefully pulled out a scalpel, then made a vertical incision just above the bikini line. He cut through the tissue, fat, and muscle to reach the uterus. Once finished, he wiped the scalpel on her clothes and returned it to the zippered compartment.

Leaving the gaping wound exposed, he proceeded back up the stairs, kicking the fallen pictures out of his way. Snatching the infant from its crib, the abrupt sudden movement startled child and it began wailing. Holding it at arm's length, his head turned away from the noise, he moved quickly back down and packed it inside the sunken space in her body. The stark difference between his crib and the temperature and texture of his mother's body only accelerated the cries.

"Shut up," he growled while opening the gas can.

He flung the majority of the contents sloppily around the room, picked up his backpack, and spilled the remainder behind him as he walked toward the back glass doors. Tossing the can back into the room, he reached into his pants pocket and pulled out the pack of matches. Striking a match, he threw it directly into the gasoline. *Whoosh!* Strolling out the door, he traced his steps along the boxwood back to his car. He did not even look back at the flames. The fire didn't seem as important as making things right did anymore. Something had flipped, and he finally believed he knew how to do that. Return the little bastard where it should have stayed.

10
DETECTIVE MCALLISTER

It was the second time in less than two weeks that Detective McAllister had to drive out to Braddock Road. Pulling into the parking space, she pulled the visor mirror down and gave her face a once-over.

"Ugh," she said audibly. She rubbed her fingertips in the corner of her eyes, then made a makeshift comb with her fingers.

The door to Dr. Lynch's office was open. He was concentrating on the screen in front of him. He was so engrossed that even the slight knock startled him. His head jerked up, and he waved her in.

"Well, this has to be a record," she said, plunking down on the leather chair across from him.

"Indeed," he said, then paused. "It's a shame this is the only way we seem to meet."

Before she could reply, he averted his gaze and instantly changed the subject. "Looks like you may have been right about there being more similar murders." He tapped a few keys on the keyboard.

"This sure wasn't something I wanted to be right about, but yeah, looked the same to me, maybe with slight variations."

"The Steckler family," he began. "The ex-husband came in yesterday. He wanted to see their bodies. Based on what I saw, I can't imagine he had anything to do with this. I didn't ask him for any details, though. I guess that would be more your job."

"We notified him and I interviewed him Tuesday morning. The guy was overwhelmed with grief and genuinely shocked. He and Jimmy were heavily involved in the Special Olympics. Jimmy ran track, and the father was one of the coaches. The divorce came about because the wife moved out and had an affair that resulted in a second child. The second father is not in the picture…" She stopped herself when she remembered the details were much the same reason for his unpleasant divorce.

"Indeed." Dr. Lynch looked down. "I think we both agree he is probably not a suspect. So, let me start with start with Jimmy. He is an eleven-year-old male with Down syndrome, as you mentioned. The same cause of death as with the prior victims of similar age. A cervical fracture."

She scrambled to get her notebook and began taking notes.

Next is Dorothy Steckler, thirty-five. She sustained blunt force trauma. Same as with the Tabor family."

"He also left the gas can, and this time, we found the charred remains of a baseball bat in the room with the woman's body," Detective McAllister stated. "Since it appears that he brings his supplies I've got several people canvasing the local sporting stores and big box stores."

"Good idea, but in this age of home delivery, he might not even need to leave his house."

"Well, who knows? We may get lucky."

"There was one significant variation. The placement of the baby's body on top of the mother. You wouldn't have been able to see it because it was hidden by her body. They were fused together, essentially. He cut a vertical line across her abdomen just above the pubis and placed the child inside."

"You mean like a C-section?" Baffled, Detective McAllister looked up from her pad.

"It was as if he were trying to put the baby back in his mother's womb."

"I wonder if that is some sign of remorse?" she said out loud, then asked, "Do you think he might have any prior surgical training?"

"My first reaction would be yes. Due to the precision of the cut, he probably had some sort of surgical training, but in this digital age, anyone can be an expert thanks to online videos, I suppose."

"He definitely took more time with the mother. He positioned her body. He's escalating." Sitting back further in the chair, lightly hitting her index finger against her head, she said, "Jeez, I took those courses at Quantico, perhaps naively I never thought I would be involved in something like this first hand.

We may just be at the beginning of understanding the motivation behind the killings."

Dr. Lynch challenged, "And that would be what? 'I hate families?'"

"To some degree, yes, but it seems only certain types of families. Think about it. A single mother with an elementary-aged child and an infant. That is what he wants to destroy. But why?"

"I know it is hard enough when I have to do an autopsy on a child, but several in such a short span is…" He drifted off. "Sometimes it is hard to understand that such evil walks around." He sighed and tapped a few keys on the computer in front of him. "In the case of Colt Steckler, this three-month-old male, the cause of death was smoke inhalation. Thankfully, he died before the fire reached him."

"Thankfully," she repeated, shaking her head. "That makes sense because Carlos said the fire was started several rooms away, and the flames had to follow the gas back to where the bodies were." Closing her notebook, she reached down to put it away. "Thank you." She added as she began getting up out of the chair.

"Hold on a minute. I want to show you something." Dr. Lynch looked under several stacks of papers on his desk with no success, he then leaned over, turning his attention to the several stacks on the floor. "Ah…here it is," he said triumphantly. When he emerged, he was holding up a hardcover book that he slid across the desk to her.

Detective McAllister took the book, scrutinizing it from front to back before the name of the author caught her attention. Kevin Richards. She opened the back jacket of the book and saw the face grinning at her. "Do you know him?" she asked.

"I don't. I had heard that he was local, but that's not why I'm showing it to you."

Leaning back in her chair, lifting her chin, and crossing her legs she said, "You have my curiosity piqued."

"My diener, Amy, read the book and brought it to my attention after we completed the autopsies on this family."

"OK." She shifted her position in the chair. "Catherine Richards is one of the psychologists we refer out to. I'm assuming that this is her husband."

"I don't know anything about that. The story is about a depraved serial killer who murders families of three. They consist of a single mother and two children. Even the ages are similar. Sound familiar?"

Perking up, she flipped the pages in the book, willing it to give her the answers.

"I believe Amy said the only difference was the way the older boy died. Otherwise, she felt like it was a textbook for these crimes".

A grim twist set on her mouth. Feeling weighted in the chair, she rested her hands on her thighs before getting out of the chair. "Fuuuck," she said. "Can I keep this?"

"Yeah."

When she was halfway out the door, he stopped her. "Um..." He paused briefly. "It would be nice to see you under different circumstances…"

"Thank you," she said lifting the book in his direction, her back toward him.

She continued walking down the hall, grateful Jack could not see the huge grin that overtook her face.

Getting into her car, she looked over at the book she had thrown onto the passenger seat. This book presented a new complication. The Police Department had used Catherine throughout the years, and she had just referred one of the potential witnesses in this case to her.

11

CATHERINE

Kevin was watching the news as Catherine walked into the room with a glass of wine. "Can I change it?" she asked, grabbing the clicker on the table between them.

"Sure, I'm not really watching it. Just had it on for noise," Kevin said, engrossed in his tablet. Clicker in hand, Catherine was ready to change the channel when the screen became ablaze with a house on fire. She stopped and wondered if this was a follow-up story from the murder last week that involved her patient. Putting her wine on the table, she paused the news story and turned to Kevin. "I haven't found the right time to talk to you, but I have been meaning to tell you about this…" she pressed the button on the controller to resume play. The local news anchor described the scene of a triple murder and arson several days earlier. Catherine watched while plucking at her lip as the new crime scene was being described on the television. This was not her patient. There had been another murder/arson.

"Holy shit," she said while blinking rapidly. "Holy shit! Not another one. I'm going to call Detective McAllister." Bouncing out of the chair, she desperately began searching for her phone.

"What do you mean another one?" Kevin asked. He perked his head up from his tablet.

Bound by confidentiality, Catherine could only say so much regarding Detective McAllister's referral. "I was told the night of your party that there was another crime just like this. Just like the one in Staunton, and just like the one in your book."

"You knew this and didn't say anything?"

"It was the night of the party, and I did not think it was the best time to bring it up, and I suppose a part of me was in denial and wished it away. But now we have this, and I don't think we can ignore it anymore." She picked up her phone and pressed some numbers. "Detective McAllister please…" she said into the phone.

Kevin looked out the window and saw a car rolling down the driveway, followed by a cloud of dirt. The car stopped and he watched as the figure got out of the car. He recognized her from the news.

"I'm thinking you can hang up," he said, flatly.

"I can't, Kevin," she snapped, pacing from room to room. Marlo began barking and racing toward the door. She flinched when the doorbell rang. Shutting off the television, she challenged, "Who in the hell is that?"

"I believe it's the detective you were calling. Catherine, she's here." He put his hand on her shoulder as he brushed past her to answer the door.

"Oh." She froze before slowly putting the phone next to the wine and the controller. The blazing fire was still frozen on the screen when Kevin came back with Detective McAllister in tow.

"I was trying to call you," Catherine said, pointing in the direction of her phone for some sort of verification.

"I was going to ask why that was, but I see this time you actually watched the news." Detective McAllister tilted her head toward the television.

"We…" Catherine pointed back and forth between her and Kevin. "We… just saw the fire on the news."

"But why would you call me?"

"Maybe we should start over," Kevin interrupted. "I'm Kevin."

Detective McAllister ignored his extended hand and instead asked, "Is there somewhere we can talk?"

"Sure, follow me," Catherine said and led them to the table on the other side of the room. She slid papers and stacked books to make room for all three of them.

The detective pulled out her notebook before she sat.

"You were about to tell me why you were going to call?" she asked once they were all seated.

"Um…well. Where to begin?" Catherine faltered.

"Let me help you." Detective McAllister planted her elbows on the table and leaned toward Catherine. "Maybe we start with this." Her mouth turned down as she reached over for one of Kevin's books.

Kevin pursed his lips and reached for his phone, but Catherine stopped him by placing her hand over his.

"My ME gave me your book after the second set of autopsies Do you know why he would do that?"

Catherine and Kevin remained wide-eyed and silent.

"You have nothing?" McAllister rolled her eyes as she thumbed through the pages of the book.

Catherine opened her mouth to speak, unsure what to say. She knew instinctively it was not smart to talk to the police, especially if they came into your home. She worked with the police. and normally they were allies, but this was different.

Detective McAllister put her hand up, preventing her from making an original statement. "Don't bother, Catherine, I'll tell you," she said, scornfully looking in their direction. "It's because these murders are almost exactly like the two recent murders in our area." She paused, "See, I think it is interesting that this book…" She slapped it for emphasis. "…comes out, and suddenly there are two almost identical murders." Her posture stiffened, and she glared at Kevin. "Do you believe in coincidences?"

"It's a terrible one," he finally said. "But that is what this is. A coincidence."

"There may be more." Catherine intervened, taking the emphasis off of her husband.

"Excuse me?" The detective spewed as she swiveled in Catherine's direction.

"It was at Kevin's book signing about five months ago, right?" she glanced over at him. He agreed, nodding, tight-lipped.

"There was a strange encounter with one of the attendees." Catherine paused as the detective began to write down what she was saying. "A disheveled man came to Kevin's book signing and made a bit of a scene about a fire and a murder in Staunton that was like the one in the book."

"It was nothing," Kevin chimed in.

"Well, initially that is what we thought, but then we looked it up online." She took Kevin's phone, pulled up the article and passed it to the detective.

While scanning the article, the detective's face became tighter as she read. She paused only briefly to write down some things. When she finished, she placed the phone on the table and said, "The incident occurred in early August, and some guy drove all the way from Staunton to your book signing to tell you about this murder?"

"That's right, isn't it?" Catherine touched Kevin's arm lightly and tried to engage him in the conversation.

"I guess…yeah." Kevin waved it off and began massaging his temples. "But geez, the murder was in Staunton. Not here."

"I'll need the exact dates of that book signing," Detective McAllister requested. She put her pen down and made direct eye contact with both of them.

"I'll get that for you," Catherine said. "The idea from Kevin's book was a case study that I learned about in graduate school, years ago. I merely told him about it, and he brought the story to life."

Jerking her head in the direction of Catherine, Detective McAllister once again picked up her pen and said, "I think it might be wise for one of you to start at the beginning."

Catherine waited to see if Kevin would explain, and when he did not, she started, "Kevin's book is loosely based on an adolescent by the name of James Martin. He was an eleven-year-old who was believed to have killed his mother and then set the house on fire. He was admitted to DeJarnette in Staunton, where he remained until his escape when he was seventeen. He was not heard from again, and no one knows what happened to him. The end. This book was just Kevin's fictional theory that after he escaped, he never stopped killing."

"So, no one knows who James Martin is? Theoretically, it could be anybody, and you are saying there is a possibility that this book could have triggered this Martin character?"

"Well, he's not a *character,* detective. He was, or is, very much a real person."

"And still another possibility could be that some sicko wants to bring fiction to life. A copycat."

"That is possible, too. The timing is suspect, I agree, but what if these aren't the first killings? What if…" Catherine continued to let her guard down and attempted to collaborate with Detective McAllister until the rug was jerked out from under her, and the severity of the conversation became apparent.

"Kevin, I am going to need your whereabouts on these dates. As well as the Staunton…"

"You have got to be kidding me," Catherine said and stood up. "I think perhaps it is time for you to go." Realizing the gravity of the situation.

"I'm suddenly a suspect now?" Kevin raised his voice, taking the cue from his wife.

"You don't see any correlation between your book and these murders?"

"This is a fucking book," he said and picked up a copy before pushing it toward her face. "I had nothing to do with any of this."

Detective McAllister held up the palm of her hand. "Calm down. You both need to understand that it would be irresponsible in an investigation not to ask your whereabouts, Kevin. You do understand that, correct?"

"I do understand." Catherine exhaled the breath she had been holding in and sat back down. She placed her hand over Kevin's stiff upper arm.

"I am going to take your suggestion and pull up VICAP to see what else we have. Either way, it seems that the magic number has been reached. We officially have a serial killer in the State of Virginia, and he's now decided to make this area his playground."

"Didn't you say you were at Quantico?" Catherine inquired. "I believe you told me that Dr. Hunter was one of the lecturers?" she cringed slightly as his name crossed her lips.

"He was…"

"Do you remember me telling you that Dr. Hunter was one of my Professors at UVA? It was in his class that I learned about this case study."

"Small world. He might be a good person to talk with. Thank you." She got out of the chair, looked down at Kevin, and asked, "Anything you have to add, Kevin?"

Straining his neck, he turned toward her. "What is it you want me to say?"

"Thank you for your time. I can see my way out. Get me those dates, Kevin, so we can clear this up."

Catherine hurried down the hall. "You can't possibly think that Kevin had anything to do with any of this. Perhaps I can help—"

"Catherine, you know you can't touch this one. I'm genuinely sorry because, honestly, I could use some psychological insight."

"But…" she pleaded. Marlo suddenly appeared, sitting next to her, looking up.

"You need to back off. This could be that real-life James Martin, or it could be a copycat," she said before nodding her head toward the porch. "Or an author trying to keep his book at Number One."

Putting her hands on her hips, Catherine returned the hard gaze, "That is way out of line, and I certainly hope that you don't mean that."

"You're the shrink. What do you want me to deduce by his evasive behavior?"

"Kevin is just in shock. Wouldn't you be after working for something for so long to have this happen?"

"Maybe, and I certainly hope it is, but you, more than anyone know that everything is on the table. I have to follow where the facts take me, Catherine. Just get me an alibi for those dates."

Locking the door behind her, Catherine watched as the unmarked car drove slowly back to the road. She understood that everything needed to be looked into, but surely no one would believe that Kevin had orchestrated something so heinous to sell books! Catherine's thoughts turned to Steve—now he was ruthless. She tossed the thought out of her mind. No way he was involved.

Catherine returned to the porch to find Kevin opening a bottle of wine. "Wine?" he smiled, pointing to an empty glass.

"That's your reaction to this, to open a bottle of wine?"

"Apparently, it is." Kevin lifted his glass and took a sip. "Would you like a glass?"

"No." Catherine left the room, not sure that she could remain civil.

She collapsed in the chair and turned on the television for a distraction. She hadn't thought of Dr. Hunter in years. She fought her initial response when she uttered his name, but he may be able to help.

Kevin eventually staggered into the den with another freshly filled glass. He sat in the chair catty-cornered, plunked his feet on the ottoman, leaned back, and stared up at the ceiling,

"What do you want me to say, Catherine? This is *my* book. It has been my life for almost three years, and now it has become a best seller. Then, out of the blue, I am told I may be responsible for nine people getting killed…getting murdered. It feels pretty shitty."

"I don't think that is what the detective was saying, Kevin."

"It sure as hell is what she was saying. Take your blinders off. You're the fucking shrink and the kid of a cop. You know damn well she was." He sat up and snatched his iPad from the table.

"This is not about you. It is about helping the police find the person responsible. The timing is odd, that's all. We just need to prove your alibi and get you off the table as a suspect."

"Whatever. Think what you want." Kevin turned his attention to his wine and iPad, freezing her out.

"Great," she said under her breath as she left the room.

In the morning, the coffee was made. Kevin was sitting at the table with a yellow legal pad, deep in thought.

Knowing better than to disturb him, she took her coffee to the other end of the room, sprawled out on the sofa, and played a few games of solitaire on her phone.

"Sorry," he said when he took the seat across from her. "I just had to get a few thoughts down. I have my writer's club later this afternoon."

"Oh, I thought maybe you would have been listing the dates to give to Detective McAllister to clear your name."

"I have to do this first. It's this afternoon."

"It is getting very difficult to defend your actions, Kevin. I know you didn't do this, but your asinine pride, or whatever the hell it is, is going to get you into trouble."

"I'll take care of it."

"You mean your Fan Club is more important?"

"That's not fair. We started this long before the book was published, and I guess I just feel an obligation now to them. Besides, right now, I feel like it's all I have left, and I need some support myself."

"Wait!" she perked up, leaning towards him. "You talked about your book to your writer's club, didn't you?"

"Of course I did. It's what we do. Bounce ideas off of each other."

"Then someone in your club knew about the premise of your book before it was published."

"Catherine, you're not accusing the guys in my writing club of committing murder now, or are you?"

"Kevin, I am just trying to put everything out on the table," she said, quoting Detective McAllister.

12
DETECTIVE MCALLISTER

The Violent Criminal Apprehension Program is the largest database of serial violent crimes since its inception in 1985. Detective McAllister had never had a reason to use the FBI tool before she entered the details from the two Fairfax County crimes into the ViCAP database and waited for the result. She hoped to find something that would link the cases together. She waited.

"Oh shit," McAllister said, unprepared for the findings. The database collected all the years of comparable crimes, with the same MO. She found that from 1995 through 2008 fifteen similar crimes in Virginia and two in the neighboring State of West Virginia fit the description of her crimes. She opened the desk drawer, tore off a sheet of paper, and feverishly scribbled down all the dates. To her surprise, the first of the original murders happened in Staunton, just as they did this time. She shook her head and circled the word Staunton before continuing with her list. The murders suddenly stopped in 2008, and there was over a decade cooling off period, with no activity until now. When the murders resumed, they began once again in Staunton. She had not expected to find anything like this.

"That can't be a coincidence," she said aloud as she held her head in her hands. She blew out a short, quick breath. "Blair," she called out to her co-worker and pointed at the screen. "I've narrowed this down to Virginia and West Virginia, so now I need you to make an Excel spreadsheet for me of the chronological timetable, manner of deaths, and anything else similar you find about the crimes."

Detective McAllister knew she was looking at the work of a serial killer, which meant that she and other law enforcement officers were going to be logging in a lot of overtime.

Admittedly, the original crimes had certainly not been set in motion by Kevin's book, but what about the subsequent murders? Pulling open the bottom drawer, she sifted through loose items in search of a single business card she had taken from one of the guest lectures at Quantico, Virginia. She hoped she had kept it. At last, she found the coffee-soaked card in the bottom drawer.

She quickly dialed the number, unsure what to expect, but was relieved when she heard him answer. "Hello?"

"Hello, is this Dr. Hunter?"

"It is. Who is asking?" The tone of his voice brought back memories of the grueling weeks at Quantico. Dr. Hunter had been one of the more challenging lecturers. A mix of brilliance and narcissism.

"Dr. Hunter this is Detective McAllister from Fairfax County. We have a situation that I am hoping you can help with." Adding quickly to keep his interest, she continued, "I took a class from you last year."

"I teach many classes, in many places, detective. You will have to be more specific."

"Quantico,"

"I see. How is it you think I might be of service?" He seemed only slightly more engaged.

"I believe that we have a serial killer—"

"You understand I am not with the FBI? What is it you want from me?"

A sudden unexpected insecurity washed over her as she bit her lip. "I'm asking for your expertise. We don't get too many serial killers in Fairfax County."

"What is it you think you found, Detective?"

"I checked with ViCAP and came up with fifteen murders in Virginia and two murders in West Virginia between the years 1995 and 2008. There was then no activity until recently…"

"You said Fairfax County, Virginia?" he queried, cutting her short again.

"I did."

"It so happens detective that you are in luck. I happen to be teaching a class this semester at GMU. I could come on Friday to discuss this with you."

"Well," she hedged. "I do appreciate that, but I was hoping we could make it sooner, if possible. There have been two murders in the past three weeks."

"As I recall, Catherine Richards is in your area, at least I believe that is her married name. Is there a reason she can't help you?" he asked, catching her off guard.

"She is not able to help with this." She paused slightly, unsure how much information to give over the phone.

"I'm sorry, Detective, but why is that?"

"Her husband has written a book about something to do with a James Martin case. I'm concerned that her husband's book inspired a copycat, if he isn't indeed a suspect himself."

"How can you possibly know anything about James Martin?" his tone abruptly changed.

"I spoke with Catherine and her husband last night…"

"I will be in touch with you, detective…McAllister, is that what you said?"

"Yes, my number is…hello…"

She looked at her phone and tried to call back, assuming they had been disconnected. There was no answer. She tried again. No answer.

"What a dick." She understood that any help would come with a price of arrogance.

13
CATHERINE

Still in her pajamas, Catherine scrunched over the computer in her home office, plugging keywords into a search engine. After several hours of laborious searches, she had compiled a list of ten such murders in Virginia.

"This can't be," Catherine repeated several times, plucking her lip and staring at what she had written down. She had not been prepared for the result.

Curious as to the most recent dates of murders in in Fairfax County, she pulled out her day timer and noted that one of those days Kevin had been on his book tour. Sweat filled her palms.

"That isn't good, Pickles," she said out loud to one of her black cats lying next to the computer. Slightly lightheaded, she stared out the window, her eyes unfocused until she saw the unexpected shape of a car speeding towards the house.

"Oh crap!" Catherine jumped up and tightened her robe before rushing into the bedroom closet. She threw open some drawers and changed into sweatpants and a heavy Kith hoodie. On her way out, she stopped at her dresser mirror, re-tied her ponytail, and put on mascara in a hasty attempt to prepare for the sudden visitor. Dutifully, Marlo began barking before the looming shadow appeared at the door and rang the bell.

Catherine cautiously opened the wooden door, let out a small gasp, and stumbled back, her face flushed to the tip of her ears. "Kem." Her voice cracked.

"Catherine." He brushed past her, stopped, sized up the layout, and strolled down the hall toward the back porch. She dutifully followed the path of his intoxicating cologne.

"Why don't we go into the den?" She stood at the door, pointing into the paneled room, not wanting him near her inner sanctuary.

He looked from room to room and said, "No, I like this room, don't you?" He stepped down through the double glass doors and made a beeline to the sofa.

Anchored in front of the coffee table, plucking her lip, Catherine unabashedly stared.

Kem smiled up at her. "I always found that to be such a perky little trait." He mimicked her plucking lip.

Instantly, she placed her hand at her side and asked, "What are you doing here?"

"Have a seat, Catherine," he said, stretching his arm next to the sofa. "It certainly is good to see you after all this time."

"I just gave your name to Detective McAllister. Did she contact you?"

"Hmm, obviously, but I suppose it is really your husband that brought me here." He looked at a photograph of Catherine and Kevin. "Is that your husband?"

"It is."

"You aren't surprised to see me at all? You really didn't think I would come?" Kem pursed his lips together, quizzing her. "Detective McAllister told me that your husband has written a book on a topic very familiar to us. Is that correct?"

Catherine's cheeks burned. "It is," she said yielding to his influence.

"I suppose I find it interesting that you would have even discussed that."

"Kem, it was based on something we talked about openly in a classroom years ago."

"And? I would have thought then that maybe you would have had the common courtesy to tell me you were using a case study that you learned about in my lecture hall for the premise of a book."

"I didn't know where you were," she lied, tugging on her lower lip. "I also don't believe that I owed you anything, considering it was public knowledge."

"I guess we will just have to leave it at that then." Kem inched his way to the end of the sofa closer to her. "Detective McAllister would like me to help her on this case. Apparently, she took a class from me at Quantico."

"Yes, I remember that she told me that."

"She must have thought I had something to offer."

"I think that would be a fair assumption," Catherine smirked before adding, "I'm fairly sure she also thought you were an arrogant ass."

He laughed. "I suppose excellence does sometimes come with a price."

"To other people," Catherine said and smiled before relaxing back into the chair. Maybe time had tempered the both of them.

"When this Detective told me about all of these unsolved murder/arson cases, my first thought was you. I asked her why you were not being consulted in this matter. That is when I was told you were somehow involved, and she does not want you anywhere near this case." He shrugged and put his hands up. "Now, I understand her reasoning, but I thought I would afford you the courtesy of being involved. Something that you did not afford to me."

"OK, I deserved that. What did Detective McAllister say when you told her you were coming here?"

His eyes flicked up. "I didn't tell her anything. I hung up and directly came over here to see you."

"Signature move." Catherine arched her eyebrows and felt a memory tug of the last time he had hung up on her many years ago.

"Perhaps it is. Old history is beside the point now."

"Wait. Go back. You said cases?"

"I am not fully up to speed, but this Detective told me she looked into ViCAP and found fifteen unsolved cases in Virginia and two in West Virginia that were eerily similar to the cases she is currently working on."

"Fifteen in Virginia and two in West Virginia? So that does not include the new cases?"

"I believe she was only referring to the cold cases. The cases you are aware of are completely separate from the others." He sat on the seat and leaned forward, his steel eyes focused. "I don't know this detective, but I know you, and I am here to tell you that I believe this is the work of James Martin."

"I can understand why you would think that. You have been somewhat obsessed with him, but I'm just not sure I believe that. It was so many years ago, and I always assumed he was dead. This has to be some copycat that has, for some reason, fixated on Kevin's book."

"I would not use the word obsesses Catherine. I think intrigued would be a better description. You think these latest cases could be a copycat? Who would they be copying? Think about it. None of these murders were linked to each other. No one knew about them until now. It is something that only the original murderer would know. Perhaps with these new cases, I would be inclined to agree with you, but it appears that the MO has consistently remained the same throughout the years."

"So, you actually believe this could be James Martin?"

"Who else could this be? He has been killing a mother and her two male children for over a decade." He paused and looked over at the picture of Kevin. "Unless these latest killings are tied to your husband and his book."

Jumping out of the chair, she protectively grabbed the picture of Kevin and stood over him. "There is no way Kevin has anything to do with this."

Kem extended his arm out. "Whoa there, tiger. You don't need to get so defensive. I am just stating a conclusion any cop would come to."

"I think she already has," Catherine said and returned to her chair. She put the picture back down on a table closer to her and away from him.

"That's better. Now, I think we need to recognize that our James Martin, despite our aspirations, has indeed turned out to be a full-fledged psychopath. I believe the only way we are going to find an unknown is to create a profile of him."

"I see that," Catherine whispered, secretly elated to be involved.

"This is our case," Kem said, sucking her in deeper.

"You're right, but, um, can we do this later? I'm just a bit overwhelmed right now."

To her surprise, he stood up, "I agree." He turned and headed down the hall to the front door.

She slipped past him and opened the door wide.

"It is good to see you, Catherine," he said as he walked by her and out the door.

Catherine quietly pushed the door hard until she heard the click of the lock, reached up to turn the deadbolt, and leaned against the door, squeezing her eyes shut. Returning to the sofa, she called Marlo by patting the couch beside her. She could still smell Dr. Hunter's residual musky odor. When Marlo joined her at last, she pulled him against her and let the tears of confusion stream down her face.

14
DETECTIVE MCALLISTER

The following morning, Detective McAllister sipped her third coffee from an oversized mug and continued to research all the areas of Virginia and West Virginia where the past murders had taken place. The spreadsheet gave her further clarity and also gave her the contact information of detectives involved in the other cases. Now, it was time to get first-hand knowledge of the cases and to update the other officers on their cases. Unlike her, they currently had no idea there was a serial killer connecting them all.

To get the work done, she needed help. So, she printed copies and assembled their team. While she waited for them to gather in the conference room, she rubbed the back of her neck and thought about all the evidence and information that was probably spread across Virginia and West Virginia. Gathering it up and putting all the pieces together was going to take some time. Time they didn't have.

"Listen up," she barked once her team was settled in front of the copies she'd laid out for them. "I need you to divide up these cases and call the detectives on them. Find out anything you can about these past homicides. They may be connected to our cases. I would appreciate it done ASAP."

The team dispersed as quickly as she'd gathered them, and within a minute or two, she was back at her desk. Almost immediately, her phone started ringing.

"Detective McAllister," she answered half-heartedly. She didn't need distractions right now, so whoever this was on the other end of her phone was a low priority.

"This is Dr. Hunter."

She could feel her neck muscles loosen slightly as she straightened in her chair. Now she was paying attention. "Thanks for calling back. We . . . got disconnected earlier."

"No, we didn't. I'm at that coffee shop down the street…Café Java…if you would like to meet."

Shaking her head at his boldness but grateful for any help, she instinctively replied, "I'll be right over. " Hanging up, she gathered everything she had, copied it, and stuffed the duplicates into a separate manila folder.

Within a few minutes, she was sitting across from him with a fresh cup of coffee in front of her.

"Thank you for meeting me, and thank you for the coffee," she said, taking the lid off.

"There is cream and sugar over there," he said, tilting his head in the direction of the condiments.

"Yeah, I'm well aware," she said and waved to the barista behind the counter.

They rehashed the short conversation they'd had on the phone the previous day, then she brought him up to date on the details of the local murders. Then, she pulled out two manila folders and set them on the table in front of him.

"This is everything I have so far," she said and pointed at one of the folders. "This has the crime scene photos in it. They might be tough to look at. At least, I have to admit, I'm having a hard time…"

He slid them over and opened the folder with the photos inside first. "I'm going to need a minute or two to look over all this," he said, patting the pile. "If you have something else you need to do, we can meet back here in a few hours or tomorrow."

"I want to get this piece of shit off the streets, so even though I'd like your opinion quickly, I want you to be able to go through it all. Plus, I have some spreadsheets to send to you as well."

"This time works well for me, so shall we say tomorrow, then?"

"Yes, thank you again, Dr. Hunter,"

The following morning, she found him in the same spot. Her papers were spread all over the table in front of him. If it weren't for his change of clothes, she wondered if he had ever left. He greeted her by looking over his bright blue pair of reading glasses. He began talking about the case before she even had time to sit down at the table.

"I believe the suspect is male, given the force with which he kills the female victim. I believe he is organized. He plans ahead by bringing a bat and gas can to the scene."

"OK, jumping right in, I see," she said.

"Well, it's what you want, isn't it?"

"Of course, yes. Go on." She sat and leaned over to pull her notebook out. He didn't wait for her to get prepared to take notes and instead plowed forward with his analysis of her case.

"I would also say that he is educated and older, given the fact that he has been doing this for over two decades. It appears that all of the cases have the same thing in common. The makeup of the family is consistent. The ages of the children vary, but only slightly, and they are always boys in late childhood with infant siblings. It seems that from 1995-2008, the cases are also similar to the recent murders: the mother was killed by blunt force trauma, the older child had his neck snapped, and the baby was left to die. The signature has remained the same. He is compelled to annihilate this certain type of family structure, but why?"

"Essentially, this piece of shit has been doing the same thing to the same type of family for a long time. Is this what you are saying?"

"Well, that would be one way of putting it. Yes, except that these last murders have been within two weeks of each other, which puts them a lot closer together than the others. That part is new. Otherwise, his signature has remained the same. This is who he is and what he does to fulfill himself, and throughout this entire time period, that has not and will not change."

"The killings stopped in 2008 and resumed again this year. Why?" she asked.

"Perhaps after a cooling-off period, he is trying to reassert himself. His age has made him more confident, or he has developed new ties in this area, perhaps? These are all factors to consider, but naturally, we won't know the real answers to these questions until he is caught, and then still maybe never."

"True," she said and pointed to the paper in front of him, "And honestly, I don't care, as long as we get this son of a bitch."

"I understand." He paused and took a sip of his coffee, "I am most intrigued by the most recent case. There is a slight variation in that one that is rather fascinating. It appeared that the baby was placed on top of the mother and her abdomen had been sliced open. Much like a cesarean section. Is that correct?"

Detective McAllister took a deep breath, looked up at the ceiling, nodded her head, and said, "Pretty weird and gruesome if you ask me. Are you implying that this change is significant?"

"Significant? I'm not so sure"," he replied. "The MO, separate from the signature, is learned behavior and can change, so it can evolve or adapt, depending upon the situation. He may be developing new fantasies–like returning the baby to the womb."

"Do you believe this is this James Martin?"

He looked up, lowering his glasses and looking over the rim. "And what do you think you know about James Martin, Detective?"

"I'm not here to have a pissing match with you, doctor. I just want you to know that I am aware of his existence and the theory of his possible past involvement."

"Hmm, then what you are saying is that you believe perhaps the latest cases are unrelated to the past ones?"

"I understand it is likely the same perp. He has been dormant for over a decade, and as far as I'm concerned, James Martin is ghost-folklore."

He piled the papers together and put them back in the folder. Arranging his glasses on the top of his head, he leaned back and crossed his arms. "There may be several explanations for that. If we go back to his signature, it hasn't changed. Think about it this way, detective. You yourself have just linked all of these murders together, so how on earth would a copycat killer know about any of these cold cases?"

"Perhaps this book has been an impetus?"

"Then, there are two totally different killers?" He added.

Briskly shaking her head, she said, "I thought—"

"Hear me out…" he said.

She wrote several things in her notebook, then put down her pen and leaned over the table. "I'm all ears." Her eyebrows knitted together as she focused on each new idea.

"You may very well be looking at two suspects. One scenario is that James Martin has resurfaced and resumed killing again. The second is that someone new is now acting completely on his own and using a bestselling book as his blueprint." Looking to his right and left, he asked, "I have not read the book—how similar is it?"

"It reads like a textbook. The only difference is that the older boy is killed by smothering him with a pillow," she said through clenched teeth.

"Then I believe you have your answer, then."

"Excuse me?"

"I go back to the signature. It has not changed, and how would a copycat know of these murders if law enforcement never put them together." He stood up and took the manila folder. "I need to prepare for my class."

He was gone before she could even tell him goodbye.

<h1 style="text-align:center">15</h1>

CATHERINE

Seated at the granite kitchen island, Catherine could hear Kevin's key turning in the lock. The front door creaked, and Marlo raced to the door with a welcoming bark. Catherine's body tensed. Darting to the refrigerator, she opened it up and began staring into it blindly as Kevin strolled down the hall humming.

"Hey," he beamed and grabbed her waist. She flinched.

"Brr…" he said as the coolant from the refrigerator drifted out into the room. Oblivious to her reaction to him, he ambled to the back porch.

Thankful for the reprieve, she moved back to her seat at the counter and waited for him to return. When he did, he carried a bottle of red wine and two glasses. He saddled up on the seat next to her, uncorked the bottle, and poured a glass. "Mmm, you're going to like this," he said, taking a sip

"No thank you, I don't want any,"

"Did you want a white? I can go get that for you."

"No," she said curtly and shifted her body toward him while avoiding eye contact. "I, uh, had an unexpected visitor today."

"That sounds mysterious," he said and took another sip, raising his eyebrows.

"It was Kem, I mean…Dr. Hunter," she quickly corrected.

"The Dr. Hunter? Your professor from graduate school? Didn't you just tell the detective about him?"

"That is the one. The one and only," she said thankful that she never told him the whole history between them.

"What on earth was he doing here?"

"Apparently, Detective McAllister did end up calling him to consult on the murders—"

"Stop, stop," he said, waving two fingers. "A Fairfax Detective can't handle two murder cases?"

Catherine's eyes narrowed. "Try twenty"

"What are you even talking about? Twenty?"

She swallowed hard as she relayed her day, beginning with her own discovery.

"There were fifteen murders in Virginia, two in West Virginia, and the three recent murders since your book came out. The two here and one in Staunton."

Kevin listened intently, drinking his wine, and when she was finished, asked, "But what does that have to do with you?"

Picking up the half-drunk bottle, she rotated it to see how much was left. Realizing how quickly he'd finished off the bottle, she shook her head and sat it back down. She bit her lip before she spoke. "You don't understand how this pertains to me, or you—honestly?"

"Whoa," he said, holding up both hands in self-defense. "I just wrote a fictional book about some whack job you studied in graduate school." His voice elevated. "*Fiction.*"

Closing her eyes, Catherine attempted to try again in a calmer voice. "*Acceleration* may be a novel, but the fires and the murders are very real, and Detective McAllister is not going to ignore them."

"You think I had something to do with this?" Kevin pulled away from her and stared at her.

She knew at this point there was no point in arguing. She got off the bar stool. "Enjoy your wine." She grabbed her car keys before adding, "And make your own fucking dinner."

Marlo trotted faithfully behind as she stormed out the front door. He jumped into the car through the driver's seat and settled into the front seat. Catherine got in, and they sped down the driveway, gravel flying up from the tires as she drove.

At the end of the driveway, she slammed on the brakes, dropped her forehead on the steering wheel, and instantly regretted her hasty decision.

Looking over at her excited travel companion, she asked, "Now where in the hell do we go?" Forcing a smile, she petted her loyal shadow as he lifted his paw in her direction. She drove aimlessly until the gas gauge read that she had used half a tank. "I guess I've made my point," she said and leaned over to pet Marlo who was curled up in a tight ball on the passenger seat.

Soon, she was turning into her driveway, and her eyes landed on the fluorescent glow of the porch light. Smiling to herself, she thought of Kevin leaving the light on for her despite her childish temper tantrum. What point exactly had she made?

Her thoughts vanished when she saw the unmarked police car in the driveway. She put her foot to the floor, churning up the gravel behind her. She drove the car onto the brick walkway and slammed on breaks, causing Marlo to lurch to the floor. She left the car door open for the dog and raced inside while calling her husband's name.

"In here," came a slurred voice.

Detective McAllister was perched across from Kevin and writing on her notepad Another Detective stood behind her. Kevin was slouched back in his chair and appeared to be in no shape to answer any questions coherently.

Dizzy at the sight of her husband being interrogated by the police in her home, Catherine took a forceful breath in and out. "What in the hell is going on here, Detective?"

"Kevin let us in so that we could just clear up a few questions…" the detective said calmly as she shifted toward Catherine. "This is Detective Blair."

Catherine ignored the second detective and focused a glare in Detective McAllister's direction. "What do you need to know, Mattei? Whether my husband is a serial killer because he wrote a book?"

Catherine rushed over to Kevin's side and placed her hand on his arm. He looked up at her bleary-eyed and gave her a weak crooked smile.

"Do not answer any more questions, Kevin," she ordered. Catherine then returned her glare to the detective. "So, I'm asking you again. What are you doing here?"

"Why don't we all have a seat? I can question him here or take him down to the station."

Catherine refused to comply, and instead began pacing. "This is my house. At what point do you think it is all right to question someone who is clearly impaired?"

"Catherine, please," the detective interrupted. "I went through ViCAP today and found there have been more murders that we didn't know about…"

"Seventeen," Catherine added without thinking and, for the second time tonight, regretted her hasty reaction.

"How might you know that?"

"I have a computer too, Detective."

"And I remember clearly telling you to stay away from this."

"You have my husband pegged as the main suspect," she said. "How am I supposed to stay away? Besides, you still haven't told me what you are doing here so how can I trust that you have his best interest in mind?

Catherine paused and glanced at Kevin whose head was bobbing from side to side. She couldn't let this interview continue. No telling what he'd already said to them. The damage might already be done, but Catherine wasn't about to sit here and let more happen.

"I think it is time for you to go," Catherine said and turned to lead them to the door. She walked them all the way outside before saying anything more. "If you have any further questions, you can contact our lawyer instead of making another pointless home visit."

"We'll be in touch when you have time to calm down," Detective McAllister said, gently. She nodded to the other detective and together they returned to their vehicles. Catherine waited until their taillights were completely out of sight before she went back inside.

Kevin was right where she'd left him, except it appeared he had fallen asleep in her absence. With a sigh, Catherine walked over to him and shook his shoulder. Hard.

"What?" Kevin's eyes bulged open, and darted from one side to the other as if he was trying to get his bearings.

Catherine stood over him, her hands on her hips, until he finally focused on her. "Do you remember what Detective McAllister asked you? Do you? Or are you that wasted?"

He pinched the bridge of his nose with his finger, and it was several minutes before he mustered a response. "She asked me where I was the past couple of Mondays. No big deal. I told her

I still needed to get the dates together for her. What's the big deal? I'll get it done! Stop nagging me about it!"

"No, it's a pretty big deal, Kevin." A chill ran up her spine. Was he trying to hide something? Was there any possible way he and Steve could be involved in this?

Rising slowly out of the chair, he wobbled past her. She cringed when he touched her shoulder briefly for support. When she didn't help him, he stumbled his way to the stairs. He dragged himself up the railing as he took one step at a time. Eventually, he disappeared from her line of sight completely.

Fatigued, she fell into his chair, which was still warm. Her palms began to sweat as she pulled out her phone. She couldn't just sit here wondering if her life was going to fall apart in a few days. She needed to get ahead of this. Her fingers shook as she dialed the number to the only person who could help her.

"Hello?" came a sleepy voice on the other end.

"Kem?" Catherine held the phone tightly, her voice quivering.

"Catherine?" All the drowsiness was gone from his voice.

"The police were here, and I think they believe Kevin has something to do with this…"

"Did they take Kevin into custody?"

"Not in custody," she said while shaking her head. She paused. "Yet. But he is definitely a person of interest because of this damn book. This fucking James Martin. I fucking hate him, and we have to find him Kem, we have to." Even though she tried to keep her composure, she couldn't help but sniffle.

An audible sigh came across the phone before he spoke. "I think we need to start at the beginning. We can discuss logistics later, but I think we need to go to Staunton. I will call you tomorrow. Goodnight, Catherine. Try not to worry."

In the morning, Catherine found Kevin at the kitchen island, slumped over a steaming cup of coffee. "Do you feel as bad as you look?"

"Worse," he groaned, holding his mug with two hands.

"That, I would believe." She gave a weak smile as she poured herself a cup of coffee.

"What happened?" he asked, staring into his coffee.

"You decided to polish off a bottle and a half of wine and, for an encore, thought it was a good idea to speak to the police while drunk."

He jolted his head up, wide-eyed. "I what?"

Catherine took a sip of her coffee and watched his face as he went over the fragmented memory he probably had of the night before. Eventually, his body slumped back down again, and he said, "The doorbell rang. You were gone, so I answered it. Detective McAllister and some other guy was there. She said she just had a few follow-up questions."

"Do you remember the questions?"

"No, but she left without putting me in handcuffs, so I guess it couldn't have been that bad."

"I came home and told her to leave. You don't seem to be taking this very seriously, Kevin. The murders started after your book was published."

"I mean, I can't help that," he argued. "It isn't like I did this, and she just had a few questions. You were the one that said I should be more helpful." He deflected.

Catherine spoke slowly and loudly, over-enunciating the syllables. "When a detective asks about your whereabouts at the time of a murder, you are a person of interest."

He took his hands from his mug to his head. "Can we just talk about this later?"

"I need to get ready for work." She slammed the coffee mug on the granite counter. It echoed so loudly she was thankful it didn't break.

Later, as she drove to her office, she looked over several times at her phone willing it to ring. If Kevin wasn't going to take this seriously, maybe Kem would. Silence followed her throughout the day. After each session, she snatched up the phone eagerly and hoped for some sort of direction from Kem. By late afternoon, she had become so frustrated that she decided to take matters into her own hands. More confident in her actions this time, she redialed his number.

"I'm sorry. I was just checking in to see if you had called," she lied.

"You could look at your recent calls."

"I did, and your number came up," she replied, knowing she was digging herself in deeper.

"That must have been from last night. I haven't called you today."

"Well, since I'm talking to you, do you think we can make plans to speak more...?"

"Calm down, Catherine," he said in the condescending tone that she was used to. "You're overreacting. I can clear my schedule on Wednesday and Thursday of this week, but I will need to be back here Thursday evening to prepare for my Friday class. I will pick you up Wednesday, and we will go interview the families in Staunton, and go to where James Martin spent a good portion of his childhood. At DeJarnette."

"I'm, um, not sure why this can't be done in one day," she said, plucking her lip and glad he couldn't see her. "I just don't think I will be able to do that."

"One of the families can only see us Thursday morning. I thought that you were concerned about how this investigation was reflecting on your husband, Catherine."

"All right, but I think we should meet at my office and go from here."

"You worried about what your husband will think, Catherine?"

"I think it would be better for all concerned," she said before giving him the address.

16
CATHERINE

"You sure you don't want me to go with you?" Kevin asked again as he wrapped his arms around her. "I can cancel my dinner with Steve."

"No, I'm fine. I think it's better if I go it alone." Catherine placed her head on his chest to keep from making eye contact.

"All right," he said and held her close. "I love you."

"I love you too," she said swiftly. She picked up her overnight bag and walked out the door he opened for her as fast as she could before the guilt could overtake her. It didn't help that with each step closer to the car, she became more and more excited. Staring at the road as she drove, she began fantasizing about how she and Kem could solve the murders together. She rationalized that it was a good thing because it would clear Kevin. As she pulled into the parking lot, her stomach dropped when she saw him leaning against his silver Audi. She parked and got out of the car but didn't move toward him. Her knees buckled slightly when he walked toward her with an outstretched hand. He took her bag and tossed it in the trunk, all without uttering a word.

"You ready?" he finally said as he smiled coyly after opening the passenger side door for her. When she climbed inside, she found he had turned on the seat warmer for her. The scent of his cologne transformed her back into the naïve graduate.

He reached behind her into the back seat and returned with a pair of manila folders that he laid in her lap. "One is what Detective McAllister gave me, and the second is a surprise." He grinned in her direction and gunned the motor in preparation. With a thrust of the engine, they were off, headed towards Staunton.

Catherine put the one from Detective McAllister on her lap and eagerly opened the second file. It was worn and somewhat tattered with old institutionalized small-faced typing: James Martin 1984-1991.

"Is this really his file?"

"It is," he said, smiling broadly at his prize.

"But how did you get it?" she asked, puzzled.

"Oh, I've always been in possession of it," he stated cryptically, "I acquired it when I worked at DeJarnette. James Martin's story was a bit of a legend at the hospital. I was always curious…between what was folklore and what was reality." He paused. "I think you used the word obsessed. It seems you may have been correct."

She smiled.

"I took the file. I wondered. What was his reality? Through the years, he has been a cross between a nemesis and a muse. So much of my work in psychology has come about because of my original fascination with him, and so, for this to be put back into my life after so many years, especially in this manner, is both disconcerting and exhilarating."

"I guess, in a strange way, you could say the same for me," she reflected. "But I didn't know you ever worked at DeJarnette."

"Catherine, I would suspect there is a great deal you don't know about me," he bantered and reached his hand over to graze her knee.

She felt a tingle run throughout her body and tried to concentrate on the conversation. She leaned against the door and twisted toward him, stretching the seatbelt to its full length. "What was it like".

"When?" A blank look crossed his face and he grew silent. Catherine let the silence linger for several minutes.

"Kem, what was it like?' she repeated, touching his shoulder.

"I only worked there from 1995 to 1996 then it closed," he said, adjusting his sunglass. "Sorry, my mind drifted."

"What was it like?" she repeated. "Kevin says that most of the institutions by then had lost most of their funding."

"He is right. It wasn't good. The money wasn't there, and most of the staff reflected that. I worked on D-J North with the adolescents. I had just completed my PhD, and believe me, they were happy to have a psychologist whom they didn't have to pay much."

"They were lucky to have had you."

He scoffed. "They relied heavily on psychopharmacology and less on therapy, which naturally, as a psychologist, I didn't necessarily always agree with. Those kids were snowed with very little possibility of ever gaining any insight into their behavior."

She nodded in agreement. "There is a balance, but unfortunately, I think it is human nature to go for the quick fix."

She pushed her seat back and began scanning the file. "James Martin," she echoed. "James Martin." Staring at his profile, she said, "Lately, hearing his name so often has brought back a lot of memories of my time at UVA. I also would sure like to be able to put this whole chapter behind Kevin and me."

"I can understand that," he said and smiled in her direction.

"Plus, I would just like to play even a small part in finding this bastard," she said, wistfully staring out as they headed on to 66W.

"This has certainly changed over the past year," he said.

"No kidding, and it probably still won't be enough," she said, shaking her head in agreement before returning her focus to the folder. "This thing is a mess. I think there are pages out of place or missing…"

"I am quite sure that is true. I haven't looked at it in years."

She shrugged and read in silence until they reached the mountains.

"James escaped when he was seventeen…" she broke the silence. "It says here that he never spoke but that he had an above-average IQ, completed his GED, and was already taking college-level classes. I'm just wondering how he was able to do that without communicating with anyone." Catherine stopped to digest the information, then continued. "It also says he was receiving psychotherapy and medication to relieve anxiety. They attempted to try speech-language therapy and other cognitive strategies, but nothing seemed to work. I guess he just created his own world."

"The medication was useless. He wasn't not speaking

because he was anxious. He was not speaking because he was a controlled psychopath." Kem added morosely, and then asked, "Have you seen DeJarnette?"

"No."

"Hmm, I would have thought, given your husband's book, that you might have snuck over for a tour."

"You can take tours?"

"The operative word Catherine is snuck." He smirked.

"Kevin did extensive research on the place, but surprisingly he never saw it."

"It's sad really. It sits abandoned and discarded on a hill. It's a stately building with an abhorrent history."

"Yes, Kevin told me that. I still find it hard to believe how this so-called doctor decided who was unfit. What happened to 'Do no Harm'?" Catherine's voice began to rise.

"He was gone a very long time before I got there. Most of those ghosts were gone, but I would agree that by today's standards Dr. DeJarnette had a God complex. But, what if he thought he was doing the world a service?" He looked over with a coy smile and said, "You don't think that the world practices a type of eugenics today? What about the constant drumbeat of the 'overpopulation crowd' who scare people into believing the world will be overpopulated if we don't do something? Who gets to decide who gets to remain on the planet?"

"That is pretty much what Kevin said," she said, shaking her head. "Really nothing has changed in all these years. We just push it forward by calling it another name. But at least we don't sterilize them and experiment on them."

"Hmm. We may not institutionalize them in a formal setting, but we most certainly are still committing social experiments on people. We don't treat people. We discard them by either jailing them or throwing them on the street."

"I never thought of it that way." She took a deep breath and whispered, "I don't know," before turning her concentration out the window to the mountains in the distance. She saw the familiar hay-bails, piling up on the farms in preparation for winter and knew exit 273 would be coming up. Mt Jackson.

She and Kevin had a house at Bryce, on the advice of her

good friend Patty, where they could retreat from the hustle and bustle of Northern Virginia. They had both learned to ski and had developed a tight network of friends. Her body tightened as she thought of happier times on their deck. She was becoming increasingly unsettled with the lie she had told Kevin. She was now beginning to question her decision to go away with another man. She yearned to be getting off the exit with her husband. Deciding to check out for a while, she closed her eyes and slept until she felt the car turn off the exit toward Staunton. She opened her eyes as Kem drove up to a Sheetz, which was not too far off the exit, and parked.

"There it is," he pointed.

"Oh, my goodness. It is right there," she said, turning to look at all the built-up construction surrounding the antiquated structure that stood alone on the hill. "I dare say it looks like DeJarnette might outlast everything around here."

"It does feel that it is mocking the new growth." He stared at the proud historic structure that stood as a monument to the troubled souls that resided there. Even though the arched windows were boarded up, the palatial columns of the entrance hauntingly beckoned with a twisted southern hospitality.

"It's abandoned in plain sight." She turned to face him. "But you said we aren't allowed to go in?"

"There's no one to stop us," he said, cutting the car engine off.

As he opened the passenger door to let her out, she glanced up. "I don't think I want to do this."

Holding out his hand, he smiled. "Where's your sense of adventure, Catherine? Is there a better way to get a tiny glimpse of what James experienced for almost seven years of his life?"

Unsnapping the seat belt, she got out, ignoring his outstretched hand, and reluctantly stepped out of the car. They walked up to Frontier Ridge and edged along the road, then down toward the building. As they stepped around short, jaggedly cut grass, Catherine tried to examine the building. The sides of the property were overgrown with shrubs and bramble, and the deer scampered away as they approached. When

Catherine and Kem finally got close enough, they briefly stopped and looked up at the front of the front doors.

"I wonder what was going through their minds?" she murmured, "It looks so stately to have had such hidden horror inside. I just can't…"

"No, you can't," Dr. Hunter remarked.

"Why is it still here?"

"That I can't answer."

"It's a shame."

"Here," he said, pointing to the overgrowth in the back. "Let's go this way. It will give us some shelter from prying eyes."

Inspecting the back and side, they found a small window in which a board had been removed and not yet re-patched by authorities. They were able to slide through and make their way inside the building.

They trudged through the broken tiles, glass, and other debris. Minimal rays of light streamed through the cracks of the boarded windows but allowed enough light in to illuminate their path. The curved archways and thick walls were mixed with old murals and graffiti.

"I haven't been here since…" Kem stopped. "It is strange to see this place desolate. The last time I was here, it was alive with voices and clatter." Pursing his lips, he shook his memories away. "This place was built in 1932, which is probably why it is still standing. It had a long history before they brought the children and adolescents over here in 1972."

She kicked some glass out of her path.

Kem was lost in thought as his eyes surveyed the corridors that he had once walked through. Letting out a distinctive sigh, he eventually continued. "Well, anyway, by the1980's, it was a full-time residential facility for both children and adolescents. That was around the time that James Martin was admitted." He began to walk again. "Come..." He guided her gingerly throughout the building. "Hmm. I don't see it."

"What is that?"

"There was a pool here," his voice trailed off. He took her hand and guided her up some stairs and down another hall. The lower half of the walls were painted in sky blue, with primitive artwork spread sporadically throughout. Like a docent, Kem strolled down the halls, pointing and discussing some of the various rooms along the way.

At one point, Catherine stopped and stared into a particular room. "What is this?" she murmured, pointing.

Intrigued, she felt the pull of the room calling her in. An eerie glow from the sun illuminated the remains of the tattered flimsy orange curtains. Tiny black handprints haphazardly surrounded the room. They covered the wall only as high as a child could reach. She stood in the middle of the room, absorbing the formidable pulsating energy of small voices that were once attached to those hands.

Had they playfully placed their hands as art projects on the wall? Before she could come up with an answer, the door slammed shut with a loud *Wham!* It made her jump. Large red graffiti blazed on the back of the door.

"HELP US."

Suddenly claustrophobic, Catherine felt a cold chill run through her as she raced toward the door and turned the doorknob. It did not open. Desperately jostling the knob, she imagined the walls and hands closing in. Panic. Now, the surrounding handprints did not feel so innocent. She fumbled several more times before she finally got the door open. She rushed out of the room into Kem's arms. Trembling, she allowed him to hold her longer than she should have. The faint aroma of his cologne, his soothing presence, and his warm embrace swept her into a temptation she had not expected. He gently released his grip, gazing down at her. His eyes penetrated her, his lips parted, and she reached up hungrily to meet them with a passion of lost years. Breathing heavily, she stepped back, looking longingly to him for guidance. Instead, he slowly licked his lips, gave her a salacious smile, and wandered down the hall. "Come on, we have more exploring to do."

Shaking her head, she hugged herself tightly and trudged down the divided hall, unsure how to recover. *What have you done?"* Berating herself, she focused on the debris on the floor.

He stopped and waited for her to catch up. "This used to be a staff station where meds were distributed."

They continued to the larger room at the end of the hall. He glanced around the room, nodding, his eyes childlike. "I almost feel like if I walk around the corner, I'll see the people who were once here." Squeezing his eyes together, he said, "Wow, it's been so many years. Hard to believe I was ever that young. We used to play pool in here. It was a good way to connect with the patients." He pointed to the apparition of where a pool table would have been. "I sometimes wonder what happened to them. Do you ever do that, Catherine? Wonder what happened to your patients after therapy?"

"I do. I guess I shouldn't, but I do." She smiled weakly.

"I don't think you would be human if you didn't." He reached out to touch her shoulder but stopped. "Come on. Let's go. It's getting too dark for us to see much more."

They walked silently and ducked out the way they came in.

Drifting to the front of the building, she looked up once again at the entrance. "Did they know what horrors waited for them?"

"It wasn't bad after the DeJarnette years, but during those years, I would say most of them did not know what to expect. For the few that did, I am sure it was terrifying."

They gave a collective sigh when they reached the car unnoticed. Kem started the car, pulled out of the Sheetz parking lot, made a right onto Frontier Drive, and then a left on Jefferson Highway towards downtown.

"The original Western State Hospital has been restored and is now the Blackburn Inn. I hear it is quite lovely."

"I heard. Kevin told me about that building…" She trailed off lost in the thought, a lump in her throat formed at the mention of her husband's name.

"I thought we would check into the hotel and then get lunch before we met with the Samsons," Dr. Hunter said.

Catherine shifted her weight toward the car door and leaned her head against the cool window. "Which family are the Samsons again?"

"They were the first family. Their daughter Emily, her son Timmy, and an infant son were killed in 1995."

"That's a long time ago. What do we even hope to get from speaking with them?"

"Hmm, I would have thought, Catherine, that you would understand the importance of interviewing the first family affected by this murderer." He gave her a glance. "This is where it all began. This is where he was born—where he developed his signature."

"If we are going to believe this is James Martin, I suppose his signature was already formed, wasn't it?"

"He could have fantasized about it, but it is not his signature until completion," he said and smiled broadly over at her. "I think it also strengthens the argument since this is where James is from, so it would be likely that the first murders would be close to home. For example, was he connected somehow with Emily Samson?"

After turning onto Market Street in front of the old Stonewall Jackson Hotel, now renamed Hotel 24 South. he parked and looked up wistfully while pointing to the top of the roof. "I remember there used to be a large red emblem that said Stonewall Jackson Hotel. It was a landmark. For years, it sat on top of the vacant hotel. Although it was burnt out, it was always a reminder of a prestigious past. I used to imagine that some of the patrons were family members visiting their loved ones at Western or DeJarnette."

"How old is this place?" she said, getting out of the car and looking around.

"It was built in 1924 and then restored in 2005. I suppose now preserving the past means changing it." He sighed.

When they entered, Catherine gazed around the lobby, which had been restored to its full grandeur while remaining admirably intimate.

"May I help you?" the hotel receptionist asked with a slight southern drawl.

"I sure hope you can. We did not make reservations, but I am wondering if you have a room for the night for us." Kem leaned over the desk, appealing to the young woman behind the desk.

Tapping her toe repeatedly, Catherine could feel the sweat drip down from her underarms as the woman checked her computer.

"Two rooms, please," she blurted forcefully, while holding up two fingers, "We need two rooms for the night."

Catherine moved past Kem, whipped her credit card out of her purse, and placed it on the marble counter.

"Yes, we do have two rooms available," the receptionist said and looked up at Catherine. "Y'all are lucky, this is a busy night for us, but it looks like we just had a cancellation."

Catherine slid the card toward the agent. "Here you go. For my room."

They exchanged information, received their keys, and took the elevator up to their respective rooms which were a mere two doorways apart. Catherine lightly tapped the key on the pad as she felt Kem moving closer, and she felt immediate relief when the door whirled open.

Placing her hand on the slightly opened door, she found the strength to say, "Kem, despite what happened earlier, I am married, and nothing like that can ever happen again."

"If you recall, it is I who stopped your mistake earlier. I was merely unsure of how many rooms they had, Catherine. I think you misunderstood my motives."

"Well, we are all settled then," She said and escaped into her room, forcing the door closed behind her. Even in the safe confines of the hotel room, her heart still raced.

She jumped when she heard him say through the door, "Fifteen minutes, and we can go get our lunch down the street." When she didn't reply, he knocked slightly, "All right?"

She muttered some sort of response and moved into the bathroom to splash water on her face. Once again, she questioned her decision to take this trip. What were her true motivations? Was it really to help Kevin or to fulfill unfinished business with Kem?

She took a deep breath when the rap on the door came fifteen minutes later. She opened it just enough to squeeze out and proceeded to avoid eye contact as much as possible with him.

When they emerged from the hotel, Catherine couldn't help but be taken in by the 1900s architecture in the City of Staunton that stood proudly repurposed for its new destiny. New bustling restaurants and shops lined both sides of the street that somehow kept the visual appeal of long-gone days while still being appealing for the modern one. Catherine glanced up at the details on the buildings and marveled at their sturdy construction as they walked down Beverly Street to Emilo's Italian Restaurant.

He pulled the door open for her and she stepped inside looking around. "They sure don't make them like this anymore."

"I think you're going to like this place." He turned his attention to the waiting host and said, "*Buon pomeriggio. Vorrei un tavolo d'angolo.*"

A big smile stretched across his face as he heard his native tongue. "*Si, seguimi.*"

Placing his palm in the middle of her back, Dr. Hunter steered Catherine forward in the direction of the table. The waiter brought water and bread before leaving them to peruse the menu. Upon his return, Kem continued his discourse in Italian and handed the menu back.

"*Grazie*," he said, taking the menus away.

"I didn't order anything," she leaned over, frowning.

"Yes you did. You ordered the pear salad," Kem said while gathering his napkin and resting it on his lap. He smiled and looked up confidently.

Flushed, she asked, "How did you know that is what I was going to order?"

"It's late in the afternoon, and most people would go for something lighter since dinner time is not that far off."

"True. I was actually going to order that."

"Deduction. 'It was quite elementary,' wouldn't you agree?"

"Holmes." She smiled.

"Realistically, Poe, without the catchphrase," he continued the banter. "There would be no Holmes without Dupin."

"You remember," she said softly. Her face reddened, and she quickly changed the subject. "I didn't know you spoke Italian?"

"It's one of the languages I speak. Yes."

Rolling her eyes back, she said, "That's right, you're a military brat…"

Shaking his head, he interrupted, holding up his hand, "No. My father was in the State Department. A big difference."

She picked up the sweating water glass and looked outside the window. "Such a beautiful city." She was thankful when the meals arrived. She hadn't realized how hungry she was.

After lunch, they walked back to the car that waited for them in the hotel parking lot. Once it was running, Kem typed the address into his phone, and they were directed through the fall colors of the matured tree-lined streets to an old colonial brick house. They followed the crooked sidewalk up to the door. A dog barked, and before Kem could ring the bell, the door opened, and an elderly man opened the door.

"I reckon you're that doctor, fella?" he said and stepped aside. He took his baseball cap off and put it on a small mahogany Chippendale dresser that sat by the door. Without the cap, he looked older. Just a few wisps of blonde hair covered his head and wrinkles floated across his face. With a slight hunch to his back, he shuffled into the living room with a white Westie close behind and pointed to the two sofas facing each other. "Have a seat; either one."

He stood and waited for them to sit before he sat across them and clearing his card game of solitaire off the coffee table. The dog jumped up next to him.

"Are they here?" a voice called out. A woman with salt and pepper hair appeared, wiping floured hands off on her apron. Pulling it over her head, she tossed it over one of the tufted wingback chairs, and began walking toward them with her outstretched hand.

She held Kem's hand and scrunched her nose while looking at his face closely before letting go. "I'm Marsha Samson, and I see y'all have met Tim."

"Thank you for agreeing to see us," Catherine said, as they all sat.

"We don't want to take up much of your time, so I'll get straight to the point," Kem said. "There have been a series of murders in Northern Virginia recently, and we believe they may be related to what happened to your daughter."

"That was almost thirty years ago," Marsha said, rubbing her hands over her knees. "That can't be."

"Yes, ma'am," Catherine said. "We know that it's tough to believe."

Dr. Hunter interrupted her, looked at both parents and said, "But it is a bit more complicated than that. There have been a total of over seventeen similar murders since her death."

Catherine bristled at how fast he brought up the serial killings in relationship to their daughter. Tim's eyebrows furrowed, and his eyes flashed. "That can't be right."

"We believe that these murders originated with Emily."

"Well, now I know damned well they didn't," Tim proclaimed. "I know the SOB that did this."

"And who do you think that was?" Catherine held her breath as Kem kept his tone measured and tilted his head slightly.

"It was that good-for-nothing second piece of shit she married."

Kem and Catherine both leaned back and respectfully waited for Tim's explanation.

"At least with the first piece of shit I got my namesake and things looked like they might be going all right." He mumbled something under his breath, got up, and stomped out of the room. Putting back on his baseball cap, he called to the dog, and the two of them walked out the front door.

Marsha's grief-stricken eyes followed her husband. "The pain never goes away."

Glancing back to the visitors in front of her, she said, "Tim didn't even want to talk with you, but my feeling is always what harm can it do. I keep hoping that one day we will get answers."

"Can you tell me what your husband meant?" Catherine asked. "Were there problems with Emily's marriages?"

"Emily, she uh, well–she didn't exactly have the best taste in men." A tear streamed down her face. "The first one drank and beat her. He left, got sober, came back, and they had Timmy. Then, after about eight years, he up and left. Never heard from him again. We were pretty surprised, but I guess people can only change for so long."

"How was your relationship with Emily?" Dr. Hunter asked.

"It was rocky. She needed us after Jeff left. I thought things were turning around for her, or I hoped they had." She smiled sadly. "She stopped drinking. She took back her maiden name. We were hopeful until she met the second one—Jacob. She started drinking again. He was mean. Then, she cut us off completely." She reached a shaking hand up to her face to brush away a stray hair. "She definitely had a type."

"Was the second child his baby?"

"Yes, and that was when he left her. I guess she wasn't fun anymore when she got pregnant. Who knows? I used to go to CoDA meetings. You know, to help with the guilt." She stopped, squinting over at Dr. Hunter. "Are you from here? I can't help but feel like you look familiar to me."

"I used to work at DeJarnette."

"That was too long ago, and it wouldn't be from there. Did you ever go to a CoDA meeting?" she asked, completely ignoring the anonymity aspect of the group that dealt with co-dependency issues. "I'm sorry," she wailed when she realized her mistake. She placed her hands over her face. "I'm sorry."

"It's all right, Marsha. I did attend several meetings back then," he replied, quelling her fears, "You have quite a memory. I was in a co-dependent relationship with my father, and without going into detail, I had some things I needed to straighten out."

"I'm sorry. I know better, it's just..." She looked down, smoothing her skirt on her lap.

"I understand. Let's get back to Emily and why your husband thinks Jacob had something to do with the murders."

"Emily went to court to sue for child support, and I heard it got bad."

"You heard?" Catherine chimed in while trying to focus on the conversation. She was still reeling from Kem's admission of attending CoDA meetings.

"We didn't speak. I think she started drinking again." Marsha looked down at her hands. "Can you even imagine what that feels like?" Tears streamed down her face. "We got all our information from Jill."

"Jill?" they asked in unison.

"Jill was Emily's best friend since they were kids. They were inseparable, but she didn't have Emily's drinking problem. Jill was…is…like a daughter to us."

"Does she still live in the area?" Catherine asked.

"She does. In fact, you could talk to her," Marsha said and perked up so she was sitting straighter. "I'm sure you could get more information from her than either of us." Letting out a mournful sigh, she popped out of her seat. "I'll be right back."

"I can't imagine," Catherine said aloud.

"Hmm, a mother's guilt…"

Marsha returned with an index card. Unsure who to give the card to, she held it between them. Kem reached up without looking at it and put it into his coat pocket. "Thank you, Marsha."

"Do you know where Jacob is?" Catherine asked in a desperate attempt to tie up loose ends.

"Drank himself to death. I think it's why Tim has such a hard time. He never felt like we got any answers." She paused. "I never thought he did it, though. Truthfully, I don't think he cared enough." Marsha got up from the sofa, signaling that she had no more to offer, and walked them to the front hall. "Whoever did this took everything from us." She lowered her head and opened the door.

Marsha reached out for Catherine's arm, her eyes pleading for information. "Do you think what happened to Emily is related to what happened to those people in Northern Virginia?"

"We do, there's also—"

"Thank you, Marsha," Kem interrupted and pushed awkwardly in front of Catherine to give Marsha an uncomfortable and uncharacteristic hug. "We will let you know if we find out anything else."

"Thank you," she said, looking out in the front yard at her husband, who was hunched and over pulling weeds. Tim kept his head down as they walked by. The only acknowledgment of their departure was a yip from the dog.

Pulling the seatbelt across her lap, Catherine asked, "Why did you cut me off?"

"I think that the less she has to think about her daughter being associated with a serial killer, the better, don't you? It's bad enough we gave her a connection to any of them."

"You were the one that brought it up first."

"I know, but I just didn't think she needed that stuck in her head after we left. It is already going to be hard enough with just our presence."

"I suppose you are right. You want to—"

He pulled his phone from his pocket and cut her off. "You up for meeting the second family today, if possible?"

"Sure, but I thought…" She shook her head and let the thought go.

He held up the phone and dialed. No response.

"Actually, why don't you contact Jill?"

He pulled the card out and dialed the number. No response. He placed it back in his pocket.

"You could try her later and see if we can see her while we are here."

"I'm wondering how much help she could really be," he said. "If Emily was an alcoholic, the chances are her best friend also had some issues, despite what Marsha says. I can't imagine that she would be a very reliable historian. I just think it would be a waste of time."

"I'm not sure I agree with you on that at all," she argued. Several of her own past relationships with self-destructive friends came to mind. She could easily recall many instances involving them that she was a part of. She didn't go down with them.

"How many people do you know remain long-time friends with people like Emily without having something to hide? Jill most likely hid her problems better. I just think Marsha doesn't know Jill as well as she thinks."

"You sound like you know her."

"No, I just know the type, and I thought you would too."

Catherine thought about Marsha's correction. "Perhaps. It's just all very sad."

"It's a murder investigation, Catherine, not sure what else it would be," he said. He started the car. Catherine caught a glimpse of Tim Samson watching them drive away in the passenger mirror.

Sorrels Lounge was just off the lobby of the hotel. Looking at the menu outside the door, Kem asked, "Want to go in and have a drink?" He had one foot up heading into the bustling lounge.

"No, I'm going to go up to my room."

"Meet here at 7 for dinner?"

She gave him a thumbs-up and headed toward the elevator. Looking back, she saw him head straight to the only empty barstool in the middle of a swarm of flirtatious women. Rolling her eyes, she pressed the up button.

After taking a nap and a quick shower, she returned to the lounge a bit before seven o'clock to find Kem still perched on the same bar stool.

"Catherine," he called, swiveling his chair in her direction. "Why don't you come join us for a drink?"

She glanced over and marched past him to an open gap at the end of the bar. "Merlot please," she called out to the bartender.

"Is house OK?"

"That's fine, I'll be over there," she said, pointing to Dr. Hunter. She left behind ten dollars to more than cover the Happy Hour price.

Taking her wine, she navigated past several women and stopped between them and their commanding suitor. Smiling dutifully and nodding at the appropriate times, she eyed the competition as he captivated them with stories of serial killers from his time teaching at Quantico. Catherine sipped her wine, wondering why she viewed this as some contest, but she was too caught up in it now for her reasoning to matter. Taking the last long sip, she stretched her arm, placed her glass on the bar, placed her hand intimately on Dr. Hunter's shoulder, and whispered something in his ear.

He properly closed his eyes, grinned, and tuned out everyone but the voice in his ear. "Hmm," he purred. Opening his eyes, he turned toward his newly established entourage. "Ladies, I need to depart you for now. It seems our table is ready."

"You'll be back?" several asked, while the others openly sighed with disappointment. "*Buonasera*," he said to them. "*Mi segui*,"

He took Catherine's hand, leading her to the table. Looking over her shoulder, she beamed a catty smile as she walked off with their prize.

Catherine saw the women gathering their purses and exiting the bar. One straggler pranced over to the table, leaned her plunging neckline eye level, and gave Dr. Hunter a slow wet peck on the cheek. "Thank you for the wine. I hope to see you later."

He followed her curves out the door, then turned to Catherine. "Now that was fun."

When the waiter came over, Catherine ordered a second glass of merlot, and Dr. Hunter ordered a cheese plate and a bottle of wine.

"Do you know what you would like for dinner?" the waiter asked.

"I believe we will both get the filet mignon," Kem said, raising his eyebrows in Catherine's direction.

"That's perfect, medium rare please."

They were well into their bottle of wine when Catherine gained enough liquid courage to ask. "You used to attend CoDA meetings?"

"You sound surprised. I told you, Catherine. There are many things you don't know about me."

"I have no doubt that is true?"

"Are you thinking that it's usually women who attend these meetings?" he goaded her. "Maybe you see it as a sign of weakness on my part?"

"No," she said, flustered. "I, um, I guess it's just nice to know you are actually human." She raised her glass and took a sip. "But I guess I am curious as to why you came to Staunton to go to meetings."

"Yes, well, I did not want to be seen going to one in Charlottesville. Small-town gossip and all. Plus, I had been to a few when I worked here and found I liked the people."

"I can understand that. Despite the anonymity, people talk."

"My father and I had a very close but codependent relationship while I was growing up," he explained. "My mother was barely a functional alcoholic. She could hold it together for all of the parties she needed to attend being the wife of someone high up in the State Department. My father was working or gone all the time, and I was in charge of making sure she showed up to the events sober. I was attuned to my parents' needs and feelings, certainly more than they were attuned to mine."

"And is that how you got into psychology?"

"I'm sure on some level it was, at least initially. But I knew the residual issues I had with my parents couldn't be resolved in the classroom, and so that is why I attended those groups," he said.

"Were you still close when you went off to college?"

"Hmmm, I would say after watching how I took care of my mother, my father believed I had a deep understanding of the human condition. I attended prestigious schools, and my father put a high price on education, but he believed that my gift should have been directed toward his line of work…diplomacy or politics. He could never understand that the two were intertwined and was very disappointed that I went into the field of psychology. He saw my career choice as a sign of weakness. So the answer would be no, we were not close."

"Where are your parents now?"

"Dead. The irony, I suppose, of their death is that they were killed by a drunk driver." He closed his eyes.

"I am so sorry," she said and put her hand on his.

"It was a long time ago." Placing his hand over hers, he smiled sadly and said, "I don't think I have ever been close enough to anyone to tell that story before, but it came up today." He leaned back in the chair, lifting his hand off hers just as their meals arrived.

"Thank you," they said in unison, both looking up to the waiter.

"Do you believe in the psychology of evil?" she blurted out halfway through dinner.

"That is quite a wine question." He laughed and filled her empty glass. Making eye contact with the waiter, he signaled for a second bottle.

"I'm just making small talk, professor," she said playfully.

"I think that early developmental factors shape us and make us who we are. I suppose if we are going to theorize, I will always go with Freud," he mused, cutting into another piece of his perfectly cooked filet.

"Do you believe a serial killer knows the difference between right and wrong?"

"I think in some instances, serial killers are displaying their compulsions and or stories." He picked up his glass and paused for a moment. "Edmund Kemper comes to mind. He started off by killing his grandparents and subsequently killed, I believe, six co-eds who were hitchhiking. He turned himself in after killing his mother and her best friend. His story was over."

"You're saying his mother was the target all along, and after she was dead, he didn't have the compulsion to kill anymore?"

"There was a family history they had with Kemper that we did not have with James Martin. Essentially, James was 'caged' for a good portion of his youth and never spoke, so we never knew if he had the trifecta of bed wetting, animal cruelty, or if he just went straight to fire starting and murder."

"They who, in essence, make a conscious decision to kill and possess a strong desire not to be caught. That is evil."

"Catherine," he said, cutting her off. "I do not want to go down this Nietzche rabbit hole with you."

"Fair enough." She smiled and picked up her wine.

"Would you like dessert?"

"Sure," she said. Taking the hint, she ordered the blackberry cheesecake.

They enjoyed their dessert and the remainder of the wine, and when the bill came, he pulled out his credit card. "I've got this."

"Thank you. I've enjoyed this."

"I have, too. It's nice to be able to intellectually talk to someone who shares the passion for my philosophy and profession."

"Yes, that's it!" She said a bit too loud. She looked around, giggling, picked up the glass, and finished with her last swallow. "I think perhaps that is why I have always been drawn to you. It's hard to find someone to get on that level with." Wiping her mouth with the linen napkin, she delicately got up from her chair and took a moment before taking another step. "Woah," she mouthed.

"You alright?" he asked and put his hand on her elbow.

"Yeah, I'm fine," she said and waved to the waiter before continuing to sway toward the elevator.

Falling into the corner, she leaned slightly forward to touch his arm, slurring, "Tttthank yoou for dinner. That was, uh, it was nice. It was good. It was good and nice."

Stumbling off the elevator, she balanced against the wall and reached down slowly to take off her shoes.

"Damn heels," she said, dangling them both in one hand and smiling at her accomplishment.

Skipping to her door, she rooted through her pocketbook, searching unsuccessfully for her key. He reached into his breast coat pocket and nimbly sprayed himself with cologne before turning toward her. "Do you need help, Catherine?"

She looked up, sniffing the air. "Mmmm," she said. Briefly closing her eyes, she touched her neck. "It's here somewhere…"

"Why don't we just use mine?" he said, reaching the door and holding up his key card.

Masterfully, he opened the door and swooped her inside. She could feel her body swell in anticipation as he grabbed her up into his arms and pressed her body into his. His hands went up and down her, exploring every curve. Taking in a deep breath of his cologne, she reflexively arched her back as he skillfully unbuttoned her blouse. With her full breasts exposed, she could feel the cool air on her skin.

Abruptly she pulled back. "Kem, I can't." She drew her shirt across her, zigzagging toward the door, repeating. "I can't." She turned in his direction, a mix of tears and mascara running down her face.

"Catherine," he said, initially trying to coax her back.

"I...I have to go…"

"Not to worry." He followed her out into the hall. Taking her pocketbook found her key, and opened her door, "Buonanotte, Catherine."

She did not look at him as she ran into her room. Once she ensured her door was shut and secured, she fell fully clothed onto the bed and cried herself to sleep.

In the morning, Catherine positioned herself by the elevator shifting her weight back and forth next to her overnight bag. While fidgeting with her purse for more aspirin, she heard Dr. Hunter's door open. Her stomach dropped in anticipation but instead of him walking out of the room in her direction, Catherine's eyes landed on the figure of a woman sashaying toward her. It was the blonde woman last night from the bar. She pressed the down button and straightened her crumpled dress as she waited.

Ding. The elevator opened, and the woman strutted past Catherine into the carriage. For the first time, she made eye contact with Catherine.

"Honey, you apparently don't know what you missed," she said before pressing the down button. She licked her lips and raised her eyebrows. "Thank you," she mouthed before disappearing into the elevator.

"That was fun," Catherine snarled, mimicking Dr. Hunter.

She waited several minutes before pressing the elevator button to avoid another awkward encounter with his paramour and made her way into the arms of the cozy cream-colored couch. While she waited, she attempted to calm herself by playing a mindless game on her phone. Her body stiffened each time she heard the elevator doors open, and a wave of nausea washed over her when Dr. Hunter did appear. Standing up, she lowered her gaze and walked at an accelerated pace past him and out of the hotel, already dreading the time she would need to spend with him in the enclosed space of his car. He followed her out the doors, down the sidewalk, and to the parking garage, the hollow sounds of their feet echoing on the cement.

It wasn't until they got onto 81 N that Catherine asked, "I thought that we were going to meet with the Wilson family today?"

He took a few minutes before answering, "Oh, I spoke with them this morning, and we both concluded that there was really nothing that they could offer."

"Nothing to offer? You're kidding."

"I think they would be better off talking with the police at this point," he said.

"What about Jill?"

"I left a message, but there was no answer. I left my number for her to return my call."

"Are you going to follow up if she doesn't call you back?"

"Hmm, I haven't thought about it."

"Why don't you give me the number so I can follow up?"

"I believe Detective McAllister has told you to stay out of this."

Pressing her lips together, she crossed her arms and gazed out the side window. "Well, then, what in the hell am I doing here if I am supposed to stay out of it?"

"I am merely saying, Catherine, that you calling someone on your own is not a good idea."

Slumping against the door, she rested her head against the cool glass as she replayed the previous night in her head. The palpable silence made her a nervous wreck as she played over and over in her head what she was going to say. "I think maybe we should talk about last night," she eventually blurted out.

"What about last night would you like to talk about?" He kept his eyes on the road.

"I'm sorry that, um, if I led you on Kem, but I am very happily married." She began plucking her bottom lip. "I, ah, just think that maybe since we have a long, tangled history together, and I can't believe I am finally saying this to you, but I used to have the biggest crush on you, and I think it just all came to a head last night." Her face burning, she turned to give him a sheepish smile.

Trucks whirled past as he silently remained focused on the road, her shame resurfacing.

"I understand." He nodded. "I suppose we can put it down as unfinished business that needed to be resolved." Looking at her, he asked, amused. "Do you have some sort of closure now?"

Blushing, she thought before answering. "I guess I do."

"Then, we shall put this whole thing behind us. We are adults, after all." He turned on the radio and for the remainder of their trip, they listened to the nineties channel both lost in their thoughts.

17
DETECTIVE MCALLISTER

Detective McAllister walked into the coffee shop and inhaled the rich, comforting coffee aromas that paired well with the dark wooden furniture. She scanned over the customers enjoying a midmorning beverage and placed her briefcase down to save the corner table before ordering a coffee.

Organizing the papers into piles, she happened to look up just as several of the female clientele shifted their position to view Dr. Hunter walking through the open door.

She stood to greet him. "Thank you for meeting with me," she said while guiding him to the small laminated square table. "I already grabbed a coffee, but I wasn't sure if you wanted anything…" She took a seat and looked up in his direction while pulling her chair closer to the table.

"Nothing. Thank you," he said. Browsing his surroundings, he combed his hair back with his spread fingers.

Drumming her fingers, she tapped the table to get his attention. "We called the precincts, and unfortunately, it has been a dead end," she said, getting straight to the point. "None of them were aware of any link connecting these crimes. Each area treated it as an individual homicide, so it went nowhere."

"Hmm," he said. He glanced down, took a seat, and focused on the organized piles assembled before him. "I can understand that. Ask yourself, detective. Would you have even looked into ViCAP if there weren't two similar crimes in your area?"

"You're right, of course, and I will pursue different avenues and work with the Cold Case Squad detectives in those jurisdictions."

"I'm sure they will be happy with any help you can give them."

"And with all these different jurisdictions…maybe that is why I keep asking…is this really just one suspect?"

"Our mind automatically wants to return to what we know, detective. The vast majority of police will not come into contact with a serial killer. I understand that it is difficult to wrap your brain around despite your experience." He paused, tilting his head toward her and flashing a smile. "It's a very different animal, but as I have pointed out before, his signature has been consistent. You took my class, detective. It is all based on data…" He tapped the papers. "…educated guesswork, and experience. Don't be so hard on your fellow law enforcement."

"You're right. Of course," she agreed. "I would say it is 'Intelligence guided by experience,' to quote Nero Wolfe."

"A well-thought-out statement to be sure. Who is Nero Wolfe?"

"It's a detective series my grandfather gave me to read when I was a little. He thought it would be more stimulating than Nancy Drew." She smiled.

"Were they?" he brought her back to the present.

"Most definitely."

"Hmm, sounds intriguing."

"I always have heard that some killers, and I guess serial killers especially, view their work as art. Do you agree with that?"

"I believe that is true for the most part." He paused in thought. "But they do not have the same compulsions. For example, a killer will most likely stage the crime scene to make it look like something different than it is to throw off the police."

"Like a murderer who takes things to make it appear that a crime of passion was a robbery gone bad. I understand that."

"That is not to say that a serial killer will not do things to throw off the police, but they are more likely to pose their victims. It is the way they tell their story."

"That would be their signature of playing to the camera, so to speak," she said.

"How and where they place their victims is one thing to look at."

"This particular bastard is leaving the older child in his room comfortable in his bed. Not sure if that would be considered a form of posing or a sign of remorse. It seems he wants him comfortable."

"I would say that is more part of his story, but you reported in the last case that there was an attempt to return the baby to the mother's uterus. To me, that is posing."

"Got it."

"To get back to your original question though, I believe that the signature could be considered their medium. Using tools and methods that are singular to their work of art. I mean, if we want to get abstract about it."

"I suppose it is," she said. "I am stuck though, on who doesn't like mothers and children."

"I don't think it is ever as simple as that, do you? You said you have called the police departments to find out about the crimes, but I would suggest now that you begin digging into the background of the victims."

"A single mother and her two children. That will narrow it down," she said, grimacing at the task at hand.

"Detective," he said, waving a finger. "You need to research the makeup of the victims to find what they all have in common. If you find a common thread, you could narrow your field down considerably. For example, one of the first thoughts that comes to my mind is it must be someone that they knew. Tim Samson believed that Emily's estranged partner killed her."

"Samson," she repeated the name and rifled through the files, stopping and holding her finger on the paper. "That is Emily Samson, the first murder victim in 1995?"

"Yes. Her father," he said casually. "I went to Staunton to interview the family."

"Excuse me?" her eyes widened, and her voice rose slightly. "This is news to me."

"I'm sorry, detective, I was not aware that I had to check in with you. I was under the impression you had asked for my help?"

Biting her lip, she looked down at the paper before she spoke, "I definitely need and appreciate your help, but that was a half-cocked move, and even though you don't need my permission, I would appreciate you keeping me in the loop."

Inhaling deeply and producing a mock smile, she said, "That being said, did you find out anything?"

Squinting his eyes, he replied, "I did not. It appears the family had been essentially estranged from Emily due to her poor choice of men and her alcohol abuse." He leaned back, flipping his hand away. "The only reason I brought it up was that her father has always believed she knew her killer. Which is why it is important to find out what, or if, these victims have something in common."

"Perhaps our suspect was originally in a custody battle? We could be talking about someone in the court system or law offices." She wrote down several things to follow up on.

"Yes," he acknowledged, patting the stack in front of him. "I think I can give you a broad profile to begin to work with."

"That would be helpful," she said while flipping the page of her notebook so she could begin writing.

"A white male between the ages of forty to fifty-five. He has not crossed racial lines; therefore, the makeup of these families most likely reflects his family of origin." He paused to give her note-taking hand time to catch up with him before he continued. "He may be taking a trophy from the scene, but with a fire, this will make it all but impossible to tell until you catch him. Killing a family is very intimate and personal. It stands to reason that he would want a keepsake or memory of his work. But not all do."

She raised her left hand as she continued to write. "Slow it down."

He waited, filling the time by surveying the room until she was caught up again. "He is educated, organized, and estranged from his family. More than likely, he has been fighting for his family through the courts, or there could be some other perceived threat. He has chosen these families as a surrogate for his anger."

"But wait. Doctor, how would that hold true, if you believe James Martin is the suspect? I mean, he was the one that killed his mother, so that doesn't sound like he wanted to keep his family together."

"Hmm…" he paused. "I may have left out some background information regarding James Martin." After apologizing, he continued. "I suppose I didn't think it made much of a difference, but I see I was wrong about that. My apologies, sincerely."

"I'm sorry, you what?" stunned by his proclamation.

"I am in possession of his original chart from DeJarnette. I worked there right out of graduate school. That is neither here nor there…" he paused. "My point is that in looking back over the file, I found some pages that were out of place in the back."

"And?" she asked, completely ignoring his admission of having evidence that might help her. "This has to do with this investigation, how?"

"I am getting to that, detective."

"It seems that James Martin killed his mother and attempted to kill his infant brother as well."

"I'm confused."

"There is not much in the file since James did not give up any information, but there is a side note that stated a male infant was rescued from the fire by someone who was passing by."

"How long have you known that, and when were you going to say something?"

"I may, on some level, remember reading it before, but put it out of my mind. After all…" He leaned toward her. "This is about a serial killer and not James Martin."

"Doctor, I believe you are the one who has been pushing this James Martin theory."

"But if it wasn't… is all I'm saying," he said, tossing his arms in the air. "It all makes perfect sense, really, now that I am thinking about it. As a juvenile, his plans were crushed. He is now able to follow through on what he was not allowed to complete: total family annihilation. He developed his deviated "love-map," which most likely fixated on his mother and saw it as a betrayal of their bond when she had the second child."

"All right, let's get back to nailing this piece of shit down, whoever he is."

"Let's begin with the fact he has killed in Virginia and also in West Virginia. This would mean he most likely has a car and is gainfully employed. Most serial killers don't initially stray that far from home. They have their anchor point or comfort zone and spread out from there. Ted Bundy was the exception, and since he was one of the most famous of the "celebrity monsters," we portray him as the norm. When or if they do branch out, they do not mind traveling for their perceived perfect target. For your suspect, the makeup of the family is so specific. It is what drives him. I believe he is not picking these areas, but the areas are choosing him. I mean that, there is a reason why he is there. Most likely for a job, and if he knew he was going to that area, then he would have to do research and, most likely, surveillance on these families. That takes time."

"So, he could be someone like a traveling salesman, a pharmaceutical rep, or anyone that travels through the state," she added.

"Yes, more than likely. These people repeatedly go to the same places, which would make that particular area familiar to him."

"What about truck drivers?"

"Probably not. As I said, the victims are targeted and stalked. A truck driver does not have that flexibility. They would need to choose more out of accessibility and convenience. I don't think I am going out on a limb in saying this, but I believe he is either from Staunton or has lived there."

"Why Staunton?"

"I was telling Catherine…" he slipped.

"Whoa." Her tone sharpened. "You were telling Catherine what? Look, I understand I cannot tell you what to do, but I think I was pretty clear in my desire not to have Catherine involved in this for obvious reasons. I don't think I need to remind you this is an active investigation to which her husband—"

"Are you going to quibble, or do you want to hear what I have to say?" He cut her off and leaned back, crossing his arms, awaiting her response. "You can certainly call someone else in to help you with this."

"I know I can, but I'm not going to start again. Plus, you have a unique vantage point when it comes to this case," she said through clenched teeth. "Go ahead. Please."

"The original murder was in Staunton, and after his extended hiatus, he resumed the murders in Staunton. These are also the only two murders that have happened within miles of this area."

"You could say that Northern Virginia only has two murders. In fact, they are both in my jurisdiction," she affirmed.

"Hmm, I see your point, but really, Detective, Northern Virginia is an anathema," he smirked. "If you agree with my premise that the original murders are close to home, then it makes sense that the murders that followed were in Waynesboro, Fishersville, and Lexington, which are all close to Staunton. It wasn't until the fifth murder that he branched out, and truthfully, West Virginia is not that far."

Taking out a map of Virginia, she arranged it between them, pointing to where the murders had taken place. "It's something to think about. Now, why?" she asked.

"The last murders may have given us the best clue. Attempting to put the baby back into the mother's womb may have just given us a clear glimmer into his rationale."

Wriggling her chair in closer, she asked, "But why wouldn't he have done that all along?"

"The murders are getting closer together. He is escalating, and many times, when the crimes intensify, so do the mistakes." He moved his chair back and rose to leave. "I hope that this has helped your investigation in some way." He looked at his phone. "I need to get to my class."

18
DETECTIVE MCALLISTER

Detective McAllister parked the car in front of the Robinson's house and stared at the empty lot across the street to momentarily relive the savagery and chaos of the events that had unfolded there. The family and their home had been replaced by a for sale sign that was stranded in the middle of the demolished lot. It was a reminder of how fast life recovered after such a tragedy. She sighed, got out of the car, and walked toward the familiar brick house.

"Detective," Judy Robinson said when she opened the door and greeted her warmly. A quilted oven mitt still covered one hand. Joey charged down the steps behind her and grabbed a lacrosse stick from the front hall. When he ran out the door, an older, slower yellow lab trailed cautiously behind.

"Time heals." She smiled weakly and watched the dog lumber down the stairs.

"Sweet dog," Detective McAllister said.

"That was David's dog, Molly." She came wandering home the next day, so we decided to keep her."

"That was nice."

"It gave Joey a little piece of David," Judy said before stepping aside when the oven timer went off. "Please come in."

Detective McAllister followed her and the wafting smell of baking cookies into the spacious kitchen. Judy scurried to the oven and pulled the next batch out as she pointed her free hand to a barstool at the marbled island in front of an already existing mound of cookies.

"Please, take one," Judy said. "Or two." She laughed at the sheer number of cookies.

"Thank you, I will," the detective replied as she was picking up the warm chocolate chip cookie. She bit into the treat and savored the creaminess as it melted in her mouth. "Yum."

"Anything to drink?"

"No, thank you." She mumbled and placed her hand in front of her full mouth.

Taking the spatula, Judy lifted the fresh cookies onto a cooling rack. "I wanted to thank you for giving us the number of Dr. Richards. She really was a big help. It was just so awful, but I think Joey is doing much better. A new boy his age just moved in up the street, and they became fast friends. I'm sure it's because Joey needed someone, but the two are inseparable."

"I'm glad to hear that, Mrs. Robinson—"

"Judy, please," she interrupted.

"Judy, I know that it has been several weeks, but I just wanted to do another follow-up to see if there is anything you can remember from that night. Sometimes after a trauma has settled, a flashback or memory may come back." She looked around the open room. "Is Mr. Robinson here?"

"He's playing lacrosse with Joey. Let me call for them. I'm pretty sure cookies will do the trick." She winked and walked over to the door to call out with the lure of fresh baked goods.

Walter and Joey came in almost immediately, sticks in hand and in search of treats. "Detective." Walter stopped short, put the stick down by the door, and extended his hand. Judy took the lacrosse stick from Joey and kneeled down to his eye level. "This is Detective McAllister. She is the one that is helping to find out what happened to David and his family."

"You mean who killed them?"

"Yes, that's right." The detective jumped off the barstool, aware of Judy's sudden discomfort. "I was just saying to your mom that sometimes after some time passes people remember things."

"I understand," Walter said, walking over to the island and grabbing a cookie. "In fact, right after we spoke last, I tried to write down everything I could remember. I'm pretty sure it is probably the same thing I told you before, but let me get it." Popping the cookie in his mouth, he slipped into the adjoining room and came back with a white sheet of paper. He gave it to her and pointed to the bottom. "I put down what Joey remembers too."

Judy's eyes widened in surprise at the comment. "Joey?" she asked and threw an accusing look at her husband. "I didn't know you did that. What could Joey remember?"

Walter dismissed his wife and grabbed two more cookies. He gave one to his son and said, "Joey, why don't you tell the detective what you told me?"

"I remember a dark car was there when we got on the school bus. It was there in the morning, and it was there when we came home." He looked up at his father before biting into his treat.

Detective McAllister said, "This is very helpful, Joey." Then, to Walter, she asked, "May I keep this?"

He smiled, vindicated, and said, "Judy has a hard time realizing he knows more than she thinks he does."

"Joey, do you remember anything else about the car? I know this is a lot, but do you remember if it had two doors or four doors?"

"Um, I just remember I never saw it before, and there was a man in the car with a baseball hat on. I remember thinking that if that guy asked us a question, we were not going to talk to him." He looked up at Judy and asked, "Right, Mom?"

"Right," she said. A tear fell down her face at the thought of her son in the same proximity as the murderer.

"Was he in the car both times?"

He shook his head affirmatively, then added, "Um, I think there were four doors." He closed his eyes tightly in thought . . . yeah," he said, nodding his head. "There were four doors. One in the front and one behind it."

"That was amazing Joey, thank you. I don't have any more questions." She looked toward Judy who released her son back outside to play.

"I have just a few more questions for the two of you please, if you don't mind," she said and pulled out her notebook before returning to the barstool.

Judy stood next to her, while Walter pulled out a Diet Coke from the stainless-steel, Sub-Zero refrigerator.

"How well did you know Mary Tabor?"

"I mean the boys were best friends, but we really didn't know her all that well. I mean, I tried, but once she had the baby, she—"

"Was all too happy to have David spend time over here," Walter cut in.

Judy narrowed her eyes. "Really Walter! Her husband was dead, and she had a baby! Geez, give it a break!"

Walter lowered his head, "You're right. He was a good kid."

"Have you ever noticed anyone in the neighborhood that doesn't belong? Like that car Joey was talking about? Have any of your neighbors said anything?" she asked quickly before an argument broke out.

"No," they said in unison.

"What about at the Tabor's house? Did you notice any unusual activity? Any visitors?"

"The only visitor was her mom. She came over at least once a week to help out, I guess," Judy added. "Margret, I believe."

"Great, Mrs. Davis is actually my next stop," she said and snapped her notebook closed. "Your information was very useful. Tell Joey, thank you."

Walter gave Judy a playful nudge. "I told you he is not a baby."

"Please take another cookie," Judy said while ignoring her husband. She went over to the counter and held up the plate.

"Thank you," the detective replied and snagged one more before following Judy to the front door.

"I'm a little bit weirded out thinking Joey was so close to a killer."

"I understand, but I don't believe Joey was in any danger." She smiled reassuringly and placed her hand on Judy's shoulder. "We are doing everything we can to get this guy off the street."

Driving to Old Town could be a short or long drive depending upon the time of day and the traffic. This afternoon, thankfully, turned out to be a short drive. She put her blinker on, turned onto South Washington, and looked for the high-end apartment complex. The next feat was to find a parking spot.

By the time Detective McAllister rang the tinny bell outside Margaret Davis's door, she was sweating. She'd had to circle the parking lot three times to no avail and ended up parking six blocks away. When Margaret Davis's petite frame and coiffed appearance finally opened the door to her, she sighed in relief.

"You must be Detective McAllister. Come in," she turned ushering her into the bright airy apartment. Margaret was a woman in her late seventies who still cared about her appearance. Even in her own home, she was dressed in high-end clothing. Detective McAllister couldn't help but admire her kitten heels as they tapped on the marble floors as she walked.

"Thank you for agreeing to see me, Mrs. Davis," she called from behind.

"Oh, please call me Margret." She waved briskly in the direction of a set of tufted damask chairs that were separated by a round wooden side table where several family pictures and a tissue box were displayed. Both chairs were faced the floor-to-ceiling windows that had a view of the water. Against the wall was a lone Italian chenille settee, which looked placed only for extra company.

"This is lovely," Detective McAllister said while looking out at the Belle Haven Marina.

"Thank you, we have enjoyed it here," Margaret replied as she spread her athletic arms in a circle around the room before sitting in the chair closest to the tissue box.

"We?" Detective McAllister asked surprised. "I'm sorry, it is just that I have only ever seen your name on any papers and contact information."

Margret nodded, obviously used to the confusion. "I get that a lot, even at our age. Ed travels quite a bit, even still. He used to work for the State Department. Very hush-hush, and he was gone all the time. I raised Mary pretty much as a single mother. She was our only child, and David and Jason, our only grandchildren." She paused and picked up one of the pictures next to her on the table and held it close to her heart. She pulled it back and began talking into it. "We took it very hard, but Ed dealt with their death by re-immersing himself in his company."

"And his company is…" she questioned.

"Detective," Margret scolded. "We are in Washington, DC."

'Hush-hush," the detective murmured while pursing her lips. She was used to the clandestine walls that halted too many investigations.

"Now tell me," Margret said as she gave the picture one more glance before placing it back on the table. "Is there anything new in my . . . my daughter's murder?"

"We have learned that this was not a single—"

"Yes, I'm aware of the murders in Clifton. You believe they were killed by the monster who killed my daughter?"

"We do. In fact, Mrs. Davis, we believe your daughter and her family were the victims of a serial killer."

"A what?" she blurted out. "So, you mean it has nothing to do with…" Margaret released an audible sigh, her posture relaxed, and her face looked suddenly years younger.

Detective McAllister tilted her head, confused by the response, but allowed the silence between them to work.

"Ed's job," she began, wringing her hands and looking down on her lap. "I secretly wondered if his past had somehow finally caught up to him." She paused. "We were not sure if the price of doing business had cost us our daughter and grandchildren." Any appearance of a steel exterior was gone, and instinctively, she reached for the box next to her. She plucked the last tissue and lightly dabbed her eyes. "I truly believe Ed thought his job had something to do with their death. It's why I think he went back to work so quickly."

"I can't imagine what you have been putting yourselves through," she said and leaned forward. "I am sorry to tell you we currently don't have any leads, and are still in the information gathering stage."

"This is going to sound very odd, but you have given us some peace. Ed can stop blaming himself, and I can secretly stop blaming him." Sadly, looking up, she said, "Isn't that awful? What an awful town we live in."

"I do have a few questions..."

"Anything," she said, eagerly.

"I understand you spent a lot of time at your daughter's."

She sighed. "My Mary recently lost her husband in Afghanistan and had two children to take care of."

"Mrs. Davis, I understand. She was very lucky to have you." She put her hand to her heart and continued, "I was only trying to say that since you were there, maybe you could tell me if there was anything out of the ordinary."

She thought about it before answering. "No. Mary was very private, especially after Thomas was killed. I used to take David to his baseball practices once a week." She picked up another frame and began talking to the image in front of her again. "I'm so glad I stayed to watch him play."

Admiring the harbor view, Detective McAllister gave Margret a few moments to relive happier memories before asking, "Did you notice if anyone had a special interest in David?"

"No, nothing. I'm sorry," she said while wiping a lone tear away and becoming lost in the picture.

Detective McAllister was not going to find any further information from the grieving woman. "I can see myself out, Mrs. Davis, and I will let you know of any new developments." She walked by, lightly touching her shoulder as she left.

Margret reached up and held her hand. "Thank you," she said and turned to look up at the detective. "You have at least given us some solace."

19
CATHERINE

Catherine unlocked the door, thankful to be greeted by the unconditional love from Marlo. Looking up, she spotted two black cats perched on the stairs that noted her entrance as she made her way inside. Once the door shut, they both gave her one more glance before dashing off.

"A dog to love you and cats to ignore you," she yelled in their direction as she followed upstairs. She carried her suitcase directly to the washroom and unzipped her bag, instantly taunted by the smell of Kem's lingering cologne. Her stomach dropped as she remembered what happened the night before.

"You are an idiot," she said to herself. She scooped up all the clothes, piled them into the washer, pressed the hot water button, and then stared blankly into the washer as the water rushed out, cleansing away her weakness.

Thinking food might help her stomach, she made her way back down to the kitchen. There on the counter were two rib eyes defrosting, along with a decanted bottle of red wine. A readied cast iron skillet waited on the stovetop.

She stepped down barefoot onto the cool brick floor and took a seat at the table. Gazing around the room, she closed her eyes and envisioned the space around her just a few short weeks ago when it was filled with laughter, well-wishers, and popping champagne. She willed herself to stay in this happier time, but her mind kept circling back to the kiss with Kem at DeJarnette. That led her to slip into the memory she now shared with him in his hotel room. Her mind was stuck on replay, and the memories were intrusive. Shaking her head, she felt as though she was crawling out of her skin. Some of her patients had described that feeling of shame, and until now, she had never fully understood it. Restless, she got up, went back into the kitchen, and addressed the stack of mail on the corner of the counter. She tried to immerse herself in the importance of the value coupon leaflets.

Such an important task. She slapped them down and rested her forehead between her arms.

Marlo barked a warning before she heard the front door open. She shot up and began absently rummaging through the mail as her heart sank and the knot in her throat grew. Exhaling loudly, she turned, ready to greet her husband's smiling face.

Tossing his keys and grocery bags on the counter, he made a beeline to her and encircled her with his arms. After kissing her on the cheek, he said, "Glad you are back."

Her body stiffened in his arms. "Me too," was all she could manage to say before he pulled away from her.

"Did you see I am making dinner for us?" he asked, proudly ransacking the bags and pulling out a prepared charcuterie board, herbs, and vegetables.

"Lovely," she mumbled while attempting a smile but shifting uncomfortably on the barstool.

Bending down, he tried to make eye contact. "You, OK?"

She could feel her face turn red as she snapped her lower lip with her finger. "Yes," she said, waving it off quickly and changing the subject. "Is that a chilled bottle of Pinot Gris I see in there?"

Taking the bait, he foraged through the last bag and held up the chilled bottle for her approval. She nodded, got two wine glasses from the cabinet, grabbed the appetizer, and took it to the back room. "You bring the wine," she called.

Centering the neatly displayed meats and cheeses on the coffee table, her eyes lifted toward the sofa. Envisioning Kem sitting there, she exhaled deeply and wiped her sweating palms on her pants.

She collapsed on the sofa, watching the ice and water sloshing in the wine bucket as Kevin joined her on the sofa. For several silent minutes, they munched and sipped silently on cheeses and cured meats.

"Are you going to tell me how your trip went?" he asked in an attempt to chip away at the stalemate between them.

"Um, yeah," she said and sat up to shift the items on the coffee table. "It was good."

"I'm dying to hear about DeJarnette, you know, and one of these days, we really need to take a trip and stay at the Blackburn," he prattled.

Plucking her lips, Catherine darted her eyes to her empty glass. She put her hand on the wine bottle before adding, "DeJarnette is just an old run-down mausoleum." She paused and poured another glass. "Not much to say about it."

"Well, sure, but…"

"We need to talk," she said, taking a deep breath.

"I thought that's what we were doing," he said jovially until he examined his wife's tightening face.

"I didn't go to Staunton alone, Kevin. I went with Dr. Hunter," she said and began crying uncontrollably as she told him of her trip.

Flinching, he clutched his fists into a ball and moved away from her. As if he were staring at a stranger, he raised his voice at her. "Did you sleep with him?"

One of the sleeping cats that had been resting comfortably on the chair darted out of the room at his raised voice.

"No, I would never," she said quietly, suddenly concerned at the sudden sternness in his eyes. "I did not, Kevin. I promise you."

Roosted in their corners of the sofa, Catherine glanced at Kevin who was staring straight ahead with a dazed look on his face. He was quiet. Too quiet. It worried her.

His lips parted several times in preparation but he did not speak. It felt like an eternity to Catherine before he made a decision. Pursing his lips, he nodded his head and released a tentative smile. Scooting toward her, he put his arm around her and brought her closer to him. Their bodies relaxed into each other, and she felt like she had her best friend back.

"Oh, Kevin, I don't know what I was even thinking. I just wanted to help." She looked up into his eyes. "Honestly."

"I suppose I have been living under a rock," he admitted. "Part of me didn't believe you were going to that place alone, but I was too caught up in my own shit to even care, I guess."

Both grateful for grace, they melted quietly on the couch.

"You say nothing happened, and I believe you," Kevin said when he broke the silence. "But I would rather you had nothing to do with him anymore."

She separated slightly from him, mindful of her next words. "I understand, and I would like nothing better, but he is working with the police, so I don't know how realistic that will be. I promise you I will keep my distance. Remember," she said and tried playful banter. She poked him in the chest and said, "It is your book that has gotten us into this mess."

"Let's get those steaks on." He got up, squeezing her leg, and changed both the room and the subject.

20
KILLER

Grasping the newly arrived box under his arm, he stormed into the garage. He kicked the blue bucket in his path and sailed it across the garage. The hollow sound echoed as he ripped the contents of the package open. Pulling out the bat, he grabbed the satchel, opened the back car door, and flung both onto the backseat. Scowling, he plucked one of the gas cans and centered it on the back floorboard. Slamming the door, he dropped into the driver's seat, clicked open the garage door, and pulled out to his next destination.

There were several houses close together that fit his needs, and he had already driven by them to get the layout. He was tired of wasting his time with surveillance. It had cost him too much time, and as he drove, he began to feel a renewed stirring that had been missing. This was a new hunt, perhaps with greater risks. Tightening his grip on the steering wheel, he set his sights on the newly established neighborhood. Street lights and uplighting of new construction created the illusion of safety. He scoffed at the illusion as he wound through the maze that led him to the only occupied house on the cul-de-sac. A yellow bulldozer gave him cover and kept him out of direct sight of the large beige stucco house.

Dragging his hand down his face, he attempted to release his clenched jaw. Eyes darting around, he opened the car doors and left them ajar as he balanced his kill kit, bat, and gas can. With agility, he maneuvered over roofing materials, pallets, and the lumber that were waiting to become transformed.

Reaching a safeguard, he paused to get a closer look at how he was going to gain entry. The only finished access to the house seemed to be the front door. He sped to the side and slid along the wall to the front before kneeling out of the sight of the windows on the front porch. Dropping the bag, he retrieved the bump key, crept to the door, and tapped it open with the mallet.

He threw the key and mallet in the bag and snatched the bat before opening the door, only enough to fit through. His senses were heightened, his heart raced, and his blood coursed vigorously through his body. In the distance, he could see the outline of the woman in the kitchen, but to get to her, he had to zig-zag through the maze of boxes that were stacked in each room. He ran into one. He stopped, crouched down, and waited to see if she had been alerted. He could still see her, so he continued adjusting the bat. Tightening his grip and getting it in a ready position, he drew closer to the kitchen.

Hands above his shoulders, he was ready to swing. He froze. She was gone. Eyes blazing, he scanned the room and located her just in time to see her pull out a gun. With the bat over his head, he lunged towards her. Placing her finger on the trigger, she fired the first shot recklessly into the air. He kept coming, but she stood firm, firing the second shot with more accuracy. This time it was aimed in his direction. The bullet grazed the shoulder holding the bottom of the bat, but he held tight. Invigorated with adrenaline, he was ready for the chase. Fixating on his target, he swung the bat fiercely in her direction. Desperately attempting to pull the trigger one more time, she found she was no match for his rage. Instantaneously, the bat cracked her head. She and the gun fell to the floor, and blood splattered on the pristine white cabinets and walls.

Immediately, his concern went to the middle child, who might have been aroused by the sound of the gunshot. He maneuvered around the boxes and raced up the stairs, frantically searching from room to room. They were all empty. Caged among the boxes, he breathed heavily, and his wild eyes darted around the room. Suddenly on the move, he bounded back down the stairs, grabbed the gas can from outside and began throwing gas haphazardly over the first floor. In the corner of his eye, he saw the unpacked knife block full of knives. It looked out of place as the only item on the granite counter.

He grabbed the largest knife, knocking the rest to the floor. Plunging the knife through her clothes into her abdomen, he clamped down and dragged it toward her pelvic bone. As the blood cascaded out from the open wound, the mixed smell of blood and gasoline incited him to act. The gunshots could potentially have spurred a neighbor into calling the police. He had to get out of here. Darting toward the front door, he paused and reached into his front pocket to grab a match, which he lit and threw onto the propellant. *Whoosh.* The fire obeyed. It jumped to life, dutifully following the path that had been made back into the kitchen. He grabbed the awaiting satchel and sprinted to the car. Eyes in front of him, he slowly drove until reaching a more established road. Stopping to turn left, he could see the billowing brushstrokes of smoke painting the night sky as he could hear the distant sounds of sirens approaching. Satisfied he had escaped, he exhaled softly, his body relaxed, and he began to feel the twinge from his shoulder. It would have to wait. He turned his blinker signal on and made a left-hand turn toward home.

The fire had shifted to the construction site, and the yellow bulldozers and forklifts that were now covered in soot, charred lumber, and black debris gave the appearance more of a movie set rather than a crime scene. Jack Lynch was the first to enter the house once given the all-clear by the firefighters. He ducked under the caution tape the local police were setting up and stepped inside.

"In here, Doc," one of the uniformed policemen called out.

Jack navigated through to the kitchen where the body lay. Setting his bag down, he leaned down next to the body.

He heard Detective McAllister's familiar voice above him. "Nice of you to show up."

"No use having too many cooks," Dr. Lynch said, looking up and cringing at his wording.

"Her body doesn't look as badly burned," she noted as she stepped across the uneven rubble and stopped to kneel next to him.

"I noticed that too." He took his index finger and floated a line above her body. "It looks like he cut into her here."

"COD, the same?"

"I can't say for certain, but I'd put a wager on it." He pointed to the area on her head.

Scanning the floor, she saw the silver tip of a knife amongst the rubble, "Here," she said and called to the forensic tech to bag the evidence.

"Did I hear there is just the one body?"

"Yes," she said while shaking her head. "Not this time."

"Interesting,"

"Oh yeah, he's got to be pissed," she said, letting out a long sigh.

"This all feels very different…"

"You haven't even seen the big-ticket item yet."

On cue, the tech reached in and pulled out a bagged handgun. Standing up, the detective took the bag and lifted it for inspection.

"Any idea where this came from?" she asked the technician.

"We won't know until we run it through and check for prints. We are looking for any casings and bullet holes now, detective."

"When someone brings a gun to a knife fight, it sure changes the dynamics."

21
DETECTIVE MCALLISTER

Several days had gone by before Detective McAllister pressed the familiar numbers on her phone to reach the doctor's office.

"Dr. Lynch," she said when he answered.

"Detective, I'm sorry, I just haven't gotten to her yet," he pronounced.

"That is actually not the reason I'm calling. I just wanted to run some things past you if you have time."

"I apologize for snapping. We are down some staff and feeling behind," he said as he walked back his unmistakable irritation. "You could come by the office this afternoon, after four…or we could grab a drink if it's not too case sensitive."

She felt herself blush and was instantly relieved by the distance of the phone. "A drink would be…" she said, searching for the right words. Placing her hand over her eyes, she decided to play it safe. "…fine."

"Indeed. How about we go to Oh George? It's got good beer, and good food, and it's just loud enough not to be overheard. Does five work?"

The remainder of her day passed in a blur, and soon Detective McAllister was walking into Oh George in search of Dr. Lynch. He'd been seated watching for her to walk into the bustling restaurant. He instantly waved to her from one of the blue booths. She smiled at the hostess and walked past her while pointing in the direction of her table.

"Great place," she said as she looked around and slid into the opposite side of the booth.

"I went ahead and ordered the shrimp and crab fondue. I'm starving," he said as the waitress arrived at the table with the food. She ordered a beer from the extensive list.

They sipped on their beers and made small talk before Jack asked, "What is it I can help you with?"

"I have been collaborating with Dr. Hunter. He's a professor at UVA who did some work at Quantico. I think I might have mentioned that." She waved it off, "Either way, he's a complete bastard, but if he helps solve this, then the collaboration will be well worth it. It's just I feel that I need all the fresh eyes that I can get on the case. You have a unique insight into the victims," she said, pulling out the manila envelope and sliding it across the table.

"What is this?" he asked as he opened up the thick folder.

"It's everything that I have gotten from ViCAP from 1995 to date."

He began shuffling through and scanning the cause of death in the cold case files while she leaned back, sampling the beer just delivered to her.

"This is interesting, an eleven-year-old male. Looks like his eyes were bloodshot, and there was bruising around the nose and mouth." Scouring the pages, he said excitedly, "Here it is, in this one too." He tapped the paper. "A feather was found in the older boy's mouth, so it looks like some of his earlier victims were probably smothered with a pillow." He kept reading. "It wasn't until the later ones that the MO changed. These reports feel hurried."

"They are old cold cases, and most of the detectives are either dead or retired. I think they are more hurried out of frustration."

"The cause of death was the same-blunt force trauma to the mother and all the smaller children had a buildup of carbon monoxide."

"So, he took more time with the older child and made sure that he was dead before the fire came in contact with him. For some reason, he did not feel protective toward the younger child."

"It takes up to three to five minutes to suffocate someone with a pillow, and that depends on if they are lying down or if they put up a fight."

Detective McAllister grimaced.

"Something wrong?"

"It's just that in Kevin Richard's book, the middle child was also killed by smothering them. It wasn't until later that he snapped their necks."

"I am not sure you need to read too much into that. The cause of death may have varied slightly, but the result was the same. Neck snapping, smothering—very personal."

"I can see that," she said, leaning back in the booth. "He subdued the mother quickly to get to his next victim. The one he wanted to spend the most time with, and then the baby seemed more of an afterthought." She pondered the older cold cases. "It wasn't until these recent kills that the baby and mother played a more prominent role."

"You do believe that this was our same guy the other night?" He questioned.

"No doubt. He just didn't do his homework. I interviewed a neighbor, and Sarah Wilson had two children both the same ages and sex as the past victims."

"So, where are the children?" he asked.

"Parents are divorced, pretty amicable. Dad is helping out with the kids while they move. The son Sam is ten, and Mark is eight months old."

"I can't imagine this bastard was too happy."

The waitress brought two fresh beers to the table. Jack picked up the beer and winced, unmistakably, as he brought it to his lips.

"You alright?

"Yeah, it's my shoulder. An old boating injury that flares up from time to time."

"Getting older is not for the weak," she said and raised her glass to him.

"Indeed." He smirked, changing the subject. "I can probably get to Sarah Wilson tomorrow, but from everything we have talked about, it looks like it should be pretty cut and dry."

22
CATHERINE

Catherine rolled over and stretched until her fingers landed on the vibrating phone on the nightstand.

"Hello?" she grumbled when she answered, but her heart skipped a beat when she heard the unmistakable voice on the other end. She sat up, reflexively pulling the sheet over her chest, grateful Kevin was not lying next to her to hear Dr. Hunter's voice.

"You're calling me so early. Why?"

"I'd like to discuss this latest murder with you."

"Not another one?" she mumbled and closed her eyes tightly. Shaking her head, she said, "Wait. Did you say murder? As in singular?"

"Yes. Early Monday morning, but this time, only the mother was killed. The children were not home."

"Praise, God," she said instinctively.

"Who?"

 "What is it that you want, Kem?"

"I just thought we should meet. I met with Detective McAllister and delivered a profile to her. I thought I would run it past you as well, and we could also go over more things I found in the ViCAP findings. You know, the one you don't have access to," he said, his voice dripping with sarcasm.

She bit the inside of her mouth.

"I can come by later today," he continued when she didn't speak. "Maybe meet Kevin. Perhaps we can all just move on and work together on this."

"That is not even close to being a good idea," she said, throwing off the covers and vaulting out of bed. "I have a full day. But I'll come in early and see you before the first patient." Before he could answer, she hung up. "So there," she said to the phone.

Halfway down the stairs, the front door opened, and a panting Marlo pranced in, wagging his tail, followed by his heavy-breathing owner. Kevin bent over and planted his hands firmly on his knees to catch his breath.

"You made it back," she smiled, skipping down the last steps and placing a hand on his sweaty back; she leaned over to taste his salty cheek.

"I did. I did make it back, but wow, do I need to do a lot more of that and a lot less of this," he said. He lifted up and mimed, holding a cup up to his mouth.

"Let's make some coffee," she said and began winding her way to the kitchen.

"Catherine," he said. Moving closer, he pulled her in and absorbed her into him. "I've been an ass." Shifting back, so he could see her face, he continued. "Nothing to say to that?"

"Not a thing," she said, a wide grin stretched across her face.

Releasing her, he continued. "Running gave me time to do a little introspection. Isn't that what you call it? I think I have just been in shock. I mean, I finally have this best-selling book. Things are going great, right?" He paused and lowered his eyes to the wooden floor. "I honestly don't want to think or believe that my book could have anything to do with the death of those families. I will do whatever else I can do to cooperate."

He started to pace around the kitchen. "I should probably go to the station and talk to Detective McAllister directly."

Jumping in front of him, she put her hand up. "Whoa, slow down there," she said. "You're a person of interest in a murder case. What are you thinking?"

"I know. You are right. It's just that I…I do feel somehow responsible for unleashing a madman. Maybe it's just the timing. I don't know." He closed his eyes, and when he opened them, Catherine could see a lone tear fall down his face.

"I know. I get it," she said and hugged him tightly. "Whoever is doing this is responsible, Kevin. Not you. Not your book. And they had been killing before your book came out."

Lifting his head back, he gave her a fake smile followed by a peck on the cheek.

"Why don't you go take a shower, and I'll make us some coffee," she said before glancing at the clock. "But then I have to get to work."

23

DR. HUNTER

"Terrific," Catherine said aloud as she saw Kem's car waiting for her when she pulled into the parking lot. Before she could park, his door opened. He smiled smugly, while holding a thick manila folder.

"Good morning," she said, briefly glancing over in his direction. Not waiting for him to follow, she walked toward the back door of her office.

She could smell his heavily applied cologne coming up behind her. "Not today," she said under her breath before unlocking the door and pushing it open.

"Excuse me?"

"I said, come in. Have a seat." She pointed to a chair next to her desk. "I need to do a few things in the other room." She walked out, unlocked the front door, and pulled back the curtains. She took a cleansing breath as she let the sunlight into the waiting room.

Once she'd taken her seat back behind her desk, he handed her the manila folder.

Snatching it from his grasp, she flipped the envelope open and began pulling the papers out and spreading them across her desk. He gave her time to look them over before he got up and moved his seat next to her.

"This is all pretty much what I've seen before. You said that you gave Detective McAllister a profile. I would be curious to hear it."

Kem relayed what he had told the detective. Catherine listened intently, turned back to the papers, and spent more time looking them over before saying, "I agree with most of it, all of it, but I'm not sure about this last murder."

"Hmm…?" Tilting his head, he sat back and crossed his arms.

"I just think there is a strong possibility that we are now dealing with two killers."

"You're grasping Catherine. All that is different is that it appears the children were not home," he said. "Otherwise, it would have been the same outcome."

"I can't believe he would make that mistake. So, perhaps if this one is a copycat, then I guess I'm beginning…" she trailed off.

"Are you saying that you do not hold the theory that this is singularly James Martin?" he questioned.

"Ugh." She put both hands on her temples. "This is all just getting way too confusing. For example, why did he start killing so long after he escaped, and why was he dormant for over a decade? That's a long time."

"We won't know the answer to that question until we meet James. There have been many serial killers that have had a cooling-off period for many reasons. Are you falling into the trap that all serial killers are between the ages of twenty-five and thirty-five?" he asked with a chuckle.

"I understand, but the timing just seems too coincidental. What I do know for sure is that it is not my husband."

"What if your husband's book set off James Martin? It is essentially a book about him, is it not?" He pushed his chair closer and leaned in. "What if, for some reason, he did stop and then started again because the book was telling his story and not him?"

"What do you mean 'his story'?" she asked while moving papers around.

"Think about it, Catherine. This book could have triggered him because he wants people to know that he is not just some fictional character portrayed in a book."

"Why now? I mean, for years, he killed without wanting notoriety. Nobody even knew he existed."

"But now he is known. People are interested in him. Perhaps he now wants to be acknowledged for what he has done."

She thought back on what he had said about the profile he had told her he gave to Detective McAllister. "You know, so many times, suspects are close to the investigation."

"That is true, which is why the police are interested in the people who help with search parties and attend funerals of those who have been murdered. They will use that to track down prospective subjects."

"If he is seeking acknowledgment, then he could very well be peripherally involved in this case or with the book somehow."

"I'm going to go back to Edmund Kemper again." He paused when she flinched from the recollection. "Sorry, I didn't mean to make you uncomfortable, but he is a good example."

"I'm fine," she said a bit too quickly.

"He inserted himself in the investigation by being a 'friendly nuisance,' as he called it, at the bar across the street from the courthouse. He would have beers with the police and ask questions about the investigation."

"I'm surprised that didn't draw attention to him."

"He probably told them that he had wanted to be a police officer. Think about it. At the time, it was all over the news. A public curiosity."

"True," she said, leaning back and looking up at the Monet for inspiration. Slapping her hand on the desk, she said, "I might just know where he could be inserting himself. Kevin has a writer's club that meets every other Wednesday."

"Hmm, how many people are in this group?"

"It keeps growing. Plus, we had a strange interaction with someone from Staunton a while back, and Kevin said there's a guy who sometimes will drive up here to attend the group."

"Same guy?"

"I don't think so, but I think we should go and talk to that club, Kem."

"Set it up."

24
CATHERINE

Singing to the radio on the way home elevated Catherine's mood. The feeling that this nightmare would soon be over began giving her a glimmer of hope. No matter what she thought of Dr. Hunter, he was brilliant, and she had no doubt that he was on the right track. She frowned when she turned down the driveway and saw a blue Tesla parked in her driveway. Trudging up the walkway, she opened the door to Marlo's paws tapping toward her on the wood floor. "We need to get those nails trimmed," she said as she leaned down to hug his neck.

Turning the corner, she saw the table was set and contained several opened bottles of red wine.

"So much for a little less of this," she muttered to herself as she picked up a bottle and took it into the kitchen. She stopped short when she spotted Kevin and Steve sitting at the kitchen counter with glasses of wine in front of them.

"Hey," they both said in unison.

"Hey back." She waved with her free hand. "What's going on?"

"I told you." Kevin poked Steve as they both laughed and clinked their glasses.

"Want to let me in on the joke?" she asked, reaching for a wine glass.

"Nothing is going on, Cath," Steve said. "I just dropped by with some tour dates and thought I would bring my two favorite people some wine and an Italian dinner." With that, he reached across the counter to a brown paper bundle and opened it. The room erupted with the overwhelming flavors the bundle contained, and the kitchen suddenly smelled as though someone had been cooking all day.

"Pazzo Pomodoro?" she asked hopefully.

"Of course! Plus, I stopped off at Victor's for some nice bottles of red."

"I'm still skeptical," she said while squinting her eyes and pointing at Steve. "But I can't argue with perfection. Let's eat. I am starving."

Half an hour later, she was patting her stomach and pushing her plate away. "Thank you, Steve. This was unexpected and delicious."

"Absolutely." He leaned over, placing his arm over Kevin's shoulder. "This guy is my family, and there isn't anything I wouldn't do for him."

"How grueling of a schedule is it?" she asked.

"Well, the book is hot, and not to sound ghoulish, but these murders have made it hotter." He scrunched his nose as he took a sip of wine. "I can't help that."

"You have heard that the police have questioned Kevin, right?"

"Yeah-yeah, he told me. Did he also tell you that when he asked me to, that I got those dates together that detective wanted? My buddy is in the clear." Leaning toward Kevin, he whispered loudly, "A small price to pay. Am I right?"

Catherine flashed him a look of disgust.

"Oh, come on, Cath, give it a couple more weeks." He gave Kevin an air high-five. Mockingly puckering his lips, he turned toward Catherine. "Don't shoot the messenger."

"You're an ass," she said as she grabbed their dishes, aggressively stacked them, and stormed off into the kitchen.

"Geez, don't break them," Kevin yelled into the kitchen.

Catherine tried to ignore the conversation they were having in the other room, but the wine was making them louder than usual.

"Seriously, dude, what the hell?" Steve said.

"Her old graduate school professor is in town trying to help the police. Plus, there's the investigation. It's just getting to be a lot on us."

"I guess," Steve said before picking up his glass and swigging the remaining drops. Finding it empty, he got out of the chair. "Well, it was fun until it wasn't."

"Don't be too tough on her. You can be an ass," Kevin laughed and slapped his friend's arm. Catherine walked back in the room just as Steve recoiled from the slap.

"Sorry about that, man," Kevin said. "Didn't mean to hit you that hard."

"I knocked it on something the other day," Steve said while rubbing his arm, "and it's still sore. No big deal, though."

"Come on, I'll see you out.

"See you, Catherine."

Catherine waved a half-hearted goodbye before returning to the kitchen. For the remainder of the evening, she spoke very little to Kevin about anything. When they finally climbed into bed together, she turned away from him.

Kevin sighed, rolling over toward her, and said, "Don't you think you overreacted a bit?"

"Sometimes, I have no problem with him. I know he is good at his job, but to openly wish harm onto others takes it too far."

"I certainly don't think he means that. He was just being flip."

"I know he has been your friend for a long time, and I am relieved he sent Detective McAllister the dates she needed, but..."

"He is like a brother to me, and sometimes it really sucks you are not more accepting of that."

She sat up and arranged the pillows behind her. "Now, who is overreacting? I understand, but at this point, we are trying to keep you out of jail, Kevin."

"I think you're being a bit melodramatic. I told you everything is fine." He rolled away from her, turning off the light.

"I met with, um, Dr. Hunter this morning," she mumbled.

"You what?" he asked and shot back up in the bed. He clicked the light back on. "What the fuck, Catherine?"

"I wasn't going to bring it up..." she murmured.

"No, but you were going to piously attack Steve and then hide the fact you saw someone I asked you not to see anymore? And then bring it up by mumbling under your breath. You're batting a thousand here, Catherine."

"I didn't say I was not going to see him anymore, and I don't like it any more than you do, but he is helping the police. As much as I hate to admit it, he does have some good ideas."

"What did this Dr. Wonderful have to say?"

"I will ignore the sarcasm and tell you that he believes this is James Martin. He thinks he was dormant for several years, but when your book was published, it sparked something inside of him—"

"Ladies and gentlemen, it was the book that made him do it," Kevin announced loudly. "I thought you were the one that believed in personal responsibility and all that?"

"Whoever is doing this is responsible, Kevin. Period. I am saying that your book may be the catalyst. You can't blame an inanimate object for your actions."

"It sure as hell feels that people are trying to, though," he replied.

"James Martin believes that he is an integral part of your story and wants people to know he is not just this fictional character in a book. He is also very likely to place himself somewhere in the investigation."

"You mean like your Dr. Wonderful?"

"Pretty sure he isn't Hannibal Lecter," she chortled before pausing. "But you are on the right track by thinking it could be anyone. So, I began to think of groups of people who were invested in some way in your book…"

"Now you are going to say Steve is a serial killer?" he asked as he began to get out of bed.

"No, no, not at all," she said and extended her arms toward him. "Kevin, please, just hear me out!"

He hesitated but ultimately returned to the bed.

"It could be someone in your writer's club," she said and braced herself for his reaction. "You said so yourself that there have been a lot of new people since your book came out."

He leaned back against the wooden headboard and stared straight ahead. "You want to come in and analyze my group now? Too late because Detective McAllister already beat you to it."

"What? When did this happen, and why didn't you say anything to me?"

"When Steve gave her the dates, she asked some questions, then called me to find out the names and numbers of the people who were in my group." His voice elevated as he said, "I wasn't too happy to have to do that. I think she's barking up the wrong tree, but I told you I would do what I could to help with the investigation."

Burrowing into the pillows, she took a cleansing breath and reflected on a way to reframe her words. "I get it, Kevin. You have become close to these people, and they look up to you, but you have to admit that is a good suspect pool. Look. I am trying to take the attention away from you."

"I'm not sure why you would have to divert attention away from me," he said. His face reddened as he leaned closer. Loudly, he said, "I have nothing to do with this."

"Obviously," she said and began plucking her lip. "I'm sorry. That came out wrong. I guess I am saying that because we have no idea who James Martin could be, we need to try to rule people out."

He slid down, turned over, and pulled the covers over him. "I'll think about it."

Beside her bed, Marlo was sitting up and gazing up at her. "I guess you didn't put the dog out?"

"Nope," he said curtly.

Sighing, she got out of bed. "I'll be back in a bit." She grabbed her phone, turned off the light, and headed back downstairs with Marlo trailing behind her.

25
DETECTIVE MCALLISTER

"You didn't have to come all the way out here. I could have just told you my findings over the phone," Jack said. He paused and smiled. "But I'm glad you did."

"I was in the area and just thought I would pop in," Detective McAllister lied. "Thank you for the other night. It was fun."

"Yes, it was." He tapped his keyboard and brought the computer screen to life. She leaned over and grabbed her notebook as he began to speak.

"Sarah Wilson, age thirty-five. Cause of death, as suspected, was blunt force trauma."

She nodded.

"He cut directly through her clothes, as there were trace elements of her clothing in her organs. He did not take the time to lift her clothing as he did in the last one, and he didn't use a scalpel. You found a kitchen knife at the scene."

"Yes, it was part of a set."

"It's just so gruesome to think and unfathomable that the knife you use to make your family's dinners is going to be used against you like that." He shook his head.

"I know. You just can't go there, Jack. It will wreck you."

"I know, and I usually don't…just sometimes, and especially with these cases, it just makes you think."

"There were two bullets found at the scene," she said, changing the subject. "So she managed to get off at least two shots. I suppose we can hope from the blood found on the one bullet that she at least grazed him."

"Too bad it didn't kill him."

"No such luck." She felt her phone buzz in her back pocket. "Hold on," she said, pulling it out and answering it. "Hello?"

Jack got out of his seat.

"I'll go get us some coffee and give you some privacy," he said, walking out the door.

"Thanks," she mouthed. Returning her attention to the phone, she said, "Dr. Hunter, what can I do for you?"

"I was speaking with Catherine yesterday—"

"What the fuck?" she yelled into the phone, suddenly glad that Jack was not there.

"Please stop, detective. She called me. I suppose she doesn't feel comfortable talking to you, but I thought you might be interested in what she had to say. Am I wrong?"

"Go ahead, please. This ought to be captivating..." She flipped her middle finger at the phone, again glad that Jack wasn't there to witness her behavior.

"Her husband is in a writing club, and she believes it might be a good idea to speak with them. Her thinking is that this suspect could very well be someone who wants to be close to Kevin. His rival, if you will."

She paused, thinking it through. "That is an interesting angle, but absolutely not. I have already spoken with several of the members."

"Hmm. I believe she is speaking with her husband about setting up a time and a date. You are more than welcome to come along."

"You would be *allowing* me to come along?" she cut him down. "How about when I get the rest of the names and numbers of everyone in this group, you can come down to the station and observe the interviews? That'd be great." She hung up, pulled up her contact list, and dialed the number before Dr. Hunter could.

"Catherine," she said as soon as she answered.

Catherine seemed reluctant to reply to her but eventually started the conversation with, "Detective I was not expecting a call from you. Is there something you need?"

"Something I need?" she repeated. She paused to take in a deep breath. She attempted to put her anger aside and remember Catherine had been a useful ally to the department in the past and that, perhaps, she would be again in the future. "I just got off the phone with Dr. Hunter. He informed me that the two of you were thinking of going to talk to a writer's group that your husband is in charge of, or attends, or whatever the fuck?"

"Yes, I thought it might be a good suspect pool," Catherine said. "The group has added several new members since the book came out. But more importantly, one of the members comes from Staunton to attend."

"That will be my job, not yours." Detective McAllister replied through her teeth, "This is a murder case. Your husband's at least been cooperative, which is more than I can say about you, Catherine. I've told you repeatedly to back off. If you keep this up, you can explain yourself to the Virginia Board of Psychology. Or, I may just arrest you for interference in an active investigation. Now, for the last fucking time, Catherine, stay out of this."

"But, I…" she stammered. "I think you are overreacting, Mattei. You know this is what I do, and we thought it would be more useful to come at it from a psychological angle."

"I am not overreacting, and I am beginning to think that you have misled me about your relationship with the good Dr. Hunter."

"No—"

She hung up just as Jack returned with two coffees.

"It's hot," he said, handing it to her. "I heard you down the hall. Sounded like you were putting someone in line."

"Just letting people know their boundaries." She blushed while thinking what he might have overheard. To avoid eye contact, she looked around the room. She noticed a spot on the wall where a section of the paint looked different than the rest. Also, one of his diplomas was missing. "Missing a picture?" She pointed the coffee in the direction of the wall, effectively changing the subject entirely.

"It fell."

"Broke?"

"Afraid so."

"Good thing it didn't take out some of the other ones with it. It was your college one? I have seen it framed up there for so many years, but I forgot where you went to school."

"Yes, I was very lucky. Those things were expensive to frame. I'm waiting for Michael's to have a sale on framing." He opened up his desk drawer and pulled out several files. "Hey, M,

I am so sorry, but I actually do need to get back to finalizing some of these reports. But I, uh, was wondering if you would like to go out to dinner sometime. No shop talk."

Placing her hands on the desk, she lifted herself out of the chair. "That sounds really nice. I would like that." She quickly moved through the door before he could see her grinning from ear to ear.

26

KEVIN

Catherine threw the phone on the chair after being scolded and marched downstairs. "Fuck him. Fuck her," she muttered with each step until she reached the den.

Kevin looked up at her. "Did you say something?"

"Yes and no. It was not directed at you if you heard what I said. How soon does your writer's club meet? Is it this Wednesday or next?"

"It is next Wednesday, but hold on. I did not say that I agreed for you to come in half-cocked and interrogate my friends."

"Oh, now they are friends? I thought they were just sycophants in the Dear Kevin's writer's club." She stopped herself. "I'm sorry. How soon can you call them together?"

Blinking several times, he said, "OK, wow. I didn't know you had such an animus toward my group."

"Oh, cut the crap, Kevin. I said I was sorry. I just need you to put it out there to your group chat or whatever that you are having a guest lecturer."

She stood with her hands on her hips and waited for him to pick up a phone or a computer. "Well?"

He got up and walked past her to the front door. "I'm going out with Steve for a bit. I'll let you know about the group later."

Within the hour, Catherine received a text. "Is tomorrow night soon enough? BTW Steve thought it was a great idea, and asked if you wanted to come to the Vienna Inn for a beer and chili dog?"

"Classy." She grinned while texting back, "Great, meet you there in ten."

Wednesday evening, Catherine and Kevin stood at the front of the room, watching the crowd spill in.

"This is preposterous," Kevin said, crossing his arms. "I can't believe I let you two talk me into this BS."

"It is pretty nonclinical. I'll give you that, but keep in mind that I'm trying to get to the bottom of this for our sake, remember."

"All right, Nancy Drew, but I just hope your half-baked scheme doesn't cost me my group."

"I don't see how this will have any adverse reflection on you. I'm just a *guest speaker*," she said, feigning innocence.

"I hope you're right."

"Now, speaking of Nancy Drew," she said and smiled at him, "Certain things I am going to mention might trigger a response, so I want you to watch everyone closely and watch their reaction."

"Got it."

"Is this size normal? There are about twenty-five people here," she whispered over at him. They observed the people grabbing folding chairs and signing the guest book as they entered.

"No, it is larger. We usually only have eight to ten people. I guess I have to hand it to the social media voyeurs." He waved as he saw a few familiar faces come in.

One of the regulars came up to Kevin, sneering, "What the hell, I thought this was our private writer's group."

"By all rights, it is Doug, but we do have drop-ins too."

Doug scowled and stormed off to sit amongst the original group toward the back of the room.

When it was time to start, Kevin scanned the room from the podium.

"Wow," he started off. "Thank you all for taking the time to come out tonight. We have a few more people than normal. I guess one of the reasons for this, you may have heard, is that tonight we have a guest speaker. So, we are going to shape this into more of a seminar atmosphere than we usually do. I thought it might help us to hear more about the subject of abnormal psychology from a psychologist. My hope is that it will also spark ideas or help with your character development." He looked at the door and saw Steve shamelessly walking in carrying a box of books. He set them by the door.

"I would like to introduce Catherine Richards, my wife, who is a clinical psychologist. She not only has a private practice but has also worked with the police department in the past." He held out an arm, beckoning her to his side. The crowd dutifully applauded.

"Thank you," Catherine said. "I want to start off by clearing something up. I have worked with the police, but I am not the police. I'm here tonight just as a guest lecturer. I thought maybe we could delve deeper into Ethan's character and how he might be tied in with these current murders that have taken place in our community."

She paused and looked around the room before continuing. "It is difficult not to see the similarity between this fictional character and the current suspect, especially because Ethan's character is loosely based on a case study that I had studied as a graduate student."

There were some murmurs in the crowd.

"James Martin was not a fictional character," she said. "He was very much real and was institutionalized at DeJarnette, a residential treatment center for adolescents in Staunton, Virginia as a child."

Catherine gave a quick synopsis of James Martin, and a brief Psychology Today version of psychopathology to the group. After she finished that part of the discussion, she pulled over the chalkboard that Kevin had found in the back.

James Martin's name appeared on the top left side of the board, and underneath she had written the dates 1995-2008.

On the top right side was a big *?-Family Annihilator*, which included the most recent murders.

Turning to face her audience, she said, "As you see here, there is quite a bit of a gap between the past murders and the most recent ones. Over a decade." She tapped the chalk in the middle of the board. "There can be many reasons for this. The first is that we are dealing with two separate murderers."

She saw many of the audience shake their heads. "Or that he was incarcerated, moved for a job and returned. Another option is that the release of Kevin's book triggered him."

Kevin was leaning against the back wall with Steve, scanning the crowd for anything that seemed out of place. When Catherine noticed his eyes hone in on a member of the audience, she followed his gaze.

A man next to one of the regulars was squirming in his chair and constantly smoothing his pants as he leaned in closer to listen to Catherine.

She continued and kept an eye on the man throughout the remainder of her speech. When she finished, there was a brief polite applause and Catherine walked off toward Kevin as Steve took over.

Holding out his hands, he said loudly, "Thank you all for coming. I hope this discussion has piqued your curiosity, and if you haven't read Kevin's book, I have a few copies available."

"Well, that's a bit tacky," Catherine said through pursed lips as Steve passed by them.

"I told you this was a good PR move," he said as he stopped and gave her a brief hug. "Let me see if we can make a few sales…"

"I need to go smooth some feathers," Kevin said after giving her a quick peck on the cheek.

As soon as he left, the disheveled man who had been so attentive hobbled toward her.

"Hi," she said in a therapeutic, calming voice and waited for him to talk.

"Hi." He stood there shuffling his feet and rubbing his hands over his face, "Um, I'm Jim, and I came here with Jerry. You know, Jerry?" he asked, looking directly out the door.

"I don't," she said with a smile. "Where is Jerry?"

"Oh, he's out in the truck, but I wanted to talk to you." More shuffling. "You're a psychologist?"

"I am, Jim. What did you want to talk about?"

"Well, I, um. You sure are prettier than any of the psychologists I ever talk to," he said, staring intently.

She smiled. "Now, what did you want to talk about?"

"I, um, I was at DeJarnette when I was a kid, too."

Catherine hoped Jim did not see the stunned look on her face. "You were? Did you know James?"

"Well, yeah, I mean everybody did," he said, looking around. "I gotta go. Jerry is waiting for me. It would be rude to keep him waiting." Scurrying toward the door, he stopped and turned. "You sure are pretty, maybe I can talk to you again sometime."

"Jim, wait," she called after him, but he was surprisingly fast and disappeared out the door.

Catherine ran over to Kevin and grabbed his arm, pointing towards the door. "Have you ever seen Jim before?"

"That guy that came up to talk to you? No."

"Do you know who this Jerry is?"

"I don't know who he is either offhand," Kevin said and grabbed the guestbook. He ran his finger down the list of names. "Here's Jerry's name, but crap, I don't see any Jim."

"Did Jerry leave his contact information?" she asked frantically. Not waiting for an answer, she flew out the door, but only in time to see the black Ram pull out of the parking lot.

She kicked the stones, swearing under her breath, and raced back inside.

"Damn, Catherine, you look like you've seen a ghost," Steve said.

"Are you alright?" Kevin asked, mimicking his friend's concern. "You look spooked."

"I might have just met James Martin," she said, blankly.

27
DETECTIVE MCALLISTER

Catherine was sitting at her kitchen table drinking a cup of coffee the next morning when a loud pounding sounded on the front door. She flinched as the cats scattered, and Marlo bounded toward the door with a loud bark.

"Who in the hell?" Still a bit groggy, Catherine put her coffee down and stumbled to the door.

Detective McAllister was positioned as though she were preparing to knock again when Catherine opened the door.

"Here," the detective hissed as she shoved the *Washington Post* in Catherine's direction. The paper fell to the floor.

"What the…?" Catherine asked, leaning over to pick up the fallen paper.

"Unreal," Detective McAllister said under her breath. She walked in, waited for Catherine to shut the door, then followed her down the hall.

"What do I owe the pleasure of this early-morning house call, detective?" Catherine asked crossly as she led the detective into the kitchen.

Detective McAllister jerked the paper out of Catherine's hands and held it up. "Care to explain this, or would you like me to read it to you?"

"Would you like some coffee? I was going to call you this morning. I have something I need to talk to you about."

"Coffee? Are you fucking kidding me, Catherine?" the detective spewed. "Coffee? Not only did you directly defy me by putting on this little demonstration, but you tainted my suspect pool. I suppose your keen observing skills did not see the reporter taking notes during your talk?"

Catherine thought back and recalled the man in the back who was frantically taking notes during her talk. "Um, I did. I actually did. I just thought he was taking notes about the case to use it for his writing or something."

"Or something," the detective nodded, sarcastically. "And you decided to name the suspect the 'Family Annihilator'?"

"I wasn't thinking, and yes," she acknowledged. "I guess I got carried away."

"That is your excuse? You and your Dr. Hunter are certainly two arrogant peas in a pod. Undermining me behind my back."

"I just wanted to help, and Kem, I mean Dr. Hunter had nothing to do with this," she said. She wasn't sure why she felt the need to protect him but the words slipped out before she could stop them.

"I don't fucking care if he was there or not. I told you to stay off the case."

"But, remember, I said there was a reason I was going to call you?" she added, desperately trying to change the subject. "I may have met James Martin."

"You what?" The detective stopped in her tracks and suddenly switched gears. "Hold on, start from the beginning."

Relieved that the diversion worked, Catherine relayed her experience. "There was this quirky guy who came with his friend. He came up to me afterward and told me his name was Jim and that he had been in DeJarnette the same time that James Martin had been there."

Catherine could hear Kevin's voice on the phone in the background coming down the stairs.

"How many more books did we sell?"

Catherine paused and cringed as the conversation continued, growing louder as he moved closer to them.

"Awesome. Yeah, I guess it did turn out to be a good idea. What? No I haven't seen any article…"

He turned the corner to the kitchen and stopped in mid-sentence. "I need to call you back."

Putting his phone in his back pocket, he put a smile on his face, and said, "Catherine, why didn't you tell me we had company?"

"Who were you on the phone with just now?" Detective McAllister demanded.

"Steve, my agent."

"Sounds like the three of you thought it was a great idea to go rogue," she said "Do you want to tell me more about this Jim, Catherine?"

"Well, he left so suddenly, and by the time I processed the information, he was gone." Plucking her lip, she added quickly, "But don't we have something, Kevin?"

Kevin flinched. "I only have Jerry's e-mail. That is who he said he came with."

"I'll need that, then."

Kevin didn't even put up a struggle and dutifully left the room to retrieve the information.

28
KILLER

His hands clutched the morning paper as he read excerpts from the article:

'Family Annihilator' is the name that Catherine Richards, a clinical psychologist, gave to the suspect who has been committing the ongoing murders that are now being played out in Central and Northern Virginia. Richards linked the murders to James Martin, a fugitive who escaped a mental institution at the age of seventeen in 1991. Martin had been institutionalized for allegedly killing his mother before setting the house on fire. Richards believes Martin had issues related to his father that led to his killing spree. She voiced concern for single mothers with a particular family type and warned for them to be particularly vigilant.

"Family Annihilator. Not very original, Dr. Richards," he proclaimed before throwing the paper and scattering it across the kitchen. "Stupid bitch."

The motion caused his shoulder to throb. "Fuck." He winced, walked into the bathroom, and pulled off his shirt. The wound was healing slowly but probably could have benefited from medical attention. That wasn't going to happen even though he could still see the red subcutaneous tissue. He reapplied a new dressing, put his shirt back on, and went into his office.

He examined the list he had made earlier and plugged in several nearby addresses. He picked one. He knew he needed to regain control after the last failure.

Before he could take care of that urge, however, he had another task he needed to take care of. Luckily, it wouldn't take long, and it was close. He looked up the information needed, and left.

He parked in the parking lot and waited. During his wait, he found a renewed patience. Finally, the woman emerged and got into her car. He started his car, initially following at a safe distance until she got into heavier traffic. Then, he moved in close.

Catherine looked in her review mirror. "What the hell? Pass me already asshole," she said out loud.

At the stop light, she attempted again to get a glimpse as to what kind of a jerk was behind her, but all she could make out was a baseball cap, and he was too close to get a license plate number.

When the light turned green, she gunned the gas and got into the other lane. The car had stayed back. Relieved, she turned the radio up and focused on the road ahead, the road rage incident, or whatever it was, had been left back at the light.

Satisfied she had outmaneuvered the moron, she turned up the volume and began singing to her Yacht Rock. Without warning...*BAM*... her car was involuntarily sideswiped and plunged into oncoming traffic. She had no control over her car, no time to think or react before she was smashed into by a Ford Explorer.

Dazed and disoriented, she slowly opened her eyes. Lying still—unable to move, she heard the scrambling sirens that signaled help was on the way. She heard muddled voices asking questions, but she didn't have the strength or understanding to answer. The last sensation she felt was her body being lifted onto a gurney.

Kevin jumped out of the rudimentary chair that had been his home for the past several days. "*She's awake!*" He ran to the door, tears streaming down his face, repeating down the hall to the nursing station, "*She's awake!*"

The following day, Detective McAllister poked her head into the room. "They said you were awake."

Catherine attempted to lift her head. "Oh, I see they're bringing in the big guns," she mumbled, attempting a smile.

"Only the best. How are you doing?"

"I really want a shower," she said, closing her eyes.

Detective McAllister took a seat next to her bed and waited.

Opening her eyes once more, Catherine she shifted her head to the side. "Did I do this Mattei? Did I hurt someone?"

"No," she said. She pushed through the cool metal railing and placed her hand on top of Catherine's.

"I have tried to remember. But it happened so fast."

"There were several witnesses that said you were sideswiped."

Catherine tried to sit up, but her head fell back into the pillow. "What about the other people?"

"They will be fine, too. Are you up to me asking some questions?"

"I don't think I remember anything," she said and stared at the ceiling for several minutes before muttering, "Wait. I remember this piece of shit little dark blue or black car riding my ass right after I left work. I tried to see who was driving, but couldn't. All I could see was that he maybe had a baseball cap on. He wouldn't pass me. After the stoplight, I thought he was gone." She winced in pain. "Until…God, that sound, I can still hear it."

"You remember more than you thought. The witness statements said it was a small dark car that hit you and then fled the scene."

"Someone did this to me on purpose. Why? Why would someone do this?" Tears streamed out of the corners of her eyes.

"Catherine," she said and took in a deep breath while remembering Joey's description of the car and driver. "I don't think this was random. I think you were the intended target, and I'd bet money on it that this has something to do with the murders."

"Why? How would anyone know me?" Her eyes brightened when she realized the truth. Squeezing her eyes shut, she said, "That article in the paper. I did this to myself, didn't I?" Digging her head deep in the pillow she grimaced and pressed the call button.

A nurse came in right away and asked, "You need more pain medication?"

"Please."

"Here you go, this should help." The nurse put the pain medication in the line and gave her a reassuring smile. "Call me if you need anything else." She scurried out and on to her next call.

"Thank you," Catherine called to the door.

"I'm afraid that the article in the paper sure put you out there front and center as the face of contact."

"You warned me, and you were right."

"Any other time I would be happy to hear that coming from you," she said as she attempted levity.

"Did you ever get hold of that Jim guy?" Catherine asked. Detective McAllister noticed how her body had relaxed in the few moments since the nurse left. It seemed as if that pain medication was taking effect quickly.

"I did get hold of him. Is he as squirrely as he sounds on the phone?"

"More so. There are most definitely some mental health issues," she said, envisioning their brief interaction.

"He is coming in later this week. Jim claims he does not drive, so his friend Jerry is having to bring him up."

She nodded, her eyes opening and closing, "Detective," she whispered. "This may be the medication talking, or it may be that someone just tried to kill me, but can I tell you something?"

"Of course," the detective said and leaned closer to her.

"You know who Steve Howard is, right?"

"That's Kevin's agent, isn't it?"

"Bingo." She pointed at the detective, then touched her nose and winked. "But did you know that Steve was from Waynesboro? Yep. You know that's close to Staunton, right? I just thought of it." Her words slurred as the medications kicked in. "Kevin told me his parents had died his freshman year of college, just like my dad, but he had nowhere to go home to so he usually went to Kevin's for holidays. They're like brothers."

"OK. I was under the assumption that you were all close friends?" Detective McAllister replied as she got out her notebook and jotted down several things.

"He's Kevin's friend." She rolled her eyes and gave a crooked smile. "And sometimes mine. I think he's an ass, and I think he would do anything for Kevin. But he would also do anything for Steve, too. Keep Kevin's book number one, for example." She held up a shaky index finger. Suddenly, she stopped talking looking past Detective McAllister.

"Anything new?"

Detective McAllister turned to find Kevin in the doorway. He gave a slight knock before entering.

"No, unfortunately," she replied. "I was just checking in." She patted the starched sheet next to Catherine. "You take care of yourself, and I will let you know if I hear anything."

"Thank you for coming by," Kevin said as he took the newly vacated seat next to his wife.

Catherine smiled up at Kevin and said, "I love you." Her eyes fluttered before she fell back asleep.

Kevin waited for his wife to wake up by passing the time reading past texts and e-mails that had piled up. When she finally stirred a few hours later, he gave her a smile.

"Hey."

"I'm sorry," she said. She sounded more lucid than she had when he arrived. "How long was I asleep?"

"Don't you worry about that." He leaned over and kissed her. "You need your rest."

Her doctor entered the room soon after and gave Kevin and Catherine a brief smile. "All good news. Your vitals are good, no internal injuries. I believe we can release you tomorrow. Your pain can be managed at home, and we will set you up with PT as well."

"That is great news," Kevin said and squeezed her hand.

"All in all, you were extremely fortunate," he told them. "You must have a good guardian angel."

"I have God," she said and pointed while looking up.

The doctor smiled broadly. "Amen."

29
KILLER

He was feeling out of control AGAIN. What was happening? Nothing was falling into place like it used to. Everything used to come so easily. Why hadn't that bitch died?

He threw the necessities into the grocery basket and gazed at everyone milling around trying to find the perfect vegetable or fruit.

"For their families," he muttered under his breath. The majority of people were women. He stopped and did a 360. His mood shifted when he remembered someone once told him that a grocery store could be a great pickup place.

Putting his basket down near the front of the store, he yanked out a cart and began sweeping through the aisles. He tossed in boxes of cookies, cereals, and sugar-laden snacks before he began wandering the store looking for potential prey. Strolling purposefully between baby food and the cereal, he was beginning to give up hope when he saw the woman with a baby seat and a young boy in tow. He quickened his pace toward her eyeing what was on the shelf next to her.

"Ah, here they are," he said aloud. He glanced at the petite blonde's ring finger as he moved closer to the shelf.

The man grabbed the items off the shelf and held them up for inspection. He leaned down to ask the young boy, "What do you think, fruit roll-ups or fruit gushers?"

The mother and child exchanged a wary glance.

Wrinkling his brow, he looked up at the woman. "I'm sorry. That was totally out of the blue. My son is coming to stay with me this weekend, and I want everything to be just right."

Convinced he was harmless she gave him a wide smile and flicked her hair back. "Jay, what do you think, sweetie? Which one?"

He smiled back at the woman before glancing down at the boy. "He's about your age, so I was wondering which one is the best one."

"Oh, I like the roll-ups," the boy said.

"Roll-ups it is." He reached up and grabbed six boxes of all kinds.

The boy looked wide-eyed as the roll-ups were being tossed in the cart. "WOW. That's a lot!"

"Don't you get any ideas," the woman said with a laugh.

"Well, thank you again," he said slowly, as he began pushing the cart away. "It's been so hard. I don't get to see him very much since his mother moved away."

"Oh, are you divorced?" she asked, rubbing her lips together.

"I am," he said and stopped the cart. He lowered his chin to his chest.

"I am, too. I sure wish my guys had a father that took an interest in them like you do."

"That's very nice of you to say…"

"Dawn," she extended her hand.

"Mark," he took her hand and held it, gazing into her eyes, "Mark Archer."

"Nice to meet you," she said and stepped into him. She touched her chest with her free hand.

"Um," he said, releasing her hand slowly, lost in her eyes, "It's nice to meet you as well."

"This might be a little forward," she said and bowed her head sheepishly, "but would you like to grab a drink sometime."

"I, I can't do it this weekend since my son is coming," he stumbled. Her forwardness both surprised and delighted him. "But, uh, yes. I would like that."

"Great. I just think life is too short." She looked up with a confident smile. "I guess we should exchange numbers," she said, scouring for her phone in her pocketbook.

He pulled out a flip phone from his pocket. "I can send you a text. What is your number?" Her eyes lingered on the phone, and he could tell she was suppressing a snicker.

"Oh this?" He gave her a broad smile and held the antiquated flip phone up for inspection. "It's my personal phone. I feel so tethered to the other one all week that it is just nice to have this. It allows me to pay attention to the more important things."

"I never thought of that," she said and gladly gave up her information to the stranger in front of her.

A ding sounded from her pocketbook, and she said, "OK then…Great!"

"Yes indeed," he said and pushed his cart down the aisle and turned the corner. Once out of sight, he peeked around the corner at her to see her reaction. She was looking down at her own phone and the message he'd sent her when he looked back.

He knew it read *I look forward to our next time together*. He gaged her reaction and was pleased when she looked up and smiled.

"Not bad for a flip phone." She laughed out loud. Then, she looked down at the baby and said, ""Mommy has a date!"

He abandoned his cart in the cleaning aisle and walked out the door.

After several steamy phone calls, they set a time to meet for the first time in a neutral place for a drink, and if all went well, she said she would cook him a homemade dinner.

30
DETECTIVE MCALLISTER

"Thank you for coming in to meet this guy with me, Dr. Hunter," Detective McAllister said as she extended her hand out to the seat in front of her desk. "Please, sit."

"No problem. I find this very intriguing. You say that Catherine met him? Where?"

"I assumed you knew. She decided to take matters into her own hands and present a little seminar to her husband's writing group."

"She what?" He jerked his head back and asked, "When did she do this?"

"Sometime last week, before the accident."

"Accident! What accident, detective?" he stammered.

"I'm surprised you didn't know about that either. I thought you two were close."

"I haven't talked with Catherine since I was read the riot act by you, Detective McAllister. I was assuming that you were handling everything."

"Catherine was in a car accident," she said, ignoring the dig.

"Is she alright?"

"She is alright. Hopefully, she should be coming home soon, but I think she was very lucky."

"I'm getting the feeling that you don't think this was an accident?"

"Not when the car plunged her into oncoming traffic and took off. No."

"Do you think the suspect had something to do with this?" He bit his lip, waiting for the answer.

"I think that her little charade almost got her killed. So, yes. Did you not see the article in the paper?"

"I don't really do media. Not my thing. Why?"

"One of the attendees was a reporter and wrote an article about Catherine's conclusions regarding the suspect, and I suppose he did not find it flattering." She forced a spurious smile in his direction.

A uniformed officer appeared behind her, bent down, and whispered, "Jim Malcovy is ready, Detective McAllister. Room five."

"Thank you." She looked up, slid her chair back, and glanced down at Dr. Hunter. "Ready?"

"How long has he been in there?" Dr. Hunter asked when he was gazing through the two-way mirror and observing Jim Malcovy as he repeatedly crossed and uncrossed his arms.

"About forty-five minutes," she answered.

"He appears to be quite agitated. If he was institutionalized, then this could be triggering for him. I think you need to go in. Time's not going to help. He has difficulty self-soothing."

"You aren't coming in?" she questioned, surprised he would not take the opportunity to possibly interview James Martin or someone who knew him.

"It will be up to you to re-focus him and assure him that he has done nothing wrong. I think I could better observe him from here than if I was in the room. He doesn't need to feel like he is being double-teamed."

"OK, got it," she said and nodded before opening the door.

"Mr. Malcovy, thank you for coming in," she said and sat across from him with the cold steel table between them.

"I, I don't like this place very much," he muttered. He scanned the room and stopped on the mirror. "Who is behind there now?"

"Mr. Malcovy, you are only here so I can talk to you. Can I get you something to drink?"

"No." he cleared his throat. "I, um I just want to know who is behind the mirror. Why won't you tell me? I'm not stupid." The chair made a screeching sound as he pushed it back and moved to the front of the mirror to look directly into the eyes of Dr. Hunter.

"No one is saying that you are stupid, Mr. Malcovy. You have done nothing wrong."

"Then, why are people looking at me behind the mirror?"

"Let me go see who is behind the mirror, Mr. Malcovy."

"I want to see them. I want to see who is behind the mirror."

"I will be right back, Mr. Malcovy."

Detective McCallister opened the door to the observation room. "I think you will have better luck with him. You were right. The time alone seems to have made it worse."

Dr. Hunter sighed and turned to follow the detective into the interrogation room. When they entered, Jim's eyes narrowed.

"Who are you? Do I know you?"

"No, you don't know me, Mr. Malcovy. I am Dr. Hunter, and I am a psychologist who is here to talk to you."

"Were you behind there?" he asked, jabbing his finger accusatory in the direction of the mirror.

"I was. I just wanted to see how you were doing before I came in," he said calmly. "You have an interesting story that we would like to hear."

"You were spying on me." He made several large circles around the table, then stopped and looked up. "You're not as nice as that pretty doctor," he said. "Why can't she come back and talk to me? I want to talk to her."

"She's busy…" Detective McAllister stated.

"She was in an accident," Dr. Hunter said, leaning his elbows into the table toward Jim.

"Is, is she o-ok?" he stuttered while biting the inside of his lip. "I have to go. Jerry is waiting for me." He got out of his chair and walked toward the door. "I have to go," he repeated.

"I understand, and it is almost time to go, but I am curious about your time at DeJarnette," Dr. Hunter said. "I was hoping you could tell me about it."

Jim whipped his head around. Squinting toward Dr. Hunter, he stood and his eyes widened. "Do I know you?"

"I understand that the nice psychologist talked about DeJarnette, and you told her that you were there."

"I was there."

"Why did you go to hear the pretty psychologist, Mr. Malcovy?"

"Jerry took me. He said I should go."

"Do you like to write? Wasn't it for writers?"

"I don't know anything about that. Jerry said I should go and I went. Now Jerry wishes he didn't take me."

"We appreciate Jerry driving you here. We want to ask you about a long time ago. Do you remember James Martin when you were there?"

"I didn't know any James Martin. I thought I was coming to talk to the pretty psychologist."

"Mr. Malcovy, you told Dr. Richards you knew James Martin."

"Nobody knew James Martin. Nobody. He couldn't talk, and he didn't like anybody. I didn't know him."

"Would you come back again if I bring back the pretty psychologist?" Detective McAllister asked, knowing they could not hold him if he did not want to stay.

Shuffling his feet, blushing slightly and looking up and down, he hesitated slightly before, he said, "I might." He opened the door and walked out.

"Shit. That was a magnificent waste of time."

"Hmm, maybe not. We did learn that he was fixated on Catherine."

She rested her head on the back of the chair. "That is true, and I think we can rule him out as causing Catherine's accident. He doesn't seem like he would hurt her, and he does not drive." She lifted her head up. "But he sure didn't like you."

"He saw me as someone who was spying on him, not being upfront. Plus, I'm not the pretty psychologist."

"Well, we at least have his information. We can do some more digging into his past and see what we can come up with."

"He may have been at DeJarnette, but he is not your guy."

"How can you be so sure?"

"You saw him. He is disheveled and does not have the mental capacity to carry out these murders, let alone maintain the endurance it has taken over the past decades."

"Perhaps he is a very good actor, Dr. Hunter. I mean the likelihood, with his initials, his claim that he knew James Martin…" She wanted this nightmare to come to an end.

"I am fairly certain we can chalk that up to a coincidence I'm afraid, detective," he stated.

She patted the folder in front of her. "Well, I do have an interview with Steve Howard, Kevin's long-time friend and agent. It seems under the proper medication Catherine believes he could be capable of doing anything to keep this book on the bestseller list. I just have to see if that 'anything' would include murder." She drew air quotes, and shrugged. "Care to join me?"

"Hmm, that would certainly be a better bet than Jim Malcovy, but I think it might be best if I sit this one out, detective."

Shifting his focus, he challenged, "Have you come up with any connection between any of these victims?"

"Nothing. Like I said, unfortunately, the precincts viewed these cases as unique to their jurisdictions, chalked them up to a cold case, and have been less than helpful, shall we say."

"Understandable, and you have found no connection here?"

"None. The only thing we know these women had in common was that they all had infants and young boys. There was no cross reference of any of them interacting."

31

STEVE

"Want to tell me why I'm here?" Steve scowled and lowered his eyebrows as Detective McAllister closed the door behind her.

"I just had a few questions for you. Thank you for coming in." She placed a thick manila folder in front of her, but it was filled with mostly blank paper. "Can I get you something to drink?"

"No thank you." He tilted his head toward the table. "What's that?"

"Oh," she glanced over at the material, shaking her head. "That's just some information we have gathered."

"Are you trying to make me a suspect?

"Look, Mr. Howard, I do have a murder investigation to conduct, and I have to interview all those who are associated with it, no matter how peripherally."

"Fine." He closed his eyes and tilted his head back. "What do you want to know?"

"You are originally from Waynesboro, Virginia?" she asked. "And that's near Staunton, isn't it?"

"And?"

"I'm just asking basic questions. I understand that you met Kevin Richards when you attended West Virginia University. Is that correct?"

"Yes."

"How did you two meet?"

"We met on the track field. We both had track scholarships."

"So, you met your freshman year?'

"There really isn't much to tell, detective. We battled it out on the track field, and after that became as close as brothers. In fact, after my parents died, I spent all my holidays with him and his family."

"How old were you when your parents died?"

"They were killed in a car accident during my freshman year."

"I'm very sorry to hear that. Didn't Mr. Richards's parents also die in a car accident?" "They did, but it was much later. I guess it ended up being just one more thing we have in common."

"Right." She nodded and scribbled some notes down. "You have been very close for a long time, and now, you're his agent."

"I'm not sure what you are trying to get at here, detective. If you're going to try to get me to implicate my best friend, it's not going to work."

"Like I said, I am just trying to get some background. When did you move to Northern Virginia?"

"After Kevin's parents' funeral. He started writing more, then he met Catherine, and the rest is history as they say."

"Well," she opened up the manila folder and looked at his portfolio. "It says here that you have done all right for yourself managing other authors, but this book has really helped you get a name for yourself."

"The book's selling. That's not a crime. Why am I here?"

"Settle down, Mr. Howard. Having a book on the best seller list is not a crime," she said as she closed the folder. "Don't make this personal. I have a job to do, and asking questions is part of the job. I will need to know your whereabouts during these past murders. I will give you the dates…"

"Don't bother," he snapped. "I have them right here because, if you remember detective, I gave you the same information for Kevin." He pulled out his iPhone. "Want to give me an e-mail so I can send this to you?"

"That would be very helpful," she said and provided him with the e-mail.

"So, you think we are all 'suspects' now?" he said, leaning back and smirking.

"I can't discuss that with you."

"Do you think I'm a suspect?"

Silence.

"You do!" His eyes widened, and his facial expression changed as he leaned toward her. "Holy shit, you do."

"There is a matter I do need to ask you about, Mr. Howard," she said, reopening the file. "It says here that in 2001 you were arrested for aggravated assault…"

"Are you fucking kidding me?" he interrupted. "A bar fight over some girl, and you bring that shit up? I'm outta here." He slammed his hands on the steel table and kicked the chair back before heading toward the door. "If you have any further questions, you can contact my lawyer."

"How important is it to you to keep this book on the best seller list?" she called out from her seat.

He froze and whipped around. "I guess Catherine said something to you? No need to answer that. I'm sure she did. Her true colors sure are coming out." He flung the door open and stormed out.

A uniformed police officer appeared and pointed in Steve's direction. "You need me to bring him back, detective?"

"No, let him go," she waved him off. "But I do need you to follow up on an e-mail he sent…"

Steve called Kevin as soon as the door to the police station closed behind him. "I just got questioned by the fucking police for an hour and a half, Kevin. Know anything about that? Did your wife have anything to do with it?"

Kevin didn't respond, which escalated Steve that much more.

"Did you just hear what I fucking said?" he continued yelling. The door to Steve's car slammed shut with a satisfying *thunk*.

"I heard you, and I'm pretty sure everyone around you heard you, too. Calm down."

"Calm down? Calm *down*." Steve slammed his fist on the steering wheel. "I just left a goddamn police station after being interviewed in a murder case! Calm down?" He tried and failed to shake the pain out of his hand. "Fuck!" he shouted.

"Steve, dude, they showed up at my house too, remember?"

He thought about it and began to calm down. His mind still racing, he took a deep breath and exhaled loudly. "It just came out of nowhere."

"I get it! Join the *Successful Serial Killer Crime Suspect Book Club!* I'm the founding member. Membership is free."

"They didn't fucking arrest me, so there's that." Steve looked down at his phone. He was getting another call. "Gotta go," he said, pressing the green button. "Hey baby…tonight?"

32
KILLER

Before he reached up to ring the bell, the door opened. Dawn stood eagerly waiting at the door with a low-cut blue dress on.

"Come in!" She motioned him in, dragging her hand down his arm as he walked by.

He could feel the heat coming off of her as he passed. Confused, he hardened as he watched her glide toward the kitchen. "*What the...*" he wondered to himself. That had never happened before. He had to maintain his composure. Maybe this was a mistake? Maybe this was not how to do it…

"Would you like some wine?" she called, interrupting his thoughts.

He stood in the doorway.

"I have a red opened, but I do have white if you prefer." She smiled and lowered her voice.

"Red wine would be nice," he said and moved closer. He reached out to her but was stopped when he heard a slight cough. He looked over to the small figure.

"Jay!" she exclaimed. "I thought you were upstairs." She paused, smoothing her dress. "You remember Mr. Archer…."

"Yeah, the one that has a kid that likes roll-ups too."

He smiled. "Great memory you have there, little dude!"

The boy smiled back.

"So Jay, what were you doing upstairs?"

"Playing," the boy said.

"OK, a man of few words. You sound like David," he chuckled. "David likes Legos. Do you like Legos, Jay?"

"Yeah!" His eyes brightened. "That's what I was playing with."

"Can I see what you're building?"

"Sure," Jay said and turned toward his mother. "Mom, is it all right if I show Mr. Archer my Legos?"

"Sure!" She smiled back in his direction.

"Come on then," the boy said and gleefully waved his arms for the stranger to follow him. He bound up the stairs.

The man followed the boy up the stairs and down the long hall. By the time he reached the playroom, Jay had already pulled down several new bins from the shelf to show his new playmate. In the middle of the room were several Lego cities, each impressively tall and detailed.

"Wow, these are awesome! You have put together a lot of really cool sets. How do you have time to do all this?" He was beginning to refocus, to feel back in control. This hadn't been a mistake.

"My mom is busy a lot of times," the boy said, his eyes looking downstairs.

The man felt the familiar rage deepening.

"I'm sorry. New babies take a lot of time," he said serenely. "Sometimes it's hard."

"It's ok," the boy said, moving the new Minecraft Lego set to the table. "I like these the best."

"Hey, we have those too," the man lied as he moved closer.

Jay instinctively backed up slightly.

"I get confused with all of these..." he picked up several pieces, examining them.

"I play Minecraft on the computer, too," he blurted out. "I'm pretty good. Does your son play Minecraft?"

"He sure does," he said, inching closer. "He loves it!"

"Maybe we can play sometime." He looked up wide-eyed at the possibility of a new friend.

"That would be great." He moved in even closer, examining Jay's handiwork. "Those are great!" He was almost within arm's length. He just needed to get a little closer.

"This is my favorite, though. Look! It's The End Battle," he said and picked it up, lifting it to show his new companion.

"Now that is appropriate," he said, leaning to the right height before reaching over and skillfully snapping Jay's neck.

The Legos fell to the floor. The man knelt beside the boy and smoothed his hair.

Dawn came into the room while he was still kneeling beside Jay. She screamed at her son's lifeless body, dropped the wine glasses, and ran to him.

"What happened?" She looked up. "*What happened?*

She picked up his lifeless body in her arms, rocking him.

"Call 911," she yelled at him.

He rose and reached into his pocket. He removed the stainless-steel scalpel he had wrapped in tissues and plunged the sharp instrument into her neck. When he picked her up, blood spurted on him and the ceiling and began pouring onto the boy's body and the Legos. He felt himself growing aroused by her body in his arms. Disgusted, he dropped her body, where she joined her son in death.

He dragged her down the hall to the room, where he smelled the pungent smell of baby powder from the nursery.

Bending down, he began to caress Dawn's neck as the baby stirred and began making gurgling sounds.

He slowly unsnapped the buttons on Dawn's dress, exposing her breasts. Methodically, he grazed the scalpel blade along her exposed body before he plunged in the blade and opened her from navel to pubis. He made the second cut into her uterus, then picked up the baby, who was now crying, and swiftly nestled it in his mother's uterus as best he could.

He suddenly became very still. He had forgotten gloves. What had he touched? This was all so different. Not as thought out as he was used to. For the first time, panic set in, and he raced downstairs to his car, mulling over in his mind all the places where his fingerprints could possibly be. The good news was, it didn't matter. By the time the police got there, all his fingerprints and DNA would be long gone. At the end of the stairs was a mirror. He examined himself to make sure no blood could be seen on him. The black hid any splattering that had gotten on him.

With a new sense of confidence, he pulled the gas can out of the backseat of his car and sped back into the house. He started by spreading a majority downstairs, and by the time he moved to the upstairs, he was laughing at himself. Why was he worrying? Fire is the great eraser. He ran up the stairs, leaving a trail for the fire to chase. Jiggling the can, he realized he did not have that much left. He sprayed what was left around the bodies in the nursery. Then, he raced down the stairs, wiped the doorknob, lit a match, and dropped it. *Whoosh*. The heat nearly singed his eyebrows.

Running to the car, he turned the engine over, willing himself to drive forward slowly, and did not look back.

33

DETECTIVE MCALLISTER

"**A**fternoon, Mattei." Jack stood up behind his desk as she entered the room.

"Sorry, I missed you at the crime scene."

"Me too," the medical examiner said. "I would have liked to have heard your initial thoughts."

"I mean, I know it's the same guy, but this one feels different. More chaotic and disorganized." She paused. "Like he's losing his shit."

"Indeed. Dawn Simpson's manner of death was completely different. She was stabbed in the neck. Her injuries were consistent with the use of a scalpel—as was the wound from the navel to the pubis.

"It was a scalpel?"

"The cut was *consistent with* ones created with a scalpel."

Detective McAllister knew that was as close to certainty as a medical examiner could come.

"This time, he lifted her dress instead of ripping through her clothes, and he exposed her breasts unnecessarily for this sort of procedure."

"I noticed that too. Maybe he wanted to spend more time with her? This is the first time I have felt that there was a sexual component in his killing of the mother. From the look of that dress and no bra, she was not expecting just anybody."

"True. She did specialize in taking care of herself, judging by her implants."

"You found that out during the autopsy?"

"No," he smirked. "Even in death, they remain at attention."

"Well, that's a vision," she said and put up her hands. "We have all the Legos in the fire packed up, and we're dusting them for prints. Possibly, we could get lucky. The downstairs was pretty much consumed by the fire, but it was put out before it did too much damage to the upstairs. We could actually get a break this time. I sure as hell hope so."

"Weren't there glasses found upstairs? Did you get any prints on those?"

"Just her prints."

"Too bad. That would have been a lucky break."

"How did the baby die?"

"I found the presence of soot in the airways. Particularly below the level of the vocal cords, meaning he died in the fire."

"The babies, Jack," she said and closed her eyes. "Jeez. I have just never seen anything like this."

"Now, what was it you said to me?"

"I know it. I need a hobby." She nodded her head towards the pictures on the wall. "It is good to have something outside of this to buffer."

"Sailing has always been a good distraction."

Pointing to the empty space on the wall, she asked, "Still haven't replaced that?"

"I still have yet to find time," he said, looking at the bare spot. Almost immediately, he turned towards her and asked, "Speaking of distractions, I was wondering if you would like to go out to dinner sometime."

"Speaking of distractions," she repeated, smiling. "I would like that."

"I'll give you a call in the next couple of days. I'm actually running a bit late, otherwise, I would set something up now."

"Just give me a call. I look forward to it."

She turned back out the door, waving her hand up overhead. She was grateful for the momentary release from this case.

In the car, she sifted through her notebook and dialed a number. She hung up and made a second call instead. "Thank you for taking my call," she said before relaying the latest murder scene and autopsy report to Dr. Hunter. "This last murder has me confused. Why would he change his behavior now?"

"I believe we spoke about the possibility and probability of escalation. If you think about it, there was a long period of no action. When he did return to the scene, the murders have been closer together than they were before. In escalation, he could be becoming disorganized, more aggressive, and careless."

"So why a different murder weapon?"

"Opportunity," he said automatically.

"Meaning?"

"That maybe he did not have his kill kit accessible and needed to use what was available. You said that it appeared the female victim could have been dressed for a date? If that is the case, then perhaps this is how he is getting into their homes. I would even go so far in saying that the scalpel has now become his weapon of choice. How do you walk into someone's home carrying a baseball bat?"

"True. It might raise one or two red flags," she said and raised her eyebrows, smiling morosely for a moment before continuing. "I spoke with Dawn's closest friend and neighbor Jan Bailey, and she remembers Dawn telling her that she met someone recently at the grocery store of all places."

"You do know a big joke is that the grocery stores are great pick-up places, especially for men, so that does not sound that atypical, Detective"

"Yes, I have heard that one. Well, she also told me that she was excited that this guy had a son roughly the same age as her son."

"Did she have any physical description?"

"That was the only information that I have so far. I'm having one of my people go to see if there is any video from the grocery store closest to her house. We are also going through Dawn's phone."

"Hopefully, that will lead to something."

"It sounds like the way he found his victims has changed."

"We don't know how he picked his past victims." He paused. "But I am inclined to agree with you. The older boy was not found in his bed, so the killer had interaction with him. That is new. We discussed that perhaps he has or had a family, which is most likely how he related to the young boy and gained his trust. You said all of the bodies were found upstairs? I don't know too many nine or ten-year-olds that would invite someone they just met upstairs to play with them."

"If this was the guy that Dawn said she met at the grocery, then it makes sense. It looks like she was killed in the playroom and that her body was dragged to the nursery, and he opened her up to put the baby on top of her." She looked around the room, silent in her thoughts.

"You still there?" he asked.

"Yeah, yeah, I'm still here. I was just thinking about another thing that points to this being a date. It appeared that she was bringing wine to him and, like I mentioned in the beginning of our conversation, she was dressed very provocatively."

"Her body was not burned?"

"No, in fact, the fire was put out before it did too much damage."

"So, you are wondering if there isn't a sexual component in some way?"

"Yes. We have seen nothing remotely intimate or sexual in the past crime scenes."

"You have been careful about what you release to the press, correct?"

"Right, we have not told them many of the details. I know you said you think the focus of his rage is the mother, but I am beginning to wonder if it isn't the infant."

"Hmm. I can understand how you can come to that conclusion, but if you think about it, the mother-child bond is still very strong with such a young child. His signature remains the same. Anything else is just a minor detail. Reread the profile and go from there. Plus, you might think about doing some grocery shopping of your own. This may be the beginning of a new pattern."

"I agree with you."

34
KILLER

He lay in bed, replaying the night before while fully absorbed and fixated on Dawn and the feel of her neck in his hands as the life drained out of her. It had all changed. He didn't know why, but it had changed. He was preoccupied with how he felt touching her and planned to begin again in the morning. He leaned back, melting in the pillows and anticipating how the next time, he would spend even more time with her. He grew harder with each snapshot in his mind. He reached down and took himself in his hands while fantasizing about the woman. When he finished, he rolled over and had a peaceful sleep.

The morning sun blazed through the window, and he groggily reached over to grab his phone. He glanced at his schedule. The day was wide open. He could take his time shopping. He might even take the time to go to several places to better his odds, or better yet, he might find more than one woman to play with.

The Giant parking lot was packed. Finding a place farther from the store, he got out, snagged a cart, and strutted into the store. He was surprised to see so many children out of school, and under normal conditions this would have helped with his hunting, but the children were almost becoming secondary as his focus shifted to his female quarry.

Meandering through the suitable aisles, he dumped the bait into the basket—cookies, ice cream, sodas, all things that made him look like a dad who needed rescuing. Up and down the aisles he went, until he saw several potential targets. At last, in the middle of an empty aisle, a middle-aged woman stared at the shelves, lost in thought. The baby cooed in a car seat while the boy sat cross-legged in the cart with a toy action figure and pretended the toy was flying in the air. The killer pushed his cart next to the distracted woman and quietly searched the shelves with her.

"Excuse me," he murmured in a hushed tone, not wanting to startle her. "This is crazy. I thought for sure that chocolate pudding cups would be here," he said, and as an afterthought looked up at the overhead sign stretched across the aisle. Lightly tapping his head with his palm, he moaned. "Oh my, I guess if I could only read, I would have known they weren't here."

"They keep changing things. It's hard to know where stuff is." She smiled reassuringly over at him.

"I know where they are," the boy chimed in. "They are down that aisle." He pointed to the right.

"Oh, you like those, too?" he asked and leaned over the cart. "I think my son could live off of them. It must be the age."

"Jonathan is ten." She gave up the information quickly.

"My son is eleven, and I'm getting ready to pick him up. He is coming to stay with me this weekend!" His face lit up at the imaginary prospect. "I don't get to see him as often as I like," he said, and then he sighed. "My ex-wife moved out of town after the divorce."

"That's awful. I am sorry about that. Divorce is rough. Trust me. I know."

"Well," he said, shrugging. "One day I'll meet my soul mate . . ." He sighed again. "I usually don't come to this store." His eyes sparkled, and he looked at her with warmth. "My name is Jim Denton."

"Joan West. I'm usually not this, well, forward, but since your son is coming into town, and our children are the same age, maybe we could get them together!"

He whipped out his phone from his back pocket. "That may not work out. I don't have much time with him, but who knows."

"Oh, I understand completely. I just thought…" she said quickly, looking down.

"Why don't we exchange numbers. If it works out that we can get the boys together, that would be great, but if it doesn't, I would like to give you a call, if that is all right?"

"Sure!"

He saw that she had dimples when she smiled.

She gave him her phone number. He tapped a few lines on his phone and smiled when, for the second time that week, he texted, *I look forward to seeing you.*

After she'd smiled at him and walked away to continue her shopping, he waited until he was sure she had left the store and driven away before abandoning the grocery cart in the fruit section. Then, he walked out, pondering as to whether or not to go to another grocery store.

35
DETECTIVE MCALLISTER

Detective McAllister had several undercover officers in the area store, but she decided she would pop into a few herself. More eyes were never a bad thing. She thought about the profile and began looking for single men between forty and fifty. Maybe we would be wearing a baseball cap to hide his face from security cameras? He would probably have children's food in his cart to show he has a child and is non-threatening.

Exasperated, she pushed an empty cart around the store aisle-to-aisle, baffled at the number of different products that were the same thing just rebranded. Buying for one, she rarely went to the larger chain grocery stores. If she did have to, she just grabbed what she needed and left. She found this shopping exercise tedious. By the third store, she was ready to leave it to the undercover officers. Then, she turned the corner, ready to take her cart back, and spotted a single man in a black baseball hat. Picking up the pace, she saw the cart was filled with cookies and other non-parental-approved snacks.

The man heard the wheels of a cart coming closer, steered his cart to get out of its way, and then turned.

"Mattei?" The man smiled broadly.

She stopped short, her heart skipping a beat. "Jack? What a surprise."

"I can say the same thing. I thought you lived further west?"

"Oh, I do. I just had a call in the area. I'm finished for the day, so figured I would stop here on the way home. I'm also doing a little reconnaissance on my own," she winked and looked into his basket. Her eyes narrowed. "That's a lot of crap in there, Jack. I thought your boys were older."

"They are, but trust me. You can never be too old for junk food," he said, pulling out a box of Chips Ahoy.

Shifting her weight, she looked up at the shelf and, grabbed the first thing she saw and threw it into the empty cart.

"Pepperidge Farmhouse cookies. Indeed, a good choice," he said with a wink.

"Never too old," she said with a smile as she began to roll away.

"Mattei, how about we set up a time to go out to dinner?"

"Sounds good," she said, pulling out her phone.

"How about Friday? After work. We could go to Bazin's."

"Yeah, sure, that works for me. I can meet you there about seven?"

"Great. I hope I don't see you before then."

"Me too," she said.

She waited for him to leave the aisle, then replaced the cookies on the shelf and deserted the empty cart.

Still shaken from seeing Jack, she walked to her car to wait for him to exit the store. When he did emerge from the store and loaded his groceries into a beige Yukon, she breathed a huge sigh of relief. She felt guilty but knew that any lead needed to be followed. Catherine's words were stuck in her mind: *"What if he's closer than you think?"*

Driving to the station, she decided to refocus her attention on Steve Howard, which would help take any further scrutiny off Jack. How ridiculous could she be for even believing Jack could be a suspect?

This was one topic she was not going to bring up at dinner, she thought as she smiled to herself.

Back in the office, she pulled out her notes from the interview with Steve. One of her officers had put in a copy of the NCIC report. She perused the report and saw the only run-in with the law was the aggravated assault.

"There's something about this guy…" she mumbled to herself. Unsatisfied, she put his name into the search engine.

"What the hell?" she asked aloud. Her mouth fell open as she read that Steve Howard's parents were still very much alive and still living in Waynesboro. She even had a number for them.

"Hello," she said when someone answered the line. "Is this, Mr. Howard?"

"What?" the raspy voice yelled back. "You're going to have to speak up. I can't hear you."

"Mr. Howard, this is Detective—"

The phone dropped, and she could hear muffled voices in the background. "I don't know!" bellowed the loud frustrated voice. "You talk to him."

"Who's calling please?" a younger female voice asked.

"This is Detective McAllister from Fairfax County, Virginia. I'm calling for Mr. or Mrs. Howard."

"Detective? What is this regarding?"

"I'd rather talk to Mrs. Howard. Is she around?

"She's even less able than my father to talk to you, but I'm their daughter, Lucy, and I'm pretty sure I can answer any questions. Now what is it you are calling about?"

"Lucy, I just have a few questions about your brother Steve."

The line went quiet.

"Hello…Lucy?" Detective McAllister said, uncertain if they had been cut off.

"Yes?" and Lucy's tone was chilly now. "What about him?"

"I was just wondering when the last time you or your parents had spoken with your brother."

"My brother? He's not my brother. My parents took in a foster kid—Steve."

Rubbing her eyes, she asked, "I am confused. How old was Steve when your parents took him in?"

"He was a teenager. I think he was thirteen or so. I was in my first year of college. I mean, why in the hell would you adopt a teenager?"

"They adopted him?"

"Oh, of course they did, my freshman year. They called me and told me."

"So he was in high school?"

"Finishing up middle school. He stayed through high school, went off to college—which they of course put him through— and then he took off."

"Have you heard from him since?"

"None of us have. It broke my parents' heart." The line went quiet again. "What did he do?"

"Steve has told everyone he knows that his parents died when he was younger."

"His bio mom drank herself to death, and he never knew his father, so yeah, I guess technically, he could legitimately can say that, but my parents adopted him. He never bothered to tell anyone that, I'm assuming. He's a piece of garbage."

"Do you know how long after his mother died that your parents adopted him?"

"All I know is that after his mother died, he went to DeJarnette for a while. My parents adopted him after he was placed in foster care. They never confided in me. For a while, I thought I didn't measure up. After he took off, I got over that one." Then she said, "Where did you say you were from?"

"Northern Virginia, Fairfax County."

"So he lives up there now? Well, rural Virginia was never good enough for him." The line went dead.

Keeping her phone in her hand, she dialed the familiar number that belonged to Dr. Hunter. When he answered, she got straight to the point. "Dr. Hunter, I was wondering if you had any time today to stop by the station."
"I am in the area and will be there after my last class."

When the doctor arrived, Detective McAllister dragged him into a conference room and closed the door behind them. Once alone with him, she began pacing around the room.

"I was going back to something Catherine said to me," she said. "What if our suspect is hiding in plain sight."

Placing his thumb and forefinger to his chin, Dr. Hunter lowered his eyes toward her. "Don't you think you have had that theory all along?"

"What do you mean?"

"You first contemplated that the suspect could be Kevin Richards. Or have you forgotten?"

Detective McAllister bristled at his tone. "I was thinking of his agent, Steve Howard. I'm sorry you've stopped taking this case seriously."

"It's you I'm taking less and less seriously. You're flailing, Detective. Steve Howard isn't James Martin."

"By my calculations, they were probably hospitalized around the same time."

"James Martin was seventeen when he escaped, and you say this Steve Howard was adopted at age thirteen, so no, the timing does not work for him to be James Martin. Maybe you should take a small vacation, then review your files."

"I am not going anywhere. I am merely bouncing ideas off of you. I haven't charged anyone."

"I wouldn't take it completely off the table, but honestly, I think it is more likely that this impressionable twelve or thirteen-year-old who just lost his mother was sucked up in the folklore that surrounded James Martin and perhaps became fixated on him. It would be the only way it would work in my mind."

"The profile fits," she said, her eyes gleaming. She lifted herself up in the chair and leaned across the desk. "Steve Howard is the correct age, he's estranged from his family, he's educated, and he's certainly involved in this case. He also has some anger issues in the past, plus he was overheard screaming into the phone—by someone outside his car." Crossing her arms, she leaned back, smiling. "I would say that makes him a person of interest."

"Hmm…You make a good point. I would have to agree with you, but I have been thinking lately about the way the suspect originally could have found his victims. All of the women had a fairly newborn child, and even though some information is easily attainable, some of it is not and birth records are one of them. I have a feeling that we are looking at someone who has direct access to medical records. That can be anyone from a doctor to any other medical staff."

Her stomach dropped as her mind returned to Jack. She shifted in her seat.

"Is there something wrong, Detective?"

"Jack Lynch. Our medical examiner," she spluttered.

"Why on earth would you think that?"

"It's little things," she said sheepishly. "He lives alone, has been in a custody battle, is highly educated, is involved in the case, and his diploma from West Virginia has been missing, which may be nothing, but it's like he wants me to forget that he lived in that area. Plus, I just saw him at the grocery store with a baseball cap and a cart full of junk food he said was for his son."

"A baseball cap makes one a suspect? That's half the middle-aged male population."

"True, but what about the other things?" She closed her eyes and forced the words through her tight lips. "Plus, he has an injured shoulder. Just like our suspect would have from being grazed by a bullet."

"Hmm…Let's look at this Stive guy first. Certainly, each one fits the profile, and each is plausible in its own way. But being a loudmouthed buffoon doesn't make one a serial killer, even if he has created a sob story for himself. Has Catherine ever mentioned him being violent?" At Detective McAllister's expression, he added, "You haven't bothered to ask, have you?"

"Maybe we need to bring Mr. Malcovy in again." He scoffed.

You arrogant prick.

"I can call Catherine, and when she is up to it, she can be here to speak with him." She said disregarding his sarcasm.

"Speaking of Catherine," Dr. Hunter said. "How is she doing?"

"You haven't called her? Really?"

"Is she all right?"

"I think perhaps you should call her rather than pumping me for information."

"I will do that," Dr. Hunter replied with a grin. "Thank you for your permission."

"My pleasure."

"As for Mr. Malcovy. I was kidding. It's pointless."

"Why do you say that? Catherine felt like he could be—"

"I thought we took care of that last time I was here," he replied with a sigh. "Mr. Malcovy has a fondness for Catherine, he doesn't drive, and the Mr. Malcovy that we met lacks the sophistication to gain access to a woman with guile. I do not think he could pick up anyone in a grocery store, no matter how good of an actor you think he could be You have two good suspects. One I'm assuming you wish was not."

She sat in her thoughts for a few minutes until she suddenly recalled her plans for that Friday. "Oh no!" Her hands flung up to her face., "I have a date with Jack on Friday."

"Keep it," he said. "His guard will be down."

"No shit."

"Anything else? If not, I will be on my way"

"Just ask about her health," she called after him, "nothing else."

36
KILLER

After three lengthy, arduous conversations, he had finally set a date with Joan West. He poured a second glass, imagining how she would feel. The scotch glass shook slightly as he raised it to his lips. His heart pumped faster. Closing his eyes, he reached down into his pants, grabbing himself tightly, and began fantasizing about what he was going to do to her. After he was finished, he was mixed with exhilaration and turmoil. He felt alive with the testosterone of a teenager, but it did not keep him in control, and if he didn't focus, this would be his undoing.

37
DETECTIVE MCALLISTER

Jack stood up as Mattei approached the table.

"Great place," she said. "I've always wanted to eat here."

"Bazin's is one of my favorites, sadly they will be closing soon." he said as he looking around. "I was a little early and went ahead and ordered a bottle of wine. I hope you like cabernet."

They were finishing up their first glass of wine when the waiter brought them a basket of steaming bread.

"I have no idea what to order," Detective McAllister said. "Everything looks so good."

"I've been here so many times," he said and looked up at the waiter, giving him a wink. "I could order for you."

"And they say chivalry is dead."

The waiter scribbled down Jack's menu choices and poured them each another glass of wine. "Is your son still visiting?" she asked, upset as the investigation popped into her mind.

"It didn't pan out," he said, ripping into a piece of bread. "My ex can be a piece of work sometimes. Instead of coming to see me on his break…his mother had other ideas, and so I'll just leave it at that." He stared out onto Church Street.

"I'm sorry."

"Me too. Hoping he can come down in a few weeks."

"Where is he in school?" she asked.

"West Virginia."

"You went to West Virginia University as an undergrad, didn't you?"

"I did. You have a good memory."

"It's funny because I feel like half the people I have come in contact with lately went there. It's nice your son is going to your Alma mater."

"It is. I grew up in York, Pennsylvania. My parents suggested somewhere closer, but I was young and wanted to get away."

"Did those murders happen while you were there?"

"In York?" He smiled. "There was nothing like that there."

"I was skipping around in thought, sorry. I meant West Virginia."

"Yes, they were fairly close to the campus. It was awful. I remember it being my first years away, and my parents were ready to pack me up and bring me home."

"If it had such an impact on you, I'm wondering why, when we have been discussing this case, you never brought them up."

"Indeed," he reflected, picking up his glass of wine, "I honestly haven't even thought about the correlation until just now."

"Really?"

"I was in college. I didn't read the newspapers or listen to the news. I just knew that there were people murdered near where I lived. I didn't ever really know the details until recently. I was young and thought it was horrible, but it didn't impact me."

He put down his wine and looked at her. "You remember those days?"

"Barely," she said with a smile. "Are your parents still living?"

"They are, thankfully. I am very lucky."

"You are." She felt her eyes well up as she thought of her deceased parents.

"It's funny you brought those murders up because even though I say they didn't affect me, sometimes I wonder." He paused. "At least subconsciously."

"How so?" She picked up a piece of crusty bread to keep herself from talking too much.

"My father is a doctor, was a surgeon. He's retired now. I was not sure I wanted to follow down that same road, but I also didn't have my own path either. So, because of indecision and to keep the peace, I ended up going to medical school."

"You do surgery."

"Indeed, but that's an odd way to put it. I like getting results and playing detective, so this was the best of both worlds."

"I guess it is. I have referred to your room as the second crime scene, haven't I?" She said and scooched to the left as their food was delivered.

"It's the final place the victim has the opportunity to make known what happened to them." He paused looking up at the waiter. "Thank you, Edwardo."

"Will there be anything else?" he asked.

"No, thank you," he said before returning his attention to their date. "I hope you like it."

"This is delicious," she said after taking a bite.

"The miso encrusted sea bass. It's one of my favorites. I am glad that you like it." They finished in relative silence.

"I have an odd question," she said when she broke the silence again. "I was wondering if you have access to medical charts?"

"If you have access to a certain hospital and their EMR, then you have access to everyone's medical chart in that particular hospital."

"Doesn't matter what department?"

"Doesn't matter. Don't let anyone tell you that this HIPPA BS protects your privacy."

"That doesn't seem right, and certainly not what it was designed to do."

"I'm wondering if it wasn't designed to do just that. Your information is everywhere, and it doesn't always fall into the right hands. One of my physician friends told me to always be careful what you tell a doctor, because it is going in that chart."

"That is being a bit skeptical, isn't it, Jack?"

"I wish it were."

"So, you can get into the OBGYN records?"

"I suppose I could if I had access to the hospital's EMR." He looked over at her. "Why does it feel like I am being interrogated? Am I suddenly on a list now?"

"Sorry. I suppose my conversational style comes off a bit intrusive." She held up her hand. "Force of habit."

"Indeed." He picked up a bite of wasabi mashed potatoes.

They finished their dinner with idle chatter and walked out to the parking garage together. "Thank you for dinner, Jack. I enjoyed all of it. The company and the food."

"My pleasure. I'd like to do it again sometime soon," he said. He took her hand and squeezed it before turning toward his car.

"Goodnight," she called after him. She wanted to put any thought of Jack as a suspect out of her head as she watched him walk to his car.

She froze when he opened the door of a small, black Toyota.

"Jack?" she called.

Smiling, he turned back as she walked toward him.

"Is this your car?"

"Yes and no," he chuckled.

She scanned it for collision marks. "Why do you have this car?"

"This is one of my son's cars, and I'm taking it into the garage to get it fixed for him. It failed inspection."

She could see the white piece of paper taped to the window.

"You have got to be kidding me.

She stepped back, and her cheeks grew warm when his eyes narrowed.

"I'm sorry, Jack," she said softly. "I can't ignore it. No matter who you are. I just had to ask."

"I'm very confused, Mattei."

"I understand, Jack and, I'm sorry. I just can't…"

"Save it," he replied, crossly. "I have to go."

When he climbed into the car, he slammed the door, started the engine, and screeched out of the parking lot onto Church Street.

"What just happened?" she said out loud before walking back to her car. Her phone rang as she was climbing inside. She groaned when she realized another officer was calling her.

"Sorry to bother you on your night off, detective," the voice on the other end of the line said. "Me and Sargent Miller went to Steve Howard's house as you requested. There's nobody here."

"Well, just sit there and wait for Mr. Howard to return. Hopefully, it will be soon."

38

KILLER

He walked up to the brick walkway, climbed the steps, and rang the bell while clenching the flowers, impassioned by his rebirth of prurience. His heartbeat pounded in his chest when she opened the door. Drifting onto the first step to meet her, he handed her the flowers.

"Here you go," he said. "They almost match your beauty."

"Thank you," she said, reaching up and hugging him. She stepped back. "Oh my." She drew her fingertips through her hair. "That cologne."

He smiled. "I'm glad you like it. I only bring it out for special occasions."

"Come in."

She extended her arm towards the living room. "I am almost sorry Evie is coming now," she whispered as he walked by.

He swung around to meet her gaze and brought a clenched smile to his face. "Who is Evie?" He brought his fingertips up and lightly brushed her neck.

She giggled. "My babysitter, silly. You do remember that I have children."

"Of course," he replied and rubbed the back of his neck. "How silly of me. Say, it was a longer drive than I thought May I use your restroom?"

She pointed to the door halfway down the hall.

Without a second look in her direction, he walked to the bathroom and closed the door behind him. After a few moments, staring at his reflection he turned the water in the faucet on. The bitch said a homecooked meal! He splashed water on his face. His mind raced. He took several deep breaths before punching in a number on his phone. When the call connected, he spoke quietly into his phone. Then, he hung up and opened the door, looking right down the long hallway and into the kitchen.

"Where did you go?" he called.

"In the kitchen! Keep walking," her sing song voice replied. "I'm putting these gorgeous flowers in a vase." She added. "Would you like something to drink before we go? I suppose it was presumptuous of me to suggest a home-cooked meal." he said as came closer to her.

"Not at all," she said, pulling out the cork from the wine bottle. She poured it into the two waiting glasses on the counter. Handing him the wine, she kept her hand on the glass as he took it.

Searching his eyes, she snuggled closer. "I should have—" She paused to take in another deep breath of his cologne. "I didn't want you to think I was that kind of girl, but now I don't care." She tipped her head back, exposing her neck. His hands reached out slowly, just as the doorbell chimed.

"Damn, what horrible timing."

Pounding footsteps came running down the stairs, and a young, excited voice called out, "Evie!"

Within moments, the young boy was bringing the intruder into the kitchen. The man forced a smile on his face.

"Can you say hi to Mr. Denton, sweetie?" the mother urged her son.

He provided a boyish acknowledgment before he grasped for Evie's hand. "Come on," he implored, pulling her out of the kitchen. "Bye, mom!" He yelled back as an afterthought.

The man's face reddened as he watched the boy walk away. Ring, damn it.

"You ready?" she asked as she grabbed her coat from the rack in the kitchen.

He stepped back toward the counter and grabbed the wine. "Let me just finish the rest of this," he said just as his phone went off. Breathing a silent sigh of relief, he said, "I'm sorry I need to take this." He made a show of answering the phone and listening to the voice on the other end. "Now? Really? But..." He paced around the kitchen, scowling. After looking down at his watch, he muttered crossly, "Fine, I'll be there."

"You'll be where?" she seethed. "You're not leaving!"

"I am so sorry, Joan, but I have an emergency."

"What kind of emergency?" her voice softened. "Is your son all right?"

He looked at her curiously, then remembered. "Oh yes, yes. I wasn't supposed to be on call but…"

"On call," she patted her chest. "Are you a doctor?" Her smile got bigger. "I can't believe I didn't even realize what you did for a living."

"Can I have a rain check?"

"Of course," she said, walking him to the door. "I'm sorry tonight didn't work out. But we will have others?"

He didn't answer and barely made it to the car without exploding. He drove away from sight before punching the back of the passenger seat, desperate for some small release.

These uncontrollable sensations were coming closer and closer. This 'testosterone' adolescent was taking over. He didn't know how to deal with this pent-up frustration. He had to find some relief. He briefly thought of a strip club but flinched at the thought. Instead, he pointed the car in the direction of home.

39
DETECTIVE MCALLISTER

Detective McAllister called the surrounding hospitals and morgue trying to find any news of Steve Howard's whereabouts. Catherine and Kevin were becoming increasingly worried and were calling constantly for any update. There was no Steve, and there had also been no new murders in the area. She did a quick VICAP search to see if there were any matching murders elsewhere on the off chance that he had moved on.

"Hey," Blair called, breaking her concentration. "He's in room two. Did you want to observe?"

"Yes, I do." Nodding, she shuffled some papers around on her desk before getting up to follow Blair to the observation room. She watched Dr. Jack Lynch shifting uncomfortably in the seat. Her heart and mind conflicted.

The door opened, and her heart skipped a beat as Blair walked in to question her friend and colleague. Taking a seat across the table, he placed the pen and paper tablet he had been writing on down. Detective McAllister flipped the switch that allowed her to hear the conversation and held her breath.

"Thank you for coming in, Doctor Lynch," Officer Blair said.

"I don't see that I had that much of a choice."

"You always have a choice." Officer Blair attempted a smile.

"Can you please tell me exactly what I am being questioned for? Where's Mattei? She couldn't make it?"

"It looks like, at this point, I just need a few details sorted out."

"Fine." He sat back in the chair.

"You are in possession of a black Volkswagen Jetta SE, correct?"

"I own the car, but it is my older son who drives it. I told Mattei why I was driving the car. Are you now going to question my son?"

"Can you tell me your whereabouts on—" Officer Blair began to rattle off the dates of the murders.

"I'm pretty familiar with those dates. What you are asking me is where I was at the time of the murders."

"I guess I am."

"Indeed." Pushing his chair back and crossing his arms and legs, he tilted his head back and admonished the Officer across from him. "I live alone. I'm fairly certain that I fit the profile. I have medical training, and I'm the right age. I have lived in the places where several of the murders have taken place. Do you need me to continue? I'm also an ME, and I'm leaving."

He reached across the table and took the pen in his hand before scribbling a name and number down.

"That is the name and number of my lawyer. You can call him the next time you need to talk to me." He slapped the paper for emphasis and got up from his chair.

"Just one more thing. Are your fingerprints on file?"

"You're printed when you get your state license," he said before making a beeline to the glass. He knocked on it and waved goodbye.

Opening the door, she watched as he marched out. She thought about going after him to explain her thought process, but she knew it would be of no use.

"That didn't go so well," Officer Blair said when they met in the hall. "I guess we will need more physical evidence the next time we bring him in."

"I'm hoping there won't be a next time," Detective McAllister said as she lowered her head and returned to her desk.

40
CATHERINE

Catherine hesitated when her phone rang, and she saw Kem's contact information on her screen. Ultimately, she answered with a simple, "Hello?"

"How are you feeling?"

"Hello, Kem. I see you heard," she said with a sigh. "I'm getting there, but still a bit weak. How did you hear about the accident?"

"I had to hear about it from Detective McAllister, unfortunately. Why didn't you call to tell me?"

"I apologize, but honestly, I didn't have the strength for you and Kevin to be anywhere near each other."

"I was wondering if we could have lunch sometime this week and discuss some developments of the case. That is, if you are up to it." He paused. "Plus, I think I want to make sure for myself that you are all right."

"I'm fine, but lunch would be nice. I haven't been out of the house, and I was going to see a few patients tomorrow if that works."

"That works for me as well."

The following day came quickly and before she knew it, she was letting her twelve o'clock patient out of her office. To her surprise, she found Kem sitting alone in the waiting room.

He stood up, passed the patient while bowing his head, and wandered into her office. He was resting comfortably when she returned.

"I don't believe I have seen you in a dress lately," he said, his eyes going directly to her legs. "You look well."

"It's easier to get dressed. I still have a lot of pain with certain movements."

"I'm sorry to hear that," he said, getting up from the couch and moving next to her.

She could smell his cologne. She inhaled it. "Why do I allow you to do that?"

"What is that?"

"Let you manipulate me?"

"Hmm, why would you say that?" He leaned closer and gazed into her eyes.

"You call, I jump," she said, plucking her lip and looking down at the floor. "I don't know if it is because I want to see you or I want to pump you for information about the investigation."

"Maybe it's a little of both." He leaned back, smiling.

"We sure do go back many years." She closed her eyes and let out an audible sigh. "I can say one thing for certain though. You helped shape me professionally. I learned so much from you. I would be lying if I didn't sometimes wonder..."

"If we couldn't have been more?" he urged.

"I think every time I see you, I become that mixed-up schoolgirl again." She blushed. "Or maybe I have made our relationship too complicated when it doesn't have to be."

"I'm not sure what you are saying?"

"I'm not exactly sure what I'm saying…" Catherine looked at the swelling of his pants and became increasingly uncomfortable. "I think what I'm saying is that we better go to lunch," she chirped and slowly got out of her chair.

"I think so too," Dr. Hunter said, rising to meet her.

"There is a place around the corner we can walk to…"

He moved closer, taking her hand in his. "Being around you…"

Catherine tried to free her hand, laughing it off when he pulled her into him. She winced in pain. "Ouch, Kem, you're hurting me!" She tried to free herself, but he drew her in tighter while whispering into her ear. No matter how cocky he had ever been, he had never been aggressive. It scared her.

"You were the one I let get away," he repeated the statement she had heard long ago on graduation day.

Fear ran through her. "No," she cried out.

"Hush, Catherine," he said. He put his hand over her mouth and threw her on the sofa. In one move, he was on top of her. Lifting her dress, he ran his free hand up and down her leg. She whipped her head from side to side in an attempt to free his hand from her mouth.

Feebly, she beat on his back with the arm that wasn't pinned down. He pivoted slightly and swatted it away like a gnat, then grabbed it and straddled her, pinning both arms down.

She scissored her legs in full panic and willed herself to remember the self-defense tactics her father taught her when she was a teenager. She could see her father's face and hear his voice. *"It might come in handy one day. I hope it doesn't."*

Drawing strength from the vision, she went limp.

He took the opportunity to begin to pull his pants down, panting.

She took the second of opportunity to knee him in the groin. He flinched enough that she was able to free her hand, reach up, and punch him in the Adam's apple as hard as she could.

Reflexively, he reached up with both of his hands while holding his neck. She screamed and tossed her body from side to side. Her pain excruciating. He was off-balance and toppled to the floor. She raced for the door, but he had somehow reached the door first and had his hand on it, blocking the way. "Catherine," he said, still in pain. "I think you misinterpreted my intentions."

"Get the fuck out of here," she hissed running to her desk to retrieve her phone. Holding it she began dialing. "NOW!"

"I thought that is what you wanted. I like to play a little rough. That's all." He opened the door walked out of her office, but turned when he was halfway through the waiting room. "I apologize sincerely for this mix-up."

She slammed her door shut and locked it.

Forcing herself to focus, she finished dialing the number. When finally, someone answered, she uttered one word. "Mattei."

"Catherine, is that you?" the detective asked. "Is something wrong? Have you heard from Steve?"

"I, I, I.." she faltered. "K-Kem tried to rape me."

"Did you say Kem tried to rape you?" she repeated.

"Yes!" she yelled into the phone.

"Are you safe?"

"I am now."

"Lock the doors and give me your address. I'm on my way."

Catherine hung up the phone and did not move from her desk until she heard a hard knock on the door to her office. Still, she was reticent to answer the door, until she was certain it was Detective McAllister. "Catherine, it's me."

The latches released, the door flew open, and Catherine lost all control. She fell into the detective's arms weeping. Instinctively, Detective McAllister wrapped her arms around Catherine.

After several minutes, she loosened her grip. "Come on, Catherine. Let's sit down, and you can tell me what happened."

Reaching for the box of tissues, Catherine threw several more onto the pile next to her before she could continue. Looking up with a puffy face and bloodshot eyes, she began, "We were supposed to go to lunch, that's all."

"Dr. Hunter?"

"Yes," Catherine growled and quickly relayed the details of her attack.

"Let me give you a ride home," she said and reached out to put a hand on Catherine. "You have been through so much in the last few weeks."

"Don't patronize me."

"I'm not. Let's just get you home." She stood up and reached for her phone. "I am going to put an APB out for Dr. Kem Hunter."

"No." She pulled at the detective's arm, "Please don't."

"He can't get away with this, Catherine."

"I don't want him to get away with this either," she said, lowering her head. "I know him, and he will turn this back on me and call it a misunderstanding. He will manipulate the situation, and nothing will happen to him. And Kevin will blame me!"

"I believe you, Catherine," Detective McAllister said. "And Kevin won't—"

"Stop it! And please don't." Holding on to the arms of the chair, she gingerly lifted herself up. "I want to go home." She shuffled into her office to gather her belongings.

When she smelled his lingering cologne, she froze and clasped her arms around herself. Taking a hesitant step forward, she held onto the desk and sat. She was not going to let him undo everything that she had worked for. Looking up, trying to center herself, she did some deep breathing exercises before stuffing her day timer and notes into her bag.

"You sure you're ready?"

"I'm OK," she mumbled as she picked up her phone to dial into her service. "I just need to cancel my patients.

They drove in silence. Catherine scrunched herself in the corner of the car, her head against the cool window. She remembered the last time she was in a similar posture. Why had she allowed Kem anywhere near her? Anywhere near her life? She was beginning to understand the cycle of battered women. She should have been stronger. *Should have…*

"Looks like Kevin's car is gone," Detective McAllister announced as she put the car in park.

"Thank goodness," Catherine said and opened her eyes. She slowly shifted her body to allow her to open the door. "Please, Mattei, not a word to Kevin either."

"Catherine, I—"

"This is my problem to deal with. Promise me, not a word. We will talk about this later."

Detective McAllister dutifully nodded back as Catherine staggered inside her home. Before moving upstairs, she moved to a window and mouthed "Thank you" to the detective before she drove away.

She moved as quickly as she could upstairs and took a long hot shower. When Catherine returned downstairs, Marlo followed her to the back-room sofa and jumped up next to her. Shaking, she held her beloved companion while her mind raced in an attempt to understand what had happened. Had she been leading him on, and it all had been a misunderstanding? She began to replay their time together in Staunton. Flinching several times at the memories, she forced herself to think of the other details. She began to question why he did not want her to contact Emily's friend Jill, or the Wilson family. Did they know something?

"Stay there," she said, petting her faithful dog before gingerly getting up and retrieving her phone from her purse to look up a number. She was grateful that she had been the one to find the Samsons' number for Kem and equally as glad she had kept it.

First, Catherine called Martha and got Jill's number. Then, she called Jill.

"Jill?"

"Yes?" the cautious tone answered on the other end.

"My name is Catherine Richards, and I am working with the police in Northern Virginia…"

"Yes," Jill interrupted, "Marsha said that Kem would probably call, but I haven't heard from him."

"Do you know, Dr. Hunter?" Catherine questioned, surprised at the familiarity of his first name in her voice.

"I guess I should say *Dr. Hunter*." A slight giggle came over the phone, "Sure I know him. We, uh, dated for a while."

"Excuse me?" was all she could manage, her head swimming.

"I was kinda surprised when Marsha told me he was in town looking into Emily's murder. I mean, uh, that was so long ago."

"Did Emily know Dr. Hunter, too?"

"Oh yeah, he knew her all right. I begged him to see her for some therapy. He wasn't going to do it, but you might say I had my ways of getting him to do what I wanted."

"I was under the impression that the two of you were good friends."

"Huh? Yeah, we were like sisters, but she was still a hot mess. Kem tried to help her, but I knew he didn't like her very much. He said she shouldn't have had her second kid. He was probably right." She let out a deep sigh. "I would be lying if I didn't say I miss some of that. Will you tell him Jill said hi, and if he is ever in town and wants to connect, to give me a call?"

"I'll be sure to do that," Catherine said and absently thanked her for her time.

She went into the kitchen for a piece of paper, her head swirling as she attempted to jot down dates and thoughts she could remember. She opened the laptop that lay waiting on the table. Fueled by confusion and betrayal, she typed in search words and read extensively about DeJarnette.

41

DETECTIVE MCALLISTER

"**B**lair!" Detective McAllister shouted out loud as she marched to her desk.

"Right here," he said, appearing next to her.

"I need your help. Dig up everything you can on Kem Hunter."

"You mean that doctor guy?"

"Yep, that doctor guy. Start digging," she snapped.

"The guy is a ghost," Officer Blair said after over an hour of searching. He placed a single piece of paper on her desk. "All I can find is some professional webpage stating that he is a tenured professor at the University of Virginia, a guest lecturer at George Mason University, and has held seminars at the Behavioral Unit at Quantico."

"That's it?" She leaned back in her chair, rubbing her temples, and thought back on past conversations she had with the illustrious Dr. Hunter. She sighed when the phone rang.

"What's up?"

"Good news. The lab has a latent print on one of the Legos."

"Legos?"

"They have methodically been sifting through a ton of Legos brought in from the latest crime scene."

"Great," she said when she suddenly remembered the clues the lab had been working on. She had put them out of her mind because she assumed they would lead nowhere. "How long will that take?"

"First, they need to develop the latent print, then compare it to IAEFS, which is the FBI's database." The voice stopped. "You know all of that. I'm sorry. I'm just rambling."

"But how long will it take?" Detective McAllister asked a little too loudly, putting the call on speaker.

"Well…" the voice stammered, "it stores at least fifty-three million prints, and it has to compare our latent fingerprint with every other fingerprint in the system. It will come up with a list of most likely matches, but then they have to develop them.”

“Days?” She waved her hands in the air in frustration.

“No, gosh no,” the voice continued. We may get our answer in a few hours. That is assuming the print is in the system.”

“Let’s hope so,” she said, crossing her fingers and looking up at Blair.

“Oh shit,” she said and shot out of her chair when she spotted Catherine standing in front of the station. “Excuse me. Keep me posted on those prints.” She hung up the phone and gave Blair a tap on the arm as she passed.

“Catherine. What are you doing here? How did you get here?”

Catherine’s hair was damp, and she had a fresh change of clothes on.

“I took an Uber to my car,” she replied. “I didn’t need those questions from Kevin. Can I sit?”

Detective McAllister directed her into an office with more comfortable seating.

“How are you?”

“I think I’m fine. I don’t know. I just needed time to process this. My dad,” Catherine reflected, “was a cop. He was practical and realistic. He didn’t portray to me what I imagined the world to be, but what it was, and I remembered what he taught me when I was younger. I think it saved me from getting raped today. I am just very thankful he taught me basic life skills, and I guess I am equally as thankful that I listened. But I also learned that I have blinders on and am pretty…”

“Stop. You’re safe, and it sounds like your father was a good man, Catherine.” Changing the subject, Detective McAllister relayed her suspicions about Jack and Steve.

“That is one of the reasons I am here,” Catherine said. “We got a voicemail from Steve. I guess, initially, he thought of promoting his interrogation with you somehow, but I think he thought better of it and said he was going to Waynesboro to see his parents.” Glancing at the ceiling, she tried to hold in her tears. “I still can’t believe he lied to us all these years. How could I have missed this?” Crossing her arms she said under her breath, “Just add it to the list.”

"Who could have predicted it? Any of it." Detective McAllister reached into her desk, pulled out a pack of tissues and put them in front of her. "Look, since your phone call, I have been trying to delve into Dr. Hunter's past, and well, there is very little of it. Honestly, there's nothing. What do you actually know about Dr. Hunter? About his past—his family?"

"Um, I only know that his father was with the State Department, which is why he moved around so much. He said he spent a lot of time overseas and he does speak several languages. But come to think of it, I have no idea where he went to college or graduate school. He had nothing on the walls in his office at UVA. At the time, I thought it was just him being quirky, and I even admired his lack of vanity as far as that went." She smiled despite herself.

"Lack of vanity? Him?" The detective shifted to the keyboard. Her fingers began tapping furiously. After several minutes, she stopped and rolled her chair back slightly to wait for the results. Biting her lip, she read what was on the screen, nodded, and flipped the computer screen toward Catherine.

"Kem Hunter worked for the State Department for the duration of his career. He died in 1991. He was not married and had no children," Catherine read. "He just stole this man's identity? He was never who he said he was."

"It looks that way."

"I know," Catherine said, "but there has to be a simple explanation. I mean, he has been helping you."

"Helping me or keeping tabs on me?" Detective McAllister waved her hands in the air in frustration.

"I went to DeJarnette with him," Catherine said. "He said he worked there from 1995–1996. Maybe there are employment records from that?"

Nothing.

She thought back to their trip. "He did seem very familiar with the place. He had been there before and mentioned something about there being a pool. Look it up." She pointed to the computer and began plucking her lips while rationalizing in her mind. "I know what I said, but I'm beginning to wonder if I said it out of haste and anger. There may be some oddities, but I mean, you don't think—"

"For God's sake, Catherine, why are you trying to protect him? He tried to rape you. By all accounts he is most likely our murderer." Detective McAllister repeated, loudly and slowly. "You sound like you are suffering from Stockholm syndrome. Snap out of it. This bastard is a psychopath!"

When Catherine didn't reply, she continued. "I told you. We can't find anything regarding his past, and even you have to agree that we can do some pretty thorough digging."

"You have to look. I mean, I just can't believe he could be …" Catherine pleaded and drifted off.

With a sigh, Detective McAllister took the screen back and used the search engine to find the History of the DeJarnette Institution. "A pool?"

"Yes, a pool, and if so, when was it there."

The detective flipped through several articles before turning the screen back to Catherine. "There was no pool when Dr. Hunter said he was employed there, but there was one when James Martin was institutionalized."

The knock on the door caused them both to jump. Blair stuck his head in, and said, "Call for you."

"Thank you," Detective McAllister said as she got out of her chair. "I'll be right back. Blair wouldn't have interrupted if it wasn't important."

Catherine nodded and anxiously waited for her to return. When she did, Catherine looked up at her expectantly.

"They developed the print," she said after returning to her chair. "It's just not on file."

"Then how can it be Kem?" Catherine contemplated. "You have to be fingerprinted to be a professor at a college or university."

"Not to mention the fact that he worked with the FBI." Detective McAllister furthered the argument. "He has evaded the law for decades. I am fairly certain manipulating his fingerprints was not that difficult for him. But it looks like we are going to have to get his fingerprints to see if they match the latent print found on the Legos."

They sat in silence for several minutes both trying to come up with a plan. Eventually, it was Detective McAllister who landed on one.

"Look, Catherine," she said. "I don't need your permission to haul his ass in here for sexual assault. I'm also going to get a search warrant."

Catherine sat up straight in the chair. "Let's get this bastard."

42

DR. HUNTER

It was the middle of the afternoon, but he poured a second Scotch anyway. His world was beginning to collapse. How had it happened? It had all begun to unravel when Catherine came back into his life. Had she sparked an undeniable desire in him that snowballed into this weakness in him? If he had been able to kill her in the traffic accident, maybe things would have been different. Maybe he could have recovered.

He glanced around the room of the rented house. He did not have that much to pack up. He would leave tonight. Calculating his next step, he heard the formable knock at the door. Opening it, he was not really surprised to see Detective McAllister and several uniformed officers.

"I suppose I have Catherine to thank for this visit. I can assure you that it was nothing but a misunderstanding, and once the three of us sit down together, we will be able to sort this out."

He continued, "She's been very emotional—nearly hysterical since her husband became a suspect. She may need to be hospitalized."

"You might have Catherine to thank indirectly, but I can assure you I seriously doubt that even you will be able to sort this one out." She shoved the warrant into his chest as the officers entered the house.

Wandering from room to room, she stepped into his den and handed his computer to one of the technicians. Thrusting open all the drawers, she paused at one with what seemed to be an excessive amount of paper clips. She picked a handful up before spilling them back through her fingers. "That's a lot of paperclips you have here, Dr. Hunter. Any reason?"

"They were on sale."

She turned to look at the bookshelves but stopped when she was called down the hallway.

"In here, detective," one of them shouted. She followed the voice to the garage. Openly, staring into the stark garage was a small black Jetta. She padded down the steps over to the car and circled it. She stopped at the grill, bent down, and saw several indentations. Upon further examination, she could see silver paint chips in the gouged area. "I need someone over here, please," she called out. Several technicians rushed over to find out what she needed them to do.

Glancing over, she saw three neatly lined red gas tanks lined up against the wall waiting to be released. She inspected the backseat of the car and saw the backpack.

"Could I get some gloves?" she called out.

She opened the car door and carefully moved the items in the bag and side pockets.

"Looks like quite the kill kit to me, Doctor," she called. She looked up and saw them standing in the doorway. He had been handcuffed and was accompanied by a fellow detective.

"I'm not sure what you think you have. That is not my car. It belongs to the owner of this house. I do not possess anything in it. The gas tanks are clearly for mowing the lawn. I suppose they are organized." She walked over to him and signaled Officer Blair to follow. "Except I see no lawn mower."

43
CATHERINE

"Are you sure you want to do this, Catherine?" Detective McAllister asked as they were going through the jail security. The hollow sound echoed as they dropped items into the bin.

"No, but I may be the only one who can. I think the only way he will talk is if he perceives the person interviewing him is someone who he views as non-threatening and not in a position of power over him. So, I guess I would be the perfect person for that, wouldn't you agree?"

"We're ready," The detective snapped and pointed to the uniformed guard to follow. Catherine stood on her tiptoes in front of the cool metal door to get a glimpse through the small window.

Dr. Kem Hunter was dressed in a bright orange jail uniform and was seated. His hands were chained to the aluminum table. His head was dropped down and bobbing slightly, but he suddenly jolted up and stared intensely in the direction of the door when he heard movement outside it.

The sudden movement spooked Catherine, and she let out an audible gasp and backed away from the door.

"He can't go anywhere. He's a caged animal," the guard reassured her.

"You do not have to do this," Detective McAllister repeated and placed her hand reassuringly on her shoulder.

Catherine waved it off. "I'll be fine."

"My shift is up in a half-hour," the guard said, "but I will go in there with you if you want. I just wanted you to know that if you don't need me, there may be a new guard when you come out."

"I think if she feels comfortable, you can step out," Detective McAllister said. "I will wait for you up at the guard desk."

"I'm going to be all right. Don't treat me like a child," she tried to reassure both of them.

"You ready?" the guard asked, pulling out the key card.

"Yes." Catherine shook her head and made eye contact. "Let's do this."

Detective McAllister backed out of sight as the guard placed his key card up to the keypad. He punched in the code and the heavy steel door released.

Catherine felt Kem's leering glance as she walked the few steps to the table. She pulled in the chair, almost allowing her knees to touch his. The proximity caused her stomach to churn.

"Hmm. I must say I am a bit surprised," he said and smiled broadly at the sight of Catherine. "Are you sure you are the best one to be conducting this interview?"

"I am. In fact, I am the only one who has any curiosity about you at all. Everybody else wants to see you fry." Catherine looked up at the guard. "I'll be all right. You are free to go."

He nodded and left.

"Some privacy. How nice. I'm glad you're not afraid of me Catherine." Kem said, sliding his chair forward until he was able to touch her knees. "How have you been? I'm sure you and your husband are relieved now that he is no longer a suspect."

"I'm not here to make small talk with you…doctor." She paused unclear how to address him.

"Oh. Doctor, it is now" He looked up pursing his lips in thought. "Hmm, it has been quite a while since you have called me that. I suppose that this almost makes this a full circle in our relationship."

"Except you are the one in handcuffs."

"We will see for how long." He shrugged. "Now, what is it you would like to ask me?"

"How did you escape DeJarnette?"

"Hmm." He leaned across the table and glared at her. His steel blue eyes corresponded with the cold surroundings. "So you believe I am James Martin?" He lifted his head and laughed out loud.

"Aren't you?" she asked.

He forcefully pushed his chair back as far as he could go, but the chain caught his wrist. Catherine flinched at the piercing echo as the chair scraped across the floor.

"That is quite a premise you have come up with." His voice boomed in the empty room.

"Is it? There is no way that you can even try to claim your innocence. The police have matched your fingerprints to the Legos, and they've found DNA." It was a lie she hoped he believed.

He looked down momentarily and avoided eye contact. "You are not very good at deception, Catherine." He looked up at her with a gleam in his eyes. "As I said…I'm not sure you are the best person to be conducting this interview. You would like to believe that it is true that I am James Martin, but you are having difficulty putting your feelings for me aside."

He tilted his head slightly and gave her a playful grin. "Maybe you are doing this to prove something to yourself. I know that you need to come face to face with what you believe is evil. But deep down, Catherine, you can't believe there is that much evil in one person and certainly not someone that you have admired." He paused. "And wanted to sleep with."

"I remember having that conversation with you," she said swallowing the lump in her throat while trying to put the last comment out of her mind and focus. "You told me that given the opportunity, the perpetrator would kill again if they had the chance. You said that's how they are wired."

"Hmm, I suppose I did say that."

"You did. So, why did you allow yourself to be caught?"

"Rhamnusia," he said, gazing at her wistfully.

"I am not sure I understand."

"It's another name for Nemesis. I have done a lot of contemplating on this, Catherine," he said with a deep sigh, "and the only conclusion that I can come up with is that once you came back into my life, it became my virtual undoing. I'm sure you know the story, so as you know, Nemesis played on Narcissus's weakness, and it became his downfall."

"You said I was the one that got away. Have you been symbolically killing me, or did you begin killing because of me?"

"Don't flatter yourself that much, Catherine. This Nemesis is something I just thought of. It may be true. It may not." He laughed scornfully in her direction. "Those women had nothing to do with you. The definition of Nemesis is 'an inescapable agent of someone's downfall.' And that downfall was mine. The stage had been set in motion, and I just allowed you to interfere in it."

"But why did you begin to kill again?

"I believe I made that perfectly clear. Do you remember our discussion about Edmond Kemper? When his story was over, he was done he turned himself in. His story was done. This is my story to tell. Not your husband's."

"You are James..." she murmured, momentarily dazed by the admission.

"I would like to get back to… us." He softly puckered his lips. Redirecting the conversation, he lowered his eyes. "I have a confession, and in a way, it gives credence to my thoughts about you. On some level, I suppose I knew I was unraveling. So, I am sorry to say I had to choose between you or me, and I thought if you were gone, I would be able to carry on."

She remained silent while staring at the door and processing what he had just said. An abrupt shiver from his words ran through her.

She had compartmentalized the murders and the attempt on her life separately. She had not allowed it to enter her mind that it was him who had tried to kill her. "You were the one who ran me off the road."

"It's a lot to take in. I know," he said, reclining back and waiting for a reaction.

She continued to look through him.

"I understand that this realization may take a little time to comprehend. But surely, on some level, you can't be that naïve." He shrugged his shoulders in a gesture of indifference, "If I say I'm sorry, would that help?"

She remained still.

"Nothing? Hmm. Then, I guess I will continue our journey down memory lane." He paused. "I am thinking now about the conversations we had about your father."

"My father?" she asked, dazed by the mention of his name.

"Yes, Catherine, your father," he said, looking up with an expression of contempt. "This little girl thing is quite unbecoming, Catherine." He paused, "Although I suppose fathers and daughters have a special bond, as do mothers and sons, and sometimes they can get…well…quite complicated."

"I'm not sure what my father has anything to do with any of this, and I…"

"I remember you telling me that he was killed." He said, cutting her off. "I believe you said it had something to do with dying in the line of duty."

"I am not sure what my father's death has to do with anything." She shook her head to focus.

"I suppose when you told me about your father all those years ago, I felt some moral obligation toward you. To help you. To mentor you. It was against all odds that our paths would ever cross." He looked down, raised his brow, and grinned. She knew he wanted a reaction, but she wasn't going to give him one.

"Perhaps I allowed my feelings to get in the way. I will have to think about that, too."

"Explain."

"It was so long ago, but I do remember your father like it was yesterday. He had a very big impact on my life." He pursed his lips together. "I was at a patient's house, and for some absurd reason, she became spooked and called the police."

"You were at a patient's house?"

"Let's not get into being self-righteous about ethics," he said with a laugh before continuing. "Besides, back then, you could make house calls, and it wasn't considered to be…"

"Unethical?" she finished.

"The policeman that happened to take that call ended up being your father."

"And you knew that how?"

"Oh, for God's sake, Catherine. I didn't know it at the time."

"The moment I saw him, I had a visceral reaction. I knew he was the bastard who took the baby out of the burning house. His face was burned into my memory." He hesitated and took a moment to think before continuing. "I have to tell you, I was blown away by the coincidence. Really. I asked him what happened to that baby. I had some pent-up rage toward your father. I see that now, too."

"You spoke to my father before you killed him. That is what you are saying."

"Yes, yes. I don't know if I would have killed another police officer, to be honest, but I hated him." He rolled his eyes back in her direction. "He told me he ended up dying at the hospital. All those years I had spent wondering…"

"He told you the baby died? Why?" she scrambled to put her thoughts in order. "That baby didn't die. My mom and dad told me that story. I'm not sure what happened to him because he was put up for adoption, but he didn't die."

Kem's eyes enlarged. His face reddened, and he roared, "ALIVE? What the fuck do you mean he's alive?"

"Alive," Catherine repeated, slamming her palms on the table for emphasis.

She slid the chair back and extended her arms while leaning forward. "Looks like your baby brother is alive and well…James." She looked at him and plucked her lip with exaggeration.

44
DETECTIVE MCALLISTER

Detective McAllister stared back at the picture of Dr. Hunter in the paper and could almost feel his eyes coming out through the page. Reading the article, she mocked the paper out loud. "Well, I guess I should be happy they got his name correct, otherwise…" She was astounded by the misinformation continually spewed out to the public. Shaking her head, she threw it in the trash. How could they get an article of a serial killer wrong?"

"Just do it," Officer Blair said under his breath as he walked by.

"Excuse me?"

"I have seen you pick up and put down that phone several times today."

"I still don't know what you are getting at."

"Come on, you're not the only sleuth in here, detective. Just call Dr. Lynch."

"Blair, how do you apologize to a colleague that you accused of murder while the whole time you were working with one?"

"I don't think you accused him…"

"Bringing someone in for questioning is not exactly giving them a vote of innocence."

"It's not a perfect profession. None of them are. We only see work that is in front of us."

"Thanks, Blair." She grabbed her coat and headed out the door. "I'll be back."

With each step down the familiar hall, she was increasingly more self-conscious of the butterflies in her stomach.

"Jack?" she fumbled when she reached his office. Her mouth twitched as she stood in the doorway, disheartened that she might be unwelcome.

"Come in, Mattei," he said, his eyes softening when they met hers. "It's good to see you."

"I don't even know what to say to you," she said.
"Have a seat and fill me in."

45

DR. HUNTER

"I am going to have to send him out for this now," the doctor told the PA, "Jim, could you do the paperwork on this? He needs to see an ophthalmologist."

"You can wait in the infirmary until we arrange for transport," he said to the patient.

"Thank you, doctor." He sat back down and held his hand over his eye. The toothpick he had damaged his own eye with was killing him. Thankfully, he knew it was just a scratch that would heal. But it was something a specialist needed to look at, which meant he would be leaving the jail to do so.

Later, Dr. Kem Hunter sat patiently alongside a new guard in the waiting room. The receptionist looked over in their direction and smiled. The guard sheepishly smiled back. Thrown off by his phone ringing, the guard imprudently went into the hallway to take the call. Kem took the opportunity to flirt with the attractive receptionist. Leaning over, he whispered into her ear. She giggled, looked in her desk, and handed him what he asked her for.

"I appreciate it," he said and crinkled his nose. "I will definitely look you up when I get out. Hopefully, it won't be too long." He returned to his seat before the guard came back. Thank God for groupies,

"I guess I wasn't supposed to leave you unsupervised in the waiting room," The red-faced guard said when looked at his prisoner. "But looks like you didn't go anywhere."

"Hmm. I'm not sure where I could have gone, do you?" He winked over at the receptionist.

"My first week on the job, and I am sure I will be written up for this."

"I wouldn't worry too much about it. I certainly won't tell anyone." Dr. Hunter smiled. "I'm sure with everything else, that will be the least of your worries."

"Sure hope you are right,"

"I'm certain of it."

When Dr. Hunter's name was called, the guard escorted him to the door.

The doctor stopped him. "It's tight quarters in here."

The guard looked skeptical and concerned due to his last faux pas.

"This isn't my first prisoner from the jail."

The guard peeked into the small room.

"Where's he going to go?" The doctor waved him out smiling in an attempt to reassure him.

The guard relented, and Dr. Hunter was led into the examination room and sat in the chair. He put his chin up to the slit lamp and began answering the doctor's questions.

"I need to pee," Kem said after a few minutes and began fidgeting in his chair. "Really bad. It's been happening a lot. I think this may be my next doctor's appointment." He looked over, biting his lip for emphasis.

The doctor got out from behind his slit lamp and reached for the doorknob. He felt the arms reaching over his neck and the cold metal on his skin before he could react.

"Oh God, please don't kill me." Before he could say anything more, he collapsed on the floor.

Kem Hunter only had a precious few minutes to execute his exit. He stood and balanced himself on the swiveled chair, reached up, and popped out one of the acoustical tiles in the ceiling. He had used his time in jail to develop his upper arm strength. Now, he easily pulled himself into the opening and slithered through the gap.

Taking the paperclip the receptionist had given him, he easily released the handcuffs. He replaced the tile and began counting as he crawled along to freedom. The moment they had entered the doctor's office earlier, he had counted the tiles in the ceiling. He knew exactly how many he needed to pass before he could escape. Once he counted to the designated number, he took a tile out, dropped to the floor, and snapped his head to the right and left to make sure he was alone. The red exit sign was before him. He went through the door to freedom and ducked into the overgrown bushes. He didn't have to wait long for a male patient to show up for an appointment in the building.

Leaping out of the bushes, he placed the unsuspecting victim in a sleeper chokehold and dragged him into the bushes. The only thing left to do was for Kem to button the man's coat to his neck and stroll down the street.

46

CATHERINE

Kevin and Catherine had invited Anne and Steve to Bryce for a long weekend. They all needed the time to reconnect and recuperate. They sat bundled in blankets, drinking wine by the fire pit overlooking the West Virginia mountain range.

"I never get tired of this view," Catherine said, holding her glass up. "Cheers."

"I am having a hard time wrapping my brain around all of this," Anne said. "So, your esteemed professor turned out to be a serial killer. Not only did he kill your father, but he also tried to kill you?"

"Shit, Kevin, there's your second book."

"Too soon, Steve." Kevin recoiled.

"It has been surreal," Catherine said, ignoring Steve's comment. "It's why I am so glad we could be here together this weekend up here where it's quiet, and we can iron some shit out and move on."

"OK, I'll start," Kevin said, his voice slightly rising. "Steve, I'm not sure why you had to lie to us. To me, man. How long have I known you?"

"You want us to go inside?" Catherine asked.

"No." Steve leaned back in the Adirondack chair. "I'm just going to claim the 'I'm a piece of shit defense.' When I met you, dude, you had it all together. You came from a good home. Your parents treated me like their own kid. I never had that. I didn't know how to ever tell you the truth. That I was a foster kid who got a second chance and royally screwed my adoptive family. I guess I wanted a fresh start, and then I got caught up in going after the brass ring, not caring who I hurt along the way." He leaned in to get his wine. "I got it, but at what cost? I went back to Waynesboro, and they didn't even know who I was anymore. I guess I deserved that."

"Steve," Catherine said. "I'm genuinely sorry about your parents. That must have been awful."

"What can I say? I have led a self-centered lifestyle and have made a living off the work that others do. I'm a parasite." He paused. "A fucking parasite."

"You're not that bad," Anne said and took her arm out from under the blanket to squeeze Steve's leg.

Kevin threw another log on the fire, and the four friends continued their evening by eating, drinking, laughing, and listening to music until the wee hours of the morning.

Eventually, Steve and Anne walked up the stairs together hand in hand.

"Well, that was a long time coming," Kevin whispered.

"Guess we will see how many beds I have to make up." Catherine chuckled.

The next day, the four friends decided to take a hike, then go for lunch at the bustling Copper Kettle at the bottom of the ski slopes. Catherine flitted from table to table visiting with friends she hadn't seen for months, finding it refreshing to make small talk. No one knew any details of what had taken place over the past several months, only that Kevin still had a best-selling book.

"We might come back down later tonight if you do the splits on the bar Michele" She laughed, hugged her friend and took a swig from her friend's beer.

"Want one of your own?" the bartender asked.

"Sure…" she was cut off by her phone ringing. "Excuse me. I need to take this." She looked at the number. By the time she reached the outside, she had missed the call. Detective McAllister picked up the line immediately when she dialed the number back again.

"Sorry I missed your call, Mattei…" she started but stopped when the detective cut her off abruptly.

"Are you sitting down?"

"What?" Catherine listened as her heart sank. "Escaped?"

As she relayed the story of Kem Hunter's escape she stopped, "Those damn paperclips. Oh my God, all those damn paperclips." She repeated to herself

By the end of the conversation, Catherine was feeling a drop in her body temperature. Not able to calm her nerves, she sat down at one of the outside tables.

When Detective McAllister ended the call, she attempted to get up and go back inside. She needed to tell the others what had happened with Dr. Hunter. She made eye contact with Kevin the moment she reached the door, and he vaulted out of his chair to meet her. Steadying her, he said, "Woah…Catherine. Sit back down." He pulled her to the nearest chair just outside the door and sat her down. "What's wrong?"

"Could you go tell Anne and Steve to come out here?" she said weakly. "It's too crowded in there right now."

Once they were all seated, Catherine told them the news. "Detective McAllister just called me." She looked around, not wanting to draw attention to their table. "Um, she just told me that Kem Hunter has escaped from custody."

"What?"

"How?"

"It seems he was at an outside medical facility where he overpowered the doctor and escaped by climbing through the ceiling. He took his cuffs off, subdued an innocent bystander for his clothes, and went on his way."

Anne attempted to console her. "I can't imagine he will be able to get too far, Catherine. They'll catch him."

"Are they going to give you protective custody?" Kevin asked concerned that Kem might come back for revenge.

"I won't need it. He will be long gone in a different direction now," she said.

"Why don't you think he will come after you now?" Anne asked, her voice brimming with concern.

Catherine shook his head. "I think he was always committing the murders because he thought he never could finish what he started."

"And what's that?" Kevin asked.

"Kill his baby brother," Catherine said. She had already told Detective McAllister her suspicions and now she was ready to share them with the others. "He's going after his baby brother to finish his story. They are not going to find him."

EPILOGUE

"Hmm, this certainly is a secluded spot you picked out," Sebastian said as he looked over at the beautiful woman lying next to him.

"I wanted you all to myself," the woman purred.

He got up and stretched. "Speaking of seclusion, I need to get back and finish up my chapter." He leaned over and kissed her.

The small room that he was using as his office overlooked the expansive coastline. Leaving the window open, he could still hear the waves crashing.

He opened his computer, searched more agencies, and got some names of hired professional researchers. The only thing he knew was that in 1980, Benjamin Martin was born. He had used his birth name to no avail. He didn't think he would find anything. He didn't think anyone knew his brother's real first name, and being adopted, he would take on his adoptive parents' name. He was at a dead end, and he sure as hell couldn't draw attention by calling any agencies or lawyers in the Shenandoah area. He would not be able to do it himself. He had to come up with a plausible story for Liza.

"I'm back," he said, kissing her neck.

"I hope you got some work done."

"Finished two chapters. Now I'm at a standstill," he looked over sheepishly, "I could sure use your legal help on how to proceed."

"Well, you will have to let me in and tell me about this book of yours…"

They grazed on appetizers in front of them and looked out at the ocean and he began to tell her about his book.

"It's about my brother," he began. "In a way, a lot of this is autobiographical."

"There are two of you? How wonderful."

"I meant to say I have a brother, but I don't know where he is."

"How can that be?" she asked as she picked up a shrimp and twirled it to her mouth.

"My parents were killed." He paused for emphasis. "Murdered."

"Murdered? Is that part of the book, or do you mean in real life?"

"I guess you could say both. But yes, in real life."

"Darling, that is awful." She exclaimed, taking his hand.

"My father had done some very shady deals that caught up to him, and they murdered them both."

"We had no other family, and we were put up for adoption in separate states. I think the authorities believed whoever was responsible would come after us. Kill the bloodline."

Her eyes remained wide open as he told her his new family history.

"This is unbelievable," she remarked. "No wonder you want to tell this story."

"We were with my grandmother at the time my parents were being murdered, or else I believe they would have killed us as well." he said, then explained quickly, "My poor Nona died from a heart attack only a few weeks later."

"How awful. Why haven't you wanted to find your brother before now?"

"I never thought about it really. I've led such a self-indulgent lifestyle."

"Yes, I know. The way you pop in and out of my life is just one example, I'm sure." She looked amused.

"I don't think I want to do that anymore," he said, taking her hand.

"What if I don't want you?" she asked smiled.

"Oh, you want me." He stood up and took her hand, leading her into the bedroom to show just how much she wanted him.

"We will find your brother," she rolled over and gently kissed him. "We will finish this story together."